My Italian Summer

For Ursula,
wishing you a good read,
Agnes
(Agnes Hirschi Várdy)

Pittsburgh, PA
April 6, 2017

Acclaim for **My Italian Summer**

"A powerful romantic tale of love, loss, and ultimately... redemption. The credibility of the characters, the setting, and the lively action make the novel a true page-turner. A riveting read for all interested in biculturalism in a constantly changing world, both in Europe and the United States."

Beatrix Detky, Vienna, Austria

"The masterful description of the unique atmosphere of the Italian Riviera -- land, sea, and architecture -- inspires plans for a future visit. A memorable story that lingers, weeks after one has finished reading."

Diane Todd Bucci, Robert Morris University,
Pittsburgh, Pennsylvania

"I loved reading about my own experiences growing up in an ethnic community -- not in Cleveland, Ohio -- but in New Brunswick, New Jersey. An insightful novel that you can't put down!"

E. K. Taylor, Los Angeles, California

"What an enjoyable novel! I learned a lot about the people of my heritage and their lives in a foreign land. I highly recommend **My Italian Summer** to anyone interested in biculturalism and transculturalism. A fitting tribute to the ideals of the 1956 Hungarian Revolution!"

C. P. Szava, Seattle, Washington

My Italian Summer

a novel by

Ágnes Huszár Várdy

Copyright © 2007 by Ágnes Huszár Várdy

ISBN 0-7414-3645-0

To order additional copies of this book, contact:
Ágnes Huszár Várdy
(412) 422-7176
AHVardy@aol.com

Published by:

PUBLISHING.COM

1094 New DeHaven Street, Suite 100
West Conshohocken, PA 19428-2713
Info@buybooksontheweb.com
www.buybooksontheweb.com
Toll-free (877) BUY BOOK
Local Phone (610) 941-9999
Fax (610) 941-9959

Printed in the United States of America

Printed on Recycled Paper

Published January 2007

For the freedom fighters
of the
1956 Hungarian Revolution

and

For Béla—now and always

Pronunciation of Some Letters in the Hungarian Alphabet

Vowels:

a   = as "o" in "come"

á   = as "o" in "obviously"

e   = as "a" in "anger"

é   = as "a" in "late"

i   = as "e" in "eve"

o   = as "o" in "omega"

ö   = as "i" in "birth"

u   = as "oo" in "good"

ü   = as "u" in the French "etude" or "ü" in the German
      "Bürger"

Consonants - single and double:

c   = as "ts" in "tsar" or "cz" in "czar"

cs   = as "ch" in "church"

gy = approximately as "dy"

j   = as "y" in "young"

ny = as "ny" in "canyon" or soft "ñ" in the Spanish
      "mañana"

s   = as "sh" in "share"

sz = as "s" in "soft"

ty = approximately as "ty"

zs = as "zh" in "Dr. Zhivago"

Tears, Idle Tears

Tears, idle tears, I know not what they mean,
Tears from the depth of some divine despair
Rise in the heart, and gather to the eyes,
In looking on the happy autumn-fields,
And thinking of the days that are no more.
. . . .

Dear as remembered kisses after death,
And sweet as those by hopeless fancy feigned
On lips that are for others; deep as love,
Deep as first love, and wild with all regret;
O Death in Life, the days that are no more!

*"Songs from **The Princess**"*
By Alfred, Lord Tennyson (1809-1892)

Contents

Acknowledgement

Although a novel is primarily the product of the author's creativity and imagination, comments by readers, editors, and other writers greatly contribute to the success of the story.

Several persons read *My Italian Summer* in manuscript form. I wish to thank them for their useful advice and critical comments. They are: Mara Bistey, Maria Cendes, Susanna Fussenegger, Magdalena Sooky, and Kathleen Wallace, all of them of Pittsburgh, Pennsylvania; Eva Baer of Blacksburg, Virginia, Klara Bessko-Várady of Fort Myers, Florida, and Helen R. Myers of Winnsboro, Texas.

I also owe thanks to Dr. Joseph Trompeter, renowned pediatrician of Pittsburgh, who provided information about Aunt Sári's peculiar illness.

Special thanks are due to Melanie Rigney, former editor of *Writer's Digest* and currently of *Editor for You* in Arlington, Virginia. Her valuable suggestions for more detail in character development, the story line, and the historical background, improved the novel and made the story more understandable to the reader.

Most of all, I wish to thank my husband, Steven B.Vardy of Duquesne University for his patience, expert advice, and for prodding me along to make *My Italian Summer* a reality.

Á.H.V.
Pittsburgh, Pennsylvania
Fall 2006

Prologue

September slipped by quickly like a child who, praised by his parents and delighted to be recognized for his good behavior, disappears into his room to finish tomorrow's homework. It was a month of golden splendor; the leaves unusually bright in their orange and yellow hues competed with the brilliant red and copper foliage all around. In September the Keller family was filled with hope, hope that Kathleen's bout with cancer would soon be over. She was in remission, Dr. Peterson told them, and everyone rejoiced.

But October was different: gloomy, rainy and sunless. It showed on the faces of those who dreaded the coming winter months. As the days went by Kathleen's condition worsened. By the end of the month she lay lifeless on the hospital bed in a private room at the Cleveland Clinic. Her beautiful face looked peaceful now, her light brown hair carefully combed, and her gown carefully arranged on her chest. Long sleeves covered her emaciated arms.

Dr. Peterson had called the family. His voice was solemn, but kind.

Michael Keller rushed to the Clinic with his son Tom and daughter Kinga. They made the trip in fifteen minutes from the family home in University Heights, whizzing through every red light. They had just left the hospital two hours before, leaving Kathleen half asleep. The once vibrant Kathleen, so full of life

1

and plans for the future, seemed barely aware of her surroundings. The morphine had eased her pain, and a private nurse was at her side if she needed anything until her family returned.

"We'll be back very soon, darling," Michael had gazed at his wife, gave her a kiss on the cheek, and forced a smile. He patted her hand and Kathleen nodded in understanding.

"She slipped away peacefully," the nurse said as the family stood motionless at her bedside. Kinga pursed her lips and squeezed her brother's hand. For two weeks Michael and his two grown children had alternated their vigil. Someone had been with Kathleen every minute of the day.

"We couldn't even say our final good-byes," Michael whispered, trying to keep his voice steady. He gazed at his wife, his eyes filled with love.

Kinga sat down on the edge of Kathleen's bed and began stroking her mother's hand. Be calm, she kept telling herself, at least she is at peace now. Crossing her legs in her Polo jeans, her glance wandered aimlessly between her brown platform shoes and her mother's bed. Where are you pain, her mother's lips asked silently. Where is all the worry and suffering? It seemed to Kinga that everything had come to naught, all the bad as well as the good. Only the memories remained.

"*Édesanyám, drága Édesanyám,* my dearest, beloved mother," Kinga whispered. "Why did you leave us so soon?" She sat still for a long time. Her father and brother waited patiently behind her, their shoulders and arms touching. Kinga looked up, noting tears flowing down their cheeks. Strong men are not supposed to cry, even in this day and age, she remembered the old adage.

"It's time to go, Kinga dear," Michael said softly. He stepped up to the bed and leaned down to his wife. He drew the sign of the cross on her forehead, a gesture he had learned from Kathleen who always asked for God's blessing every time a family member embarked on a trip. He caressed her cheeks once more. As he stood up, Kinga noticed tear drops glistening on her mother's lifeless face.

But Kinga did not move, as if her presence could chase death away.

"It's time to go, dear," Michael repeated, and Kinga heard his voice as if coming from a distance hundreds of miles away. Finally, her father and brother took her gently by the arm and raised her from the bed. For what seemed like hours, the three stood clinging to each other for a last look at Kathleen, beloved wife and mother, admired and loved by all who knew her.

"We'll miss you so much, so very much," Kinga heard Tom's quivering voice as he took a last look at his mother.

Kinga walked down the long corridor between the two men, looking straight ahead. Everything was a blur. This is not happening to us, she thought. This is a movie I am watching, but I am also part of it...

"*Édesanyám,*" she savored the word, delighting in its sound. When they were alone, she always called her by that name. Her mother had been determined to teach them the Magyar language and expected her children to attend weekly Hungarian Scout Meetings and Saturday Morning Hungarian School. "You should know where you come from. Be proud of your heritage," she would often remind them. But it was not easy. No matter how hard Kinga tried, she spoke Hungarian with a distinct American accent.

"You're not Hungarian, you Yankee. Go and play with your own kind," she remembered kids taunting her at the Hungarian School. But she went, because it was important to *Édesanya.* Kinga adored her, and made every effort to please her. Theirs was not a typical mother-daughter relationship: they were soul-mates, sharing their innermost feelings as Kinga was growing up. But she often wondered about the special sadness in her mother's eyes, a look that became more frequent with the passing years.

She recalled a late summer afternoon several years ago, when she caught her mother standing by the front window, watching the sunset. Kathleen's slender figure cast a dark shadow on the imported lace curtains. Kinga stepped up to her and put her arms around her shoulder. She gathered enough courage to pose the question she had wanted to ask ever since she was old enough to note that far-away look in her mother's eyes:

"*Édesanyám,* why are you sad? So melancholy? You often stare into the distance with a strange look in your eyes. Is anything wrong?"

"No, nothing is wrong." Kathleen had replied quickly, shrugging her shoulders. She caressed her daughter's cheeks and smiled wanly.

"Oh, it's really nothing, dear," she sighed. "But maybe... maybe I'll tell you some day..."

Now, that day will never come.

Who will offer me comfort when things look dark and hopeless, Kinga pondered, as she clung to her father's and brother's arms. Who will advise me when I'll meet that special someone to share my life?

The immense void deepened in her heart. Questions about her parents' past began to plague her. She remembered her father's expression two weeks earlier as he stood by the table in the front hall. His face alternated between snow white and dark red, as he held a long white envelope in his hand. He tore it open and removed the letter Kathleen had written before her final trip to the Cleveland Clinic. His voice was shaking as he read his wife's words:

"*Please scatter my ashes in the Mediterranean Sea at San Bartolomeo al Mare, on the Italian Riviera. Please do not ponder why. I have loved all three of you immensely, more than I can express with words. But that is my final wish. I hope you'll forgive me.*"

Kinga and Tom looked at their father with questioning eyes, but no sound escaped from their lips.

*   *   *

The Memorial Mass was exceptionally moving. There was a small table in front of the altar covered with a white embroidered tablecloth. On it stood two large bouquets of red roses, two photos, one of Kathleen, the other a family portrait, and a marble urn. It had been Kathleen's wish that in place of flowers, her friends send money to the Hungarian Orphanage and School in Déva, Transylvania. She had shown a great interest in the work of the Franciscan Friar, Brother Csaba Böjte, who had set up numerous schools and orphanages in Transylvania, a province that had been part of the Kingdom of Hungary until 1918. It still has a large Hungarian population.

St. Emeric Roman Catholic Church on the West Side was crowded; so many people, so many scouts and community leaders made speeches, eulogizing Kathleen Mátrai Keller. As a final good-bye, scouts and close friends held hands and formed a circle around the small table. They sang the popular song, "*Szellö zúg távol, alszik a tábor...* The wind is rustling far away, the camp is fast asleep...*"

Now Kathleen was fast asleep. Never to wake again.

Kinga heard a whisper behind her, "Does breast cancer run in her family?"

What happened afterwards was like wandering around in a nightmare, blindfolded. The three of them stood at the church entrance, nodding politely to people offering condolence. "Thank you, thank you very much," her father's weary voice rang in her ears while Kinga just stood there, trying hard to appear composed.

The family made every effort to thank in writing each person who had sent a sympathy card or made a contribution to the Orphanage and School in Déva. There were hundreds. One stood out because of the fine quality and size of the envelope. It was from a place called San Bartolomeo al Mare, in Italy. On the return address stood "Villa Tokay," and the card was signed *"Aunt Sári"* in elegant long-hand letters.

Oh yes, the mysterious Aunt Sári, Kinga remembered. Kathleen's aunt had often come up in family discussions, but the mere mention of her name brought a sense of foreboding to her father's eyes, while *Édesanya* quickly changed the subject.

*   *   *

Life went on. Kinga continued her studies at Case-Western Reserve University where she met Zoltán Ráday, a Fulbright student from Hungary. He was unlike those Hungarians who had recently come to America and heaped endless criticism on the United States. After a few months' stay these types often felt they knew everything about America and its people. In fact, they were convinced they were better informed than those who had lived here all their lives. Kinga didn't much care for them, and had a hard time adjusting to their ways and becoming their friends.

But Zoltán was different. He and Kinga often ran into each other in the library or at the Café Leroy nearby. She invited him to meet her father and brother. He made a good impression, and their meetings became more frequent. They spent a lot of time together and began making plans for the future. One evening in late May, Zoltán asked Michael for his daughter's hand in marriage. But Kinga wavered. Where would they live? Who would have to give up his lifestyle and country? Their dilemma increased, but no solution came to mind.

"Your mother's room will have to be cleared out," Michael reminded his daughter months after Kathleen's funeral. "I know it's terribly difficult, but it would be best if you would take care of it, Kinga. The sooner the better."

"I know," Kinga nodded, but several months passed before she gathered enough courage to step inside her mother's room.

Everything was the way Kathleen had left it before taking her final trip to the Cleveland Clinic. Kinga stood motionless, reluctant to touch anything; each piece of furniture, each object had a certain sacredness... because it had been hers, *Édesanya's.* Kinga knew she had carefully selected every item and every piece of furniture with the utmost care. It was as if the touch of her delicate fingers were everywhere, as if she had just left for a European vacation, to return a few weeks later.

She pursed her lips and shivered as she stepped up to the dresser filled with Kathleen's personal belongings. She started with the bottom drawer, and pulled it out carefully, curious about what she would find. One by one, she removed each item. Her eyes widened when she noticed a black binder at the bottom, with hundreds of typed pages inside. There was also a cache of envelopes from Italy, tied together with a blue ribbon. Kinga saw that the top one had been mailed last September. There was no return address. They must be from Aunt Sári, Kinga concluded as she put the envelopes aside. She was more curious about the manuscript in the binder.

With trembling hands she opened it to the first page. The title "*My Italian Summer* by Kathleen M. Keller" stared her in the face. She had read some of her mother's articles and stories, but never realized that she also wrote longer pieces. Was this a novel, a non-fiction piece, or a diary of her travels?

Her heartbeat quickened as she knelt on the plush carpet, staring at the manuscript. What will she find in those pages? Should she read it? What secrets will it reveal?

For a moment she wavered, then slowly slipped off her shoes and settled on her mother's bed. She stuck two pillows under her head, turned on the light on the night stand, and began to read.

1

Arriving in Genoa

Cleveland and Italy   *Spring 1983*

"Well, Luciana," Kati turned and smiled nervously at the heavy-set woman sitting next to her during their trans-Atlantic flight. "I hope you'll get to see all your relatives and friends." Kati's eyes gleamed knowingly, as she pushed a stubborn curl back from her forehead. "Especially Giorgio."

"OK, girl. Now, you have a good time too, you hear? I'll see you in a month," Luciana Fabriani returned Kati's smile and winked. "And don't be so shy. European men don't like bashful girls..."

"But Luciana, you know I'm engaged. I am not interested in meeting men."

Kati's stomach growled. She had been unable to eat all day. Michael's words of the night before kept popping into her head. "Think of me sometimes, Kati, if you'll have the time." He had looked her straight in the eye. "But I have a feeling you won't. I know you won't think of me at all." His face darkened and Kati noted the apprehension in his eyes.

"Of course I'll think of you. You know I will. And I'll write often," Kati promised with forced cheer in her voice. They were standing in the doorway of her apartment in Shaker Heights. It was almost midnight and Kati still had packing to do. Their good-bye kiss was long, but Kati knew that Michael sensed her heart was not in it, that her mind was wandering thousands of miles away.

At first Michael had encouraged her to accept Aunt Sári's invitation to attend the three-day reunion with family and friends, and to stay a month to get to know her aunt better. But a few weeks later Kati noticed that he had changed his mind. He became more distant, and one evening he told Kati that his colleagues at work teased him about his fiancée finding someone else in "romantic Italy."

"No way," Kati protested, "You know I love you."

"Well, you do now, I know and feel that," he sighed, "but what if you meet someone else?"

"How can you say that? You and I are meant for each other. You should know by now."

But Michael's doubts intensified with the passing weeks. "Why don't you go to Africa?" he demanded once, as his eyes narrowed in annoyance and his face turned a deep pink. They had been engaged for three months. The wedding was planned for next spring, but Kati's trip to visit her Aunt Sári was hanging over their head like an ominous cloud before a violent storm.

"Please don't go, Kati," Michael pleaded one evening. "Forget about the reunion. You don't know anyone there anyway." He swallowed hard. "We can go to Italy on our honeymoon and you can meet your Aunt Sári. We'll save enough money by then for both of us."

Kati had a hard time making up her mind. She finally told Michael that if her boss agreed to a leave of absence from the office, she would go. "I really would like to get to know my aunt better, and here's my chance. After all, I don't have that many family members left," she insisted, fighting her tears. "Don't you understand?"

Michael frowned. "I'll soon be your family. Isn't that enough for you?" he asked turning away in anger.

He had driven her to the airport in silence. He's making me feel guilty for visiting my aunt, Kati thought. He has no right; I am not his wife yet.

"I'll be back in a month, you'll see. I promise. And don't worry so much," she assured him, patting his knee as he tightened his grip on the steering wheel.

Michael's possessiveness had gotten worse since their engagement. "I know you love your heritage, and I respect that. But you're too caught up in those Hunky things," he told her. "You're an American. You were born here!" Kati felt offended by the word "Hunky." It was definitely a derogatory term, a negative label used for immigrants from Eastern Europe.

To avoid an argument, Kati did not reply. Michael was often annoyed when she went to her weekly scout meetings on Friday nights, and he didn't attempt to control his anger when the Hungarian guys asked her to dance at the annual Veteran's Ball in January. Sulking, he sat at the table, and hardly spoke to anyone, while Kati had a fabulous time chatting and dancing the whole evening.

"You aren't really going to marry that Yankee, are you?" her partners teased her, when Michael was out of hearing distance.

"But I am. He's a great guy. He is so caring and unselfish. He's helped me through many hard times. And, above all, I love him very much." The Hungarian boys were more like brothers, buddies she grew up with. No romance, just a lot of fun.

The storm across the Atlantic made for a disastrous flight, and no matter how hard the pilot tried, the ride on the spacious 747 Alitalia jumbo jet was bumpy. Kati was petrified. Maybe this was God's way of punishing me for leaving my fiancé behind, she thought in panic. There had even been an emergency landing in Madrid which delayed their arrival by four hours. By then, the passengers were exhausted, nervous, and distraught.

They were finally landing at the Genoa airport. Kati fidgeted in her seat. Every bone of her body felt sore and heavy. She could not sleep a wink all night, even after the lights were turned off for the in-flight movie. The moment the jumbo jet touched the runway, she sighed in relief, and joined her fellow passengers as they broke into exuberant applause, laughing loudly.

"Thank you for flying Alitalia," Kati could hardly make out the words on the squeaky microphone. She stood up and reached for her and Luciana's hand luggage in the compartment above. She handed Luciana her bulging, red canvas bag.

"Don't worry so much, dear. Michael will be OK, and your aunt or someone will be there to meet you. I'm sure," Luciana said as she glanced up between powdering her nose and putting on bright orange lipstick. She seemed rejuvenated and her dark eyes had a special glow.

As traveling companions thrown together by fate, Kati Mátrai and Luciana Fabriani became instant friends. "What a coincidence," Luciana had said after they settled into their seats before take-off from the Cleveland Hopkins International Airport, "You and I are almost neighbors; we both live on the East Side. We're both foreigners in America, and we're visiting relatives in the old country."

"Not quite," Kati said. She had already told Luciana that she was born and raised in Cleveland, but Luciana would not believe her.

"But Luciana, I was born in Cleveland," Kati repeated, smiling. "It was my parents who came to America in 1956."

"You still look like European girl," she insisted.

Although Luciana Fabriani was more than twice Kati's age and had left her native village near Genoa when she was twenty, they hit it off instantly, holding similar views about the world. But Luciana had a large family on both sides of the Atlantic, while Kati only had Aunt Sári and an elderly great uncle in Hungary, whom she had never met. And of course, there was Michael.

"Oh, everyone, everyone will come to meet me," Luciana gloated, her eyes filled with anticipation. Although her family had been adamant when she gave up her home and country to marry an Italian-American construction worker, they had kept in touch through the years, and loved her nonetheless.

"I make big mistake," Luciana admitted to Kati, after two small bottles of Chardonnay during the in-flight dinner. "Shoulda' listened to my Mama and Papa. Now I have two big boys. My husband Waldo is OK, a good guy. But he more American than Italian. You know what I mean?"

Kati nodded. She understood, but she could not put her fingers on it. She was about to ask Luciana the question often asked of foreigners who complained about Americans and the American way of life: "If you don't like it here, why don't you go back?" But she learned from her father, whom she called "*Apuka,*" that newcomers were annoyed by that question. "Once you settle in America," he had told her, "there's no turning back."

It had not been easy growing up as a first generation Hungarian-American. Expected to feel comfortable in two worlds with different customs and traditions, Kati's generation was torn between two contradictory value systems. Although her parents and their friends felt at home in their ethnic community, members of her own generation had a hard time fitting in. Some of her friends' parents even failed to learn English, and expected their children to follow the strict rules of the old country. Yet, they wanted their offspring to succeed in the New World and become part of the upper echelons of American society.

What made people who stuck to their ethnic backgrounds different from those who assimilated quickly into mainstream America? Kati had often wondered. They lived and worked in the same cities, drove the same cars, attended the same schools, shopped at the same stores, and saw the same movies. Was it the language they spoke at home, the church they went to, or the company they kept?

Turning to her present predicament, Kati recalled the problems she had faced trying to notify Aunt Sári about her arrival two days later than originally planned. Since she had telephoned several times without reaching her aunt, she sent a telegram. If Aunt Sári didn't get it in time, how would she get to San Bartolomeo al Mare? It was pretty far from Genoa.

She had heard stories about the Italian mail service, and doubted its reliability. Someone even related that from time to time Italians stuffed letters, postcards, and even telegrams into large bags and dumped them into the ocean, thus avoiding the work that went with delivery. Kati hoped such rumors were malicious propaganda circulated by those intimidated by the Mafia.

Even the brilliance of the Italian sun failed to lift her spirits. She walked down the steep exit stairs and dragged herself to the rickety bus that stood in front. Several passengers began to push and shove as they scrambled to find room on the run-down vehicle. Annoyed, Kati took her time and began to doubt the wisdom of her decision. I should have stayed at home, she told herself. Maybe Michael was right. She missed him already. He was someone she could always rely on, so helpful and understanding. Except for this trip.

In the meantime, Luciana had already pushed ahead and boarded the bus. She was waving toward Kati to join her in the front. "Stop grumbling," she reprimanded Kati as she moved closer. "Living on the Italian Riviera for a month isn't the worst thing that can happen to a girl from Cleveland."

"I know. I know. But still..."

Kati recalled the words of her best friend, Kriszta. "You'd be crazy not to go. Just think of all the fun and excitement. I wish I had an aunt in Italy!" She urged Kati to accept the invitation. But then, Kriszta's life was different. She was already a wife and mother, and worked at the same boring job since high school. Kati's prospects were much brighter. She had a B.A. from Case Western Reserve and was considered one of the rising stars at the Thompson & McKee advertising agency. And, of course, there was Michael... Not seeing him for a month was not something she had really wanted.

"Come on, Kati! You're acting as if visiting Italy was a punishment!"

Kati forced a smile, not wanting to offend Luciana and her native land.

The bus stopped, and the passengers scurried toward the doors of the airport terminal, like ants toward a piece of chocolate cake. "Go ahead. I'm in no hurry," Kati patted Luciana's shoulder. She knew that her new friend was eager to see her family and friends.

She let people get ahead, surveying them with nonchalance as they fought for a place in the lines to the passport control booths. The Italians seemed a friendly lot, and their olive-skinned faces broke into a smile of welcome at the sight of their returning brethren and tourists from abroad.

Kati stood out from the crowd in her blue silk suit. Her shoulder length light-brown hair, blue eyes, and faultless complexion drew the approving glance of males always on the look-out for female beauty. Although exhausted from the long trip, she looked fresh and alert, as if she had a good night's sleep in her own comfortable bed.

She was the last one to go through passport control. She sauntered to the luggage dispenser only to find that her suitcase was nowhere in sight and most of her fellow passengers had already left. She stood alone, wondering what to do next.

A few minutes passed and a new group of excited travelers emerged through the revolving doors. Kati thought of the worst possible scenario: a lost suitcase and no one to drive her to Aunt Sári's home in San Bartolomeo al Mare, on the Riviera Ligure.

She rummaged through her purse, searching for her aunt's letter. It was written in Hungarian, with a sophisticated, elegant handwriting. She read it for the tenth time.

"My darling Kati! Now that your Uncle Tibor is gone and you're alone, come and visit me in Italy. I have been planning a little celebration for years, and I would love to have you join us.

It will be a reunion of sorts, for family and friends, both old and new. Plan on staying at least a month. I sincerely hope you'll come. Please reply as soon as possible.   With love and kisses,
Your Aunt Sári. "

Kati realized that Aunt Sári could not have known about her engagement to Michael, since there had been no contact between them for years. But she was right. Kati was alone. She had been devastated by her parents' auto accident three years ago, when she was twenty. For a while she only had Uncle Tibor, *Apuka's* younger brother. Some gossipy women even speculated that the attractive womanizer had more than a fatherly interest in his young niece. But they both ignored such ridiculous accusations, and Uncle Tibor tried his best to take over her parents' role.

She could still hear the shrill ring of the telephone at midnight. When the police told her the horrible news, she dropped the receiver and left it dangling by her bedside. The somber voice on the other end informed her that Tibor Mátrai had a serious ski accident. They called her because she was his nearest relative. With Michael's help she immediately made arrangements to fly to Boulder, but by the time she arrived at the hospital the next afternoon, her beloved uncle had died. This happened just a few months ago, leaving Kati totally alone, without any relatives in America. She recalled Michael's sympathetic words: "I'm so sorry, Kati. Please don't forget I'll always be there to help you. You can count on me." But now Michael was so far away...

"This is all Kriszta's fault," Kati murmured. She felt apprehensive, and looked for a scapegoat. "She talked me into coming here..."

She stood apart, scrutinizing the two luggage dispensers from other flights. Suddenly she spotted her suitcase. Relieved, she grabbed it and joined the tourists who stood in line for customs control. Ignoring the clerk's look of admiration, she straightened her shoulders, took a deep breath, and resolved to face the world. Here I come, Aunt Sári, she sighed in relief. I just hope someone will be here to pick me up.

As she stepped through the automatic door marked *Uscita,* the sight of the multitude of faces overwhelmed her. People were craning their necks to get a glimpse of the friend or relative they were expecting. She noticed Luciana in the center of a large group, deluged by hugs and kisses of exuberant Italians. She waved to Kati, and pointing to a well-dressed middle-aged man, she whispered, "Giorgio." But Kati could not take a good look at him since both were swept out of sight by Luciana's welcoming party.

Kati searched for someone looking for her. There was no one in sight. Trying to hide her disappointment, she made her way through the narrow passage left open by the waiting crowd. She felt the stares of curious eyes as she walked over to the nearest refreshment stand. Why do these Italians keep gawking at me, she wondered. Don't they have any manners?

Directly opposite the stand, the sliding doors were kept in perpetual motion by travelers on the go. Kati leaned against one of the high stools, her luggage safely close by. She searched for the slightest sign of someone who may have come to take her to Aunt Sári's.

What do I do now, she asked herself. Her misgivings about the trip returned. Besides Michael's apprehension, there had been problems at the office. She had worked at Thompson & McKee's for only eight months, but her supervisor Mr. Johnson granted her the one-month leave only because of her unique family situation. He was reluctant at first, but now that Uncle Tibor was gone, the well-meaning boss felt she needed peace of mind and some rest. Having been in a similar situation in his youth, David Johnson understood Kati's plight. He hoped that visiting a member of her family would restore her spirit and her zest for work.

But at the last minute, Kati's immediate supervisor insisted that she work two more days, so her departure date had to be changed. Good thing it was still low season, the middle of May. Although reluctantly, Alitalia honored her request without changing her Apex fare.

Kati grew up speaking two languages, English and Hungarian. She picked up German and French in high school and college, but her Italian left a great deal to be desired. Making a phone call in Italian was a challenge. Besides the horror stories about the Italian mail service, she heard that Italians were not keen on learning languages. They delighted in a tourist's attempt to speak their *lingua bella*, but they rarely spoke another language themselves.

Perched on a high stool and still looking bewildered, Kati searched the crowd to find someone with whom she could leave her luggage. She planned to exchange some money, find a phone booth, and call her aunt.

A well-dressed lady in white, wearing a wide-brimmed hat, and two teenage girls sipping Coca-Cola and munching salami sandwiches stood out. Maybe she could ask one of them to watch her suitcase and carry-on.

She was just about ready to walk over to the woman when she heard an announcement in Italian, French, and finally English. She could barely make out even the English words, but the name "László" caught her attention. It was unmistakably a Hungarian name. A good omen!

She searched the faces of tourists and businessmen seated on the far side of the counter, and wondered if anyone would respond. So far there was no sign. Then she noticed two men sitting at the other end of the open café. Their backs were to Kati, but she could see that the younger one with dark hair was lean and tall. His athletic built was visible from the back.

The two men were clearly expecting someone since they stopped talking when they heard the intercom announcement. Maybe she should go up to them... Maybe they were the ones waiting for her...

Before she could gather enough nerve to walk over, the two men stood up, paid for their coffee, and grabbed their leather briefcases. They hurried toward the escalator and disappeared from view. She saw only their profiles, noting the taller man's good looks. *Too bad he wasn't the one who had come to pick me up,* Kati thought.

By this time, the woman in white and the two teenage girls were gone. Kati turned back to her glass of warm coke and fiddled with her straw. *They sure don't believe in ice in Italy!* She began sipping the warm liquid which hardly quenched her thirst. She glanced at the clock whose hands barely seemed to move. Still sitting on top of her high stool, she spotted no one in the area who could be looking for her.

Soon the area marked *"International Arrivals"* became completely deserted. The excited hugs and joyful words of recognition were part of the past.

Kati contemplated her next move.

She finally decided to walk over to the nearest phone booth, but soon learned she needed a *gettone,* a telephone token to make a call. Frustrated, she looked around wondering where she could get one. She noticed that the bartender was eyeing her from a distance. Seeing her distress, he stepped over to the phone booth, and handed her a shiny new *gettone.*

"Grazie mille," Kati smiled in appreciation. *Boy, are these Italian men nice!*

She dialed Aunt Sári's number. *If she could only talk to her aunt, everything would be all right.* She let the phone ring for a long time. No answer. Drops of perspiration rolled down her forehead and her hands were wet as she held the receiver. Still, no one picked up the phone on the other end.

With all hope gone, she walked back to the refreshment stand and ordered another coke. Annoyed by the bartender's stare, she felt like screaming out loud.

Why in God's name did I come here? What a horrible mistake!

2

Surprise on the Riviera

Genoa Airport

Kati kept looking at her watch. The minutes seemed to drag. She had already spent over an hour and a half sitting on the high stool at the refreshment stand. The bartender, who had given her the *gettone,* tried to strike up a conversation, but to no avail. Kati sighed in relief when his shift was up and he finally left. The girl who replaced him showed no interest in Kati, and soon began making eyes at her male customers. But her smile seemed fake, ready to be turned off when her gaze fell on females. Are all Italian bartenders such flirts? Kati wondered.

Totally exhausted, her nerves were on edge. She had already called Aunt Sári several times, but there was no answer. She resorted to chewing her nails, a habit she had conquered years ago. What did I come here for, she pondered. What an idiot I am!

She was about to walk to the ladies' room with her suitcase and carry-on in hand, when she noticed a man in his mid-thirties bolting through one of the sliding doors at the opposite end. He looked out of breath as he glanced around uneasily. When he spotted Kati, he headed straight toward her.

"Mátrai Katalin?" he called across the counter in a demanding voice. He pronounced her name in flawless

Hungarian, placing her last name first as customary in the language.

He circled around the refreshment stand while Kati turned around in her high stool and took a good look at him. He was dressed in gray flannel slacks, blue shirt and a navy blazer, and wore no tie. His unbuttoned shirt revealed a muscular neck tanned copper by the sun. An air of nonchalance exuded from his every move. Truly "a man of the world," Kati concluded. She noted two pock marks on his forehead which seemed to be his only flaw.

"Yes, yes. *Igen, igen, én vagyok.* I am her," Kati stammered. Surprised by his sudden appearance, she didn't know which language to use.

"All right, little girl, here I am. I'm Miklós. Dr. Kemény Miklós. I'm the one delegated to pick you up." He stared at Kati with apprehension, looking her over from head to toe. His Hungarian pronunciation may be perfect, Kati thought, but there's something about him that rubs me the wrong way.

"Kati Mátrai," she introduced herself and extended her hand in greeting. Feeling relieved, she conquered her uneasiness and added, "Thank God you're here." She tried to hide her feelings behind a smile. "I was so worried," she admitted, blushing.

"Well, we were worried too," he replied, clearly irritated. "Two days ago, we organized a welcoming party for you, and even Sárika came to the airport. It's not often that a young lady from America comes to join our humble company..." His tone drove her up a wall. Her feeling of relief began to fade.

"Didn't Aunt Sári get my telegram?" She asked. Italian efficiency! Kati was beginning to believe the rumors about Italian communication technology.

"She got it all right, little girl," Miklós sneered, pronouncing every Hungarian word with deliberate slowness.

"You don't have to talk to me that way. So slowly, I mean. I'm quite fluent in Hungarian," Kati said with a frown, resentful about his presumption that she was one of the thousands of young people whose parents failed to teach them the language of their ancestors.

"Oh, you are? Well, anyway, your telegram took two days to cross the Atlantic," Miklós continued. "When we didn't hear from you, we assumed that you would arrive a day later than we expected. So I drove to the airport yesterday, but there was still no sign of you. Finally, your telegram arrived early this morning. So, this is the third time I've had to drive to the airport to pick you up."

"Well, I'm certainly glad you're here!" Kati said, trying to appease him.

"You should be," he answered as his eyes flashed.

Kati was taken aback. He acted as if everything were her fault. It was clear this guy thought only of himself. What an obnoxious person!

"Did someone force you at gunpoint to come and pick me up?"

She was not going to let him speak to her that way. "Who are you anyway?" She demanded as she raised her voice, herself surprised by her sharp tone. A moment later she collected herself. I should be glad that someone came to pick me up... But it was too late. "Calm yourself, Kati," her mother's frequent admonition echoed in her ears.

"No one forced me! I happen to know your aunt pretty well, and I'm doing her a favor," Miklós replied, staring at her in disbelief. "You know, that tone doesn't suit you, little girl. And don't be so upset. You'll ruin your pretty face." He shook his head and wagged his finger at her. A derisive smile crossed his face.

Kati hated being called a "little girl." How dare he talk to her this way? The gall! She forced herself not to say something nasty. After all, he came to pick her up and drive her to Aunt Sári's.

"Are those your bags?" Miklós pointed to her suitcase and carry-on.

"They're mine! Obviously," Kati retorted, losing her patience again.

"Then follow me," he commanded as he picked up both pieces and led the way to the parking lot. She could hardly keep up with him as she watched his muscular frame sway gracefully, swinging her heavy suitcase and hand luggage as if they had no weight at all.

"It's that gold Mercedes sedan, over there," Miklós pointed with his head toward the far end. He opened the trunk and swung the luggage inside, then walked over to the front and opened the door for Kati.

"Here you are, *Signorina* Mátrai," he said in a mocking tone and bowed deeply. Kati made an effort not to show any emotion as she settled into the luxurious bucket seat. At least she was on her way to Aunt Sári's. It was a move in the right direction.

Miklós got into the driver's seat. He started the motor, opened the sun roof and turned on the radio. A romantic tune filled the air. *"Buona sera, Signorina,"* the vocalist sang in a deep baritone. A perfect song, welcoming me to Italy, Kati thought. She leaned back in her seat and was glad Miklós had not said a word since they had settled into the Mercedes.

He finally broke the silence. "You know, Sárika was worried to death about you. For a while we had absolutely no idea what happened to you, where you were, and what not."

Kati was puzzled. What was his relationship to her aunt? Surely, he could not be her husband; he was much younger. Was he one of her so-called "friends?" Her parents had often hinted that Aunt Sári was a woman of the world, and Kati sensed early on that her mother, whom she called *"Anyuka,"* had harbored a deep resentment toward her younger sister. Was it because Aunt Sári was popular and well-liked, and had many male friends?

Having maneuvered the car out of the airport parking lot, Miklós no longer seemed to concentrate on the road. At the first toll booth marked *"Alt Stazione,"* he reached for the ticket and turned to Kati.

"Hold this for me," he commanded. He stuck the ticket into Kati's left hand, and accelerated to a speed of 140 kilometers. Kati held her breath. She grabbed the handle above her right shoulder and clutched it tight. She was not used to such a high speed; in America a 65 mph was the law, about 40 kilometers below the speed Miklós was driving.

Miklós leaned back in the driver's seat, and turned toward Kati. "Well, I dare say, little girl, you certainly had us worried. Your aunt was a nervous wreck for two days. And that's not good for her. Not in her condition."

In her condition? Kati was puzzled. What was he talking about?

"You know, I must admit, you don't even look tired," he continued slyly, "considering the long flight and the delays. At one point Alitalia even told us you were not on the New York-Genoa flight."

"Sorry I created so much commotion. I worried a lot about Aunt Sári not getting my telegram in time." Then she added quietly, "And... I... I... also had a few problems of my own..."

A moment later she regretted her comment. Cleveland already seemed far away, and how could her situation matter to a stranger? She didn't want to give the impression she needed sympathy. Not from a nasty guy like this Miklós.

In spite of her misfortune during the last three years, Kati had proven she could take care of herself. This trip was a duty toward her family and her parents, a month to get to know her Aunt Sári. She hoped to put the unpleasant past behind her and return to her career and her new life with Michael.

Thoughts of Michael overwhelmed her and she suddenly felt guilty for not having listened to him, the one person who had always been there to comfort her and ease her pain. Please don't be angry with me, she begged him silently. Looks like everyone is upset with me, for some reason or another. I must be strong, she told herself as she straightened up in the comfortable bucket seat.

"So, this is what Hungarian-American young ladies look like," Miklós remarked, as he stared at the gold cross that had slipped out from her blouse. "By the way, that's a nice suit you're wearing," he continued. His blue eyes had a provocative look.

Kati blushed and slipped her cherished cross back in place. It had been a gift from her parents on her sixteenth birthday. "Well, I hope you didn't expect me to wear an old sweatshirt and jeans, did you?"

"Not really, but I see so many American girls dressed in ..." Miklós began.

Kati interrupted. "European men have strange notions about American women." She pushed her hair back and turned to him, anger rising in her eyes.

"Yes, this is what we look like, Dr. Kemény. Although I doubt we all look alike." She said "Dr. Kemény" on purpose to annoy him. She was aware of the custom of using first names by both males and females at the first meeting among those of the same social class; not using first names could be easily interpreted as a sign of disdain, even insult.

"Well, you're certainly an exception from what I've seen..."

His approval annoyed her. He was clearly a ladies' man, obsessed with women, and convinced that the female sex could not exist without him. He thinks he is a demigod, God's gift to women. Kati remembered a few guys like him in Cleveland, and they had always gotten on her nerves. She shifted her position in the bucket seat as she smoothed down her skirt.

"You know, Kati," Miklós began again after a few moments of silence, "When we found out that Sárika had invited her American niece to the reunion, we burned with curiosity. Especially the single, unattached males. Boy, were they excited! The married ones too. They should have some fun! Why should they suffer just because they got caught?"

Kati glanced at his hands on the steering wheel. "It looks like you got caught," she said. Funny it had not occurred to her that he might be married. There was a gold wedding band on his middle right hand finger, and a signet ring with a family crest on his left.

Miklós ignored her comment, while he peered at her through his sunglasses that slid down his nose. She was about to tell him to keep his eyes on the road, when he turned back to his driving.

"Naturally, the women were curious too," he continued. "They'll probably take a good look at you and watch your every move. And they'll be so jealous! I know women. They're afraid of competition. At the reunion..."

Kati almost forgot about the reunion. Besides getting to know her aunt, attending the reunion was the reason for her visit. What will it be like? Who will be there, she wondered. And what will they do for three weeks after it's over? Lying on the beach from morning till night was not her idea of fun.

I'll never fit in, Kati thought. These people probably live like the Italian *La dolce vita*: playboys and playgirls searching for pleasure, having a good time at any cost. Her resentment toward Aunt Sári's friends grew, yet she had only met one of them.

Miklós picked up where he had left off. "Well, anyway, our friends wondered what you looked like. Did you resemble your mother whose portrait hangs in Sárika's drawing room at the Villa Tokay? Or did you take after your aunt?"

He took a hard look at Kati as they were nearing the next tunnel. "And some others were curious about the *type* of girl you were..."

Kati noted how he emphasized the word "type." She felt like a model whose every move was on public display, scrutinized by hundreds of pairs of eyes. The fellow is clearly trying to embarrass me, to make me feel ill at ease. Kati wondered who these "others" were, but was more curious about her mother's portrait. She'll get to see it soon enough, she hoped.

"Tell me more about the reunion," she said after they emerged from the tunnel.

"For quite a while now your Aunt Sári had this *idée fixe* of a three-day celebration, a kind of reunion. She wanted to invite her old and new friends, and the few relatives she had left to her place in the sun. She wanted to see them once more, after all these years. And now that her condition..."

Miklós bit his lips and a dark shadow crossed his face, but he continued. "She tried to track down everyone she wanted to invite. You see, they scattered everywhere after the 1956 Revolution. She sent out invitations several months ago. When she heard about your Uncle Tibor's ski accident, she decided to invite you too. She told me she had the feeling your uncle didn't approve of her either. Just like your parents..."

He stopped talking as they entered another tunnel. Kati gulped when she was reminded of the estrangement between her mother and Aunt Sári. Even this stranger, this Miklós knew about it. I'm so embarrassed, but I am not going to discuss our family with this guy, she thought in defiance.

"Good thing you're only two days late," Miklós continued after they emerged into the radiant sun, "the reunion starts two days from today, on Saturday."

"It's a great idea to have a reunion. Will there be people from around the world?" Kati tried to sound excited.

"Oh, yes. So many Hungarians settled all over Europe, America and Canada, and even in Australia. As you probably know, they were fleeing from the Russians and the communists."

"Of course I know. Some even left the country after World War II." Kati wanted Miklós to know that she was familiar with the fate of the people of her heritage.

"Now they're destined to live out their lives in foreign countries," Miklós continued, sounding like a know-it-all. "Some still yearn for their homeland and the past, but going back is out of the question for most. Not until those damn commies and Russians leave. And there is little hope for that." For the first time he sounded serious.

"There would be no jobs for them in Hungary, anyway," he went on. "And I have a feeling that those who left the country would not be welcome." He paused, but continued before Kati could put in a word. "But maybe most wouldn't even want to go back." He pursed his lips. "Once you get used to the freedom of the West, our 'beloved homeland' is too narrow and confining."

"When did you leave Hungary?" Kati asked.

"I left when I was a student, back in 1968. We took a short trip to Vienna with some of my friends and I just 'forgot' to go back."

"Really?" Kati heard of numerous Hungarians, especially young people, who defected to escape from the communist regime.

"It was really hard at first. I want to forget those days. But then, your Aunt Sári was a great help to me. If it weren't for her..."

"Really?" Kati repeated, glad to hear that her aunt had been helping her compatriots. She obviously had a good heart.

"Maybe I'll tell you about that sometime." Miklós clearly did not wish to go into the details.

"Nowadays, many spend their vacations in the old country," Kati remarked, fishing for another topic.

"Oh yes, they go to visit friends and relatives, they say. Actually, I think they're showing their approval of 'goulash communism,' where everything is supposed to be fine and dandy. I suppose you've heard that expression."

"Of course I've heard it."

"I even know parents who send their foreign-born kids to camps on Lake Balaton, or to Summer School at the College of Sárospatak to learn about their roots," Miklós continued. "But what they get is communist propaganda." He shook his head. "I would never do that. And I would never return, not even for a visit. Not until those commies and Russians are out of there." It was clear he would not accept other opinions about the subject.

Kati fondly recalled the summers she had spent around Lake Balaton with her parents' friends and their children. Captivated by its special atmosphere, she felt at home in the lush environment of the largest lake in Central Europe. She knew of Hungarians in Cleveland who refused to set foot in their homeland, and even forbade their curious children to visit. Like Miklós, they declared, "not while the communists are in power."

But *Anyuka* and *Apuka* were different. Although they had escaped from Hungary during the 1956 Revolution, they wanted Kati to learn about her heritage first hand. She was grateful for those summer trips when the whole family spent three weeks visiting relatives and childhood friends. She had often felt sorry for some of her friends whose parents did not allow them to visit the land of their ancestors. How could they relate to a country and culture they only knew through hearsay? Kati's thoughts soon returned to the present as she looked out the window, admiring the Italian countryside with its verdant hills and valleys.

"I think this get-together, this reunion is a fabulous idea. I'm so glad Aunt Sári thought of me," Kati repeated, hoping to steer the conversation away from this touchy subject. She had heard from her parents that Hungarians who visited the country were often labeled as communists, or conspirators who were duped by the communist regime. This was a very controversial issue in the Hungarian-American community, and vitriolic newspaper articles were directed against those who went back for a visit.

"Oh yes. Sárika really wanted you to come. You know, she has friends everywhere. Some old friends from her acting days, and the new ones she'd made since. She doesn't have much of family, though. Not any more. Just you and your great uncle, the old Count Miskolczy de Baranya. As you know, he still lives in Hungary. He refused to leave in '56, despite what he had to go through. You've heard of Recsk, haven't you?"

"Recsk?" Kati recalled hearing that name before. *Apuka* had mentioned it, but she never bothered to find out more. She remembered *Anyuka* talking about an uncle and his wife, but somehow they never made an effort to look them up while visiting Hungary. For some reason, her mother ignored all her relatives, and it bothered Kati that she hardly knew her Aunt Sári. Dear *Anyuka,* Kati thought with apprehension, why did you lose contact with our relatives? If I knew them, I wouldn't feel so alone now.

"Tell me about the guests, so I won't be so lost. All of them will be total strangers to me."

"Don't worry about that. You won't be a stranger for long, believe me. Not if the men have their way," Miklós's gaze fell on Kati again and his eyes gleamed with approval.

"In fact, you'll be the *belle of the ball.* As you probably know, Sárika is planning a ball for Saturday night."

A ball? Kati knew nothing about a ball. Good thing she packed one of her summer evening gowns at the last minute. Just in case, she had thought then.

"There will be some pretty interesting people, Hungarians from Germany, France, and Switzerland, and some even from California and New York, your fellow Americans." Miklós took a deep breath. "Then there's the foreign aristocracy, and some other big shots in business and politics. All of them friends of your aunt," he added, frowning.

Kati was overwhelmed.

"And I shouldn't forget our own circle of friends, Italians and a few of our own countrymen living in Italy. László, for example."

"László?" Kati's eyes widened.

"Yes, there is the handsome and elusive László von Temessy. The darling of all," Miklós said wryly. "He is the only bachelor in our group, and many *signorinas* and even *signoras* are after him. But they haven't succeeded in catching him yet. He lives in Rome and happens to be one of your aunt's favorites."

"Oh, and by the way, they're related by marriage," he added as an afterthought.

But Kati hardly took note of his last sentence. She remembered a "László" being called through the intercom at the Genoa airport. There was no way he could be the same László that Miklós was talking about, she thought. László was a common Hungarian name.

"Yes, he's definitely one of your aunt's favorites," Miklós repeated shaking his head and biting his lips. "And not married."

Kati wondered how many "favorites" her aunt had. Was Miklós one of them? Maybe Aunt Sári deserved her reputation.

"Will there ever be an end to all these tunnels?" Kati asked, feeling more light-headed each time they entered one. She had been counting them since they entered the first tunnel.

"Like everything else, even the tunnels must come to an end," Miklós replied.

The pungent fumes of the trucks and the high speed made Kati dizzy and nauseous. Each time they passed through a tunnel she could barely recover to enjoy the countryside. But the tunnels had one advantage: Miklós had to look straight ahead, and Kati did not have to put up with his annoying stare and snide remarks.

Finally, they drove through the seventeenth tunnel, and Kati noticed a huge green sign to the left of the road, marked *"San Bartolomeo al Mare."*

"We'll be there in a few minutes." Miklós said as he pulled up to the toll booth, and gave the man several thousand liras. He had already paid thousands for a previous stretch.

"It will be so hard to get used to such large numbers," Kati remarked.

As they left the *autostrada* and Miklós carefully maneuvered the sharp curve to the left, the vast panorama of San Bartolomeo and neighboring Cervo came into view. It seemed to Kati that she was looking at a postcard of gargantuan size, the scene of a fairy tale that exists only in a romantic never-never land.

"This is like a dream," she gasped, overwhelmed by the magnificent landscape. The soft waves of the blue-green Mediterranean stretched far into the background. The azure sky was broken by an occasional white cloud and Cervo's four church steeples towered high above the closely-packed houses of the medieval village. Built on the mountain side, the condo roofs and terraces gleamed in hues of pale gold, green, and terra cotta under the caressing softness of the Italian sun.

"Do you know why the shutters are closed?" Miklós asked.

"No, not really."

"It's not the tourist season yet. Tourists start flocking to the place in late June, and stay until the end of August. Then they are everywhere." He shook his head, showing his displeasure.

"But there must be people who live here year round," Kati remarked. There were signs of life where the wrought-iron terraces were lined with geraniums and roses in various shades of pink and red.

A few minutes later they passed under a small bridge, and at the next intersection, turned right to Via Aurelia, the main thoroughfare of San Bartolomeo. It was lined with tiny shops, restaurants and cafés that catered to the everyday needs of the population. There were signs everywhere, some in bold and colorful letters, while others were painted in more discreet colors. Kati could not help reading them on her side of the street, *"Pizzeria," "Trattoria," "La Terrazza al Mare," "Rosticerria," "Ristorante chez Francois"*-- they were all intriguing names. But there was no sign of life anywhere. The shutters on the windows and doors of the shops and cafés were all closed.

"I guess you're right. Not too many people live here now." Kati was surprised to see so few people on the street. The place had an eerie feeling, like a ghost town in the American West, in Texas or New Mexico. She glanced at her watch.

"Ah, but it's siesta time," she exclaimed. She had heard about Italians closing their shops, banks, and offices around 12:30 each afternoon. They went home for lunch and a nap, and resumed work around 4:30 or 5:00. Their activity continued into the late evening, often until 8:00 or 9:00 when they either went home or enjoyed a late dinner with family and friends.

After a few short blocks of driving on Via Aurelia, Miklós made a left turn to the Via della Repubblica, and Kati read *"Hotel Stella Maris"* on a large yellow sign painted in red and black. They were heading toward the sea, passing several buildings on a wide street lined with palm trees. They turned right on the Via Europa, past the back entrance of the *Hotel Stella Maris.*

Miklós slowed down in the back of a three-story structure in white stucco. A high wrought-iron gate separated its grounds from the street. A sign, *"Passo Corrabile,"* warned the unsuspecting passers-by not to enter. The place was practically shut off from public view. There was a brick wall on the left, and a green wrought-iron fence on the right. Meticulously trimmed trees, bougainvillea hedges, and exotic shrubs were visible on the inside grounds while the back terrace was covered with red clay pots brimming with geraniums, begonias, petunias, and zinnias. They glowed in a myriad of colors, and cheered Kati's heart. She was so immersed in the surrounding beauty, that she barely heard Miklós's voice.

"Here we are, Mátrai *kisasszony,* Miss Mátrai." He jerked the brakes as he brought the gold Mercedes to a full stop. He stepped out of the car, pushed the tall gate open and parked in the back of the magnificent villa.

Startled by his voice, Kati felt as if she had just been awakened from a dream.

"Your Aunt Sári's seaside cottage," Miklós motioned toward the building. "It's just one of her seaside residences, the Villa Tokay."

3

The Villa Tokay

San Bartolomeo al Mare, on the Riviera Ligure

"Let's go inside through the front gate," Miklós motioned to Kati. "We'll have to go around the house. The front faces the ocean."

"You mean all this belongs to my aunt?" Kati's eyes widened in disbelief. She made no effort to conceal her astonishment. Like many of her countrymen, Aunt Sári escaped from her native land after the 1956 Revolution without a penny to her name. How in the world did she acquire such wealth?

Miklós raised his eyebrows and made a sweeping gesture with his right hand. "Oh yes, all this! And there's much more, ah, so much more! Just wait till you see what else she owns." He paused for a moment and sneered. "Oh, come on, little girl, don't tell me you're surprised."

"Of course I'm surprised. Who wouldn't be?" Kati tried to recover from her shock.

"You mean you didn't know?" He looked straight into her eyes. "I don't believe you," he stated with conviction.

Kati was taken aback. How dare he talk to her this way!

"This is just one of her seaside cottages," Miklós had casually remarked. What a cottage! Kati knew that many Hungarians had done well in America, especially those who escaped after the Revolution. They were welcomed as heroes, and those of college age received scholarships to the best colleges and universities. Many earned degrees in science, technology, and engineering. Even the older ones like her parents were given a chance. Once they learned English they continued their education, rapidly adjusting to the unfamiliar environment of their adopted country. With hard work and motivation to improve their lot, they soon became well off, bought their own homes and drove new cars. Although both her parents had been trained in the humanities they had done well. At the time of their accident *Apuka* was Head Librarian at Cleveland State University and *Anyuka* taught German and French at Shaker Heights High School.

But nothing Kati had ever seen could match this villa. She recalled the magnificent homes in Shaker Heights and University Heights, but few were as striking as this one. She had never known anyone who lived in such a place, let alone have the opportunity to go inside.

"Wow! I'm certainly not used to such luxury," she said, shaking her head, trying to forget Miklós's insinuating remark.

"My parents' house was a three-bedroom bungalow. I remember how proud they were when they saved enough for a down payment."

In order to reach the front entrance, they had to walk through a meticulously kept public park with wooden benches under palm trees. There was a fountain at the center and a profusion of rose bushes in shades of pink and white added color to the lush environment. The park was almost deserted; only a few tourists sauntered on the wide quay along the sea shore. Most were tall, fair, and blonde. Probably Scandinavians and Germans from the North, Kati thought. Funny, how easy it is to guess people's nationality by their looks, just by the way they dress and carry themselves.

The Mediterranean soon came into full view. Kati listened to the sound of the waves, mesmerized by the incredible beauty of the scene. She wondered what was awaiting her in Aunt Sári's villa. Will she ever feel comfortable in this luxury? She'll never be able to fit in.

As they reached the wrought-iron gate that matched the green of the gigantic one in the back, Kati noticed the stares of nearby tourists. They eyed her and Miklós with interest, not in the least trying to hide their curiosity. She remembered how often she had wondered about the lives of those who lived in such magnificent homes. Could their wealth and worldly possessions shield them from pain and tragedy so common in the lives of ordinary mortals?

"These tourists are probably spinning romantic tales about us," Miklós remarked smiling with satisfaction.

"About us?" Kati pretended to be shocked. He must have read my thoughts, she reflected and smiled back.

Miklós rang the bell. A few minutes later, a short, square-shouldered man opened the gate. His complexion was burned copper and the lines on his face reminded Kati of a freshly plowed field that had lain fallow for years. The bright sun and salty air had carved dark furrows into his complexion. Despite the deep grooves that seemed to have been there for centuries, his expression was jovial and full of life. He greeted the visitors with a friendly grin.

"*Buon giorno, Dottore Kemény. Buon giorno, Signorina.*" He pronounced Miklós's last name perfectly.

"*Buon giorno, Gino. Come Sta Lei?*" Miklós asked in Italian. "Our long-awaited guest is finally here," he announced. "Is the Contessa at home?'

"*Si, si, Signor*. She's resting," he said anxiously.

"Gino is Sárika's gardener, and his Hungarian wife, Aunt Juli, is her cook." Miklós explained and made a sweeping gesture toward the grounds. "As you can see, he's an expert gardener, and your aunt's friends simply adore Aunt Juli's cooking."

Miklós asked more questions which Gino answered in rapid Italian. He moved both his arms as he spoke, but Kati could only make out the word "*Contessa.*" At one point the gardener's expression turned so grim that she wanted to interrupt to find out what was going on. But she was a total stranger here, how could it be her business? She was impressed with Miklós's ability to converse in Italian, as he switched from one language to the other with ease. He must have lived in Italy for a long time, she concluded.

It seemed that Gino and Miklós had a lot to talk about, so Kati decided to step aside and take a good look at the garden. It was how she had imagined paradise on earth. A wide, gracefully winding path covered by pink pebbles led to a circular area and to two front entrances. Kati wondered which one they would use. Palm trees, blue-green firs and pines stood on the lawn in an organized fashion. Gardenia bushes with pale yellow blossoms in clusters grew close to the wrought iron fence, shielding the house and its residents from curious stares. A life-size statue of the goddess Juno stood in the middle. Kati recognized it as the replica of the one in the Vatican Museum, having seen it in one of her art books. Behind the statue, there was an array of well-kept, neatly laid-out flower beds with a mixture of exotic plants, many she had never seen before.

She took a close look at the villa. It was much more impressive from the front. Its three stories were designed to resemble the front of a sailing vessel. Each floor was surrounded by a wide terrace, the rails painted a gleaming black, in stark contrast to the white stucco walls. The balconies were lined with a profusion of flowers and shrubs, but the planters on the front terraces displayed only red geraniums and white petunias. Two large curved picture windows covered one side of the front on the first and second floors. The blinds were drawn, although it was easy to peer through the ones on the main floor. Kati detected signs of an indoor swimming pool, the hand rails of a ladder, and reddish-brown ceramic tile on the floor.

Having ended the conversation with Gino, Miklós walked up the entrance that led to the winding marble staircase at the main entrance. He rang the bell forcefully, betraying his impatience.

Kati stood apart, still bewitched by the magic garden. She turned around once more and faced the Mediterranean. The huge expanse of water glistening in hues of gray, aqua, and purple held a mysterious power over her. Ever since she was little she had felt drawn to the ocean. A scene of fifteen years ago flashed through her mind. It was her first time on the seashore walking on the beach on Longboat Key, Florida, feeding seagulls and watching sailboats with her parents. There, the sea was emerald green, broken by the rapid ripples of the waves. Here, the Mediterranean displayed a myriad of colors and the quiet rhythm of the waves added to the warm mellowness of early afternoon.

Suddenly the front door flew open and a large woman appeared in the doorway. A head scarf, tied in the back of her neck matched her red dress with white polka dots. Her gray curls peeked out on both sides, framing her friendly face.

"*Miklóskám,* my dear Miklós, " She exclaimed in a boisterous voice. "Hello, *Katikám édes,* my sweet little Kati. I'm Aunt Juli. Welcome to the Villa Tokay."

She gave both of them a hug. "Let me look at you, little Kati." She grabbed Kati again, and holding her at arm's length, she looked her up and down. "You won't stay skinny like this for long. Not with my cooking," she said and her brown eyes twinkled with mischief.

"As you can see, Aunt Juli's idea of feminine beauty is that of women in her village," Miklós remarked wryly. "Girls are deemed pretty only if they carry several extra pounds. Not like you." He scrutinized Kati, as if he had seen her for the first time.

Kati blushed and tried to ignore his stare.

She liked Aunt Juli. She acted as if she had known Kati all her life, and made her feel welcome. "I prepared a tray of light snacks for you, *Katikám.* Gino will take it up to your room."

Aunt Juli led the way to the front hall and Kati felt self-conscious as her high heels clicked on the Carrara marble floor, partially covered by a large antique Shiraz rug.

Kati took a quick look around. The walls were done in beige brocade. Two mirrors in gilded frames hung on the left wall, and a larger mirror between two doors decorated the back wall. Several exotic plants and carved chests of drawers stood in front of each of the three mirrors. Kati glanced toward the magnificent French door to the right. Its massive wings were slightly open, barely enough to give visitors the chance to peek inside. Kati was dumbfounded; never before had she seen such luxury and elegance.

"Your room is on the third floor with a gorgeous view. You can see Diano Marina and Cervo from the terrace." Aunt Juli's voice woke Kati from her reverie. "Miklós will show you upstairs," she added as an afterthought.

"Whatever you say, Aunt Juli. You know I always do whatever you say," Miklós replied eagerly.

"Oh, I have so much to do, I must go now," the housekeeper sighed. She disappeared through one of the back doors.

Kati found Miklós's behavior peculiar. He moved around the place as if he lived here. What was he doing in this house? Was he Aunt Sári's lover? Kati had read about wealthy women keeping young men around... But she dismissed the idea. Not in her family! Her upbringing found such arrangements unthinkable and totally unacceptable. But then, she reminded herself that this was not the solid middle-class community with strict moral values in which she had grown up in Cleveland.

"Go ahead, little Kati," Miklós instructed, as Kati started up the marble steps that matched the floor of the entrance hall. He followed close behind.

Suddenly Kati felt a pinch on her backside, and when she turned around, Miklós grabbed her by the arm. "Oh, I'm sure you'll like it here, little girl," he grinned and pulled her close.

She could feel his breath on her face. His blue eyes sparkled with desire.

"What are you doing? Let me go," Kati screamed. Frightened and her heart pounding, she started beating on his chest, trying to free herself from his grip. But the more she fought, the more forceful he became. He grabbed her again, and held her by the wrist.

"Oh, you'll get used to our ways. It just takes time. We know your *type!*"

Kati was in shock. Who was this guy, and what was he trying to do? Her whole body trembled as she managed to free her right hand and gathered enough strength to punch him in the nose with her fist. Miklós was taken aback. He finally eased his grip and let her go. Relieved, she ran up the steps as fast as she could. But Miklós was close behind.

After reaching the third floor landing, he suddenly stepped in front of her and led the way through the hallway. He stopped in front of one of the bedroom doors. With a careless movement of his arm, he pushed the door wide open and grinned sheepishly.

"And this is your room, at least for a month, *Mátrai kisasszony*, Miss Mátrai. I hope you'll find it suitable and adequate." His eyes sparkled in frustration and anger, but he acted as if nothing had happened just a few moments ago.

Kati stepped inside the room as fast as she could. Her heart still pounding, she avoided looking at him, having sensed that he planned to follow her inside.

"Leave me alone!" She screamed as loud as she could. She slammed the door in his face and quickly turned the key. Breathing a sigh of relief, she leaned against the closed door, still trembling.

She stood there for a while, out of breath, her hair disheveled, her palms sticky with sweat. The left sleeve of her silk jacket was ripped at the seams.

Oh my God, what am I going to do with a guy like that around, she pondered. What kind of a man was this Miklós? He thought her easy prey! His impertinence caught her off guard. Did he think she was game for an affair? He thinks I am a slut and a fortune hunter, hoping to inherit Aunt Sári's wealth, this beautiful villa and her other residences. But I hardly even know Aunt Sári. A half hour ago I didn't even know she had money, she thought helplessly.

It took several minutes to calm her nerves. Oh Michael, Michael, you were right! I should have stayed in Cleveland...

She plumped into one of the easy chairs and looked around the spacious room, admiring the white streamlined furniture with gold-leaf design on each piece. A large baldachin bed in the middle dominated the room. There was a mirrored dresser on the left wall, surrounded on either side by book cases filled with books of all kinds. The dressing table was on the right, next to the door that led to the private bath.

Her eyes fell on a small writing desk that stood in front of the glass wall facing the ocean. There were stacks of papers and documents on it.

Then she noticed a sliding door leading to the terrace. She stood up and stepped outside, admiring the pale yellow outdoor furniture and Kentia palms, perfect shields against the penetrating rays of the sun. She leaned her arms on the wrought iron railing and gazed toward the sea, overawed by its multitude of hues. Gathering all her will, she fought her tears, tears of anger, confusion and helplessness.

Watching the rhythmic movement of the waves as they merged into each other in perpetual motion finally cleared her mind and soul. The proximity of the huge expanse of water restored her sense of balance.

She stepped inside and took another look at the room. Three comfortable *fauteuils*, upholstered in blue and white chintz, graced one corner, with a round glass table between them. The blue of the upholstery matched the hand-made bedspread. White, beige, and blue chintz pillows, several dolls dressed in regional costumes of Hungary and stuffed animals were neatly arranged on top of the bed. Kati noticed a pair of *Matyó* dolls and a cuddly white dog of unknown breed, both of which reminded her of home. The plush wall-to-wall carpet was white with blue print, complementing the dominant blue of the room.

Despite Miklós and his impudence, Kati felt immediately at home. The room had a girlish prettiness mixed with unique sophistication, hard to pinpoint. It was apparently furnished with the needs of a young girl, and Kati wondered whose room it was. There were no photographs, and she noticed only a few modern prints and a large but empty bulletin board on the wall.

Having unpacked her suitcase which Gino had left inside her door, she felt exhausted. Losing a whole night's sleep was taking its toll. After a quick shower in the luxurious blue, beige and terra cotta tiled bathroom, she put on her baby doll pajamas. She nibbled on Aunt Juli's array of snacks, but could hardly keep her eyes open. She threw herself on the wide luxurious bed, cuddling up to the soft little dog. Her life in Cleveland flashed through her mind. What a difference! She'll have so much to tell Kriszta and her other friends.

Before she dozed off, she thought of Michael. She could see his eyes, hurt and angry, filled with a myriad of questions. But he seemed so far away... She wondered whether she would always feel that he had been right in discouraging her trip...

*   *   *

When Kati woke up, she felt completely refreshed.

What next, she wondered. Where was Aunt Sári? Will they meet tonight? She really didn't expect to sleep this late. As she surveyed the room her eyes fell on a white envelope under the door. She slid out of bed, grabbed the envelope and read the short note, written in the familiar handwriting of her aunt:

   "Kati darling, dinner is at eight. Hope to see you then. Lots of kisses, Your Aunt Sári."

She took a quick glance at her watch on the night stand. It was already half past seven. Relieved that she had not overslept, she wondered what to put on. She wanted to make a good impression on Aunt Sári. If she was at all like *Anyuka*, she probably put a lot of emphasis on dressing right for every occasion.

She decided on her favorite beige georgette dress with a simple line and a round scoop neck. The front of its slim bodice and its sleeves were embroidered with white silk thread in a design from the *Sárköz* region of Transdanubia in Hungary. *Anyuka* had sewn and embroidered the dress just before the accident, and even after all these years it was one of Kati's favorites. She arranged her hair in a loose chignon, a hairdo that made her feel sophisticated. With her thick light-brown hair pulled back on both sides, her delicate features and her high cheekbones became more pronounced. *Anyuka* had always been annoyed when she wore her hair covering part of her face, she remembered wistfully. "Don't hide your high cheekbones, Kati dear. We inherited them from our Asian ancestors," she used to say.

Kati put on light make-up and chose her white pearl earrings, the ones with the two pearls attached by a delicate gold chain. They went well with her gold chain and cross that came into full view in the low decolleté of her dress.

She walked down the stairs to the front hall. An eerie silence greeted her everywhere. But soon she heard soft romantic music coming from the room that was separated by large French doors. She found one wing slightly open, and entered quietly, her heart pounding and her hands shaking. Will Aunt Sári like her? How will they get along? They had met only once or twice when she was a little girl, a long time ago.

For a few moments she stood at the door, taking in all that she saw. The large drawing room was furnished in various shades of beige, gold, and rust. The right wall was covered by built-in cabinets, some with colorful stained glass doors, while others were left open to hold books, magazines and works of art. A light beige curved sofa stood directly in front of the all-glass wall on the left, with sliding doors leading to the terrace. There were several easy chairs of the same design in rust and gold on both side of the sofa. An antique coffee table with art books strewn all over stood on an exquisite Persian carpet. Three unique lamps caught Kati's attention. The lamp shades were held by colorful porcelain bases of Chinese design. Plants of all sizes were arranged in copper planters. The room gave the impression of comfort combined with high elegance, a rare combination, Kati thought.

A large crystal vase with a bouquet of red roses drew Kati's glance to the far corner, and she noticed that it stood on a Bösendorfer piano of dark mahogany. A second later she noticed the erect figure of a dark-haired woman sitting on the piano bench. Her back was to Kati. She sat motionless with both hands slightly touching the keys.

"Aunt Sári?" Kati asked timidly. She was startled by her own voice. "Aunt Sári, it's me, Kati." There was no answer.

The silence felt like eternity. The figure on the piano bench did not move. Finally, Aunt Sári stood up, and with a graceful movement of her head she turned toward her niece.

For a moment they both stood motionless, mesmerized by the significance of the moment.

Kati broke the spell. She ran across the room with her arms opened wide.

"*Katikám, drágám,* my darling little Kati." She heard her aunt's throaty but melodious voice. "I'm so happy to see you again. After all these years."

A Cleveland meeting with her aunt flashed through Kati's mind, as she recalled *Anyuka's* words: "Sári really likes our little Kati. She's really drawn to the child. But I'll never allow my daughter to associate with the likes of her." Kati remembered her father's wry smile, but he had made no comment.

"Oh, Aunt Sári, I'm so glad to see you, and I'm so happy to be here," Kati exclaimed, smiling.

Aunt Sári's warm hug made her forget Miklós's outrageous behavior and suspicious stares. Tears of joy flowed down their cheeks as they embraced.

"Let me look at you," Aunt Sári whispered, as she held Kati at arm's length. Kati noticed a deep sadness in her eyes, as she tried to hide her feelings behind a welcoming smile.

Aunt Sári pulled nervously on the long strand of pearls that she wore with her navy blue silk dress. Her dark, chestnut colored hair was done in an elegant fashion, every strand in place, as if she had just come from the hairdresser's.

"My dear little Kati," she repeated several times. "I don't have much of a family anymore. I am so glad you're here."

She took Kati by the arm and led her to the bar. She opened the door of the liquor cabinet along the wall.

"What would you like to drink, darling? Sherry, cognac, or a little *Tokaji Aszú?* Do young ladies drink in America? Or don't you drink at all?"

Kati settled for a small glass of *Tokaji Aszú*, a golden sherry she had tasted many times before. It was the drink served on special occasions back home in Cleveland, on Thanksgiving, Christmas, and at birthday celebrations.

Kati longed to relax a little, to enjoy her new surroundings. The more she thought about it, the more she regretted the lack of contact between her parents and her aunt. Why had there been such a deep rift between them?

She was immediately drawn to her aunt. Aunt Sári's elegance combined with a natural kindness appealed to her. Yet, the glint of sadness in her aunt's eyes puzzled Kati, and she had the feeling that in days of old Aunt Sári had an especially cheerful nature that attracted many people, especially men, to her side.

"I'm so glad you're here at last," Aunt Sári smiled. "I'm really sorry I couldn't make it to the airport. Miklós probably told you that I did go with him the first time."

"Oh yes, he mentioned it."

"Well, I felt a little tired, so I thought it would be better if I am all rested up when you finally arrived."

"All that matters now is that I'm here."

"That's exactly right. Tonight I just wanted the two of us to have a cozy dinner, so that we could talk about old times. The others will be arriving tomorrow," Aunt Sári said, somewhat out of breath. "I've invited many people, although some simply out of obligation. I don't want to make any more enemies."

Kati wondered how someone like Aunt Sári could have enemies. Then she remembered her own parents, especially *Anyuka*.

For a while they stood in front of the bar, chatting and sipping their drinks. Kati noted Aunt Sári frequently glancing at her watch. She had become pale, and it seemed that her attempt at cheerfulness was wearing off quickly.

"Let's have dinner now," Aunt Sári finally suggested.

They entered the spacious dining room. The long table was set for three, and Kati recognized the Herend porcelain tableware with her favorite Rothschild design, in light green. The damask tablecloth was of a delicate apple green and a gigantic silver candelabra with green candles graced the center.

After taking her place at the head of the table, Aunt Sári rang the bell next to her plate. Kati sat, admiring the exquisite Sterling silverware with the monograms "*M.S.*" etched in elaborate letters on the back of each piece, with a nine-pronged crown above the initials. A symbol of the aristocracy with the rank of a count, Kati remembered *Anyuka* telling her many years ago.

A man of medium height dressed in a dark serge suit and white gloves entered the room. Kati guessed his age to be about fifty. His dishwater blonde hair was turning gray at the temples and the forced smile on his lips made Kati feel ill at ease.

"Kati darling, meet Walter Friedmann. Walter helps me out when I have dinner guests. Otherwise he stays at San Remo."

"*Küss die Hand, Katika.* I kiss your hand, Miss Kati," Walter nodded politely, the fake smile never leaving his face. He eyed Kati with suspicion. His small, well-trimmed mustache was barely visible, and his pale blue eyes were perpetually squinting. He stood behind Aunt Sári's chair, at a loss about what to do next.

"Good evening," Kati nodded, but before she could say anything else, Walter was gone. Kati wondered about the third setting on the table. It couldn't be for this Walter, or could it?

Suddenly, Kati's thoughts turned to László, the man Miklós mentioned on their way from the airport. Miklós said that he was Aunt Sári's favorite and a relative to boot. Was he the other guest?

Walter soon returned with a large soup terrain on a silver tray, and placing it directly in front of Aunt Sári, he removed its elaborately decorated lid with measured but elegant movements. Then he left the room.

The third setting was obviously not for him! Kati felt like kicking herself for being so naive. Walter was obviously a servant.

The fragrant aroma of *húsleves*, beef bouillon, filled the air and Kati felt a sudden pang of hunger. She had learned from *Anyuka* that it was inappropriate to serve soup with an evening meal, but Kati was glad of it now. Evidently, Aunt Juli must have felt that both women needed the strength one usually derives from such soups, especially the way she prepared it. The unusually strong beef flavor, the small, delicate carrots, with long thin noodles floated appetizingly in the golden liquid.

"Help yourself, Kati darling," Aunt Sári said with forced cheerfulness. She took two ladles of soup, and did not begin eating until Kati also helped herself.

"You're probably wondering about Walter," Aunt Sári said between spoonfuls of soup. "He has been with me for years. He tells everyone that his father was a general in the German armed forces, the Wehrmacht, and was later forced to earn a living way below his social standing. But everyone knows that his father was a corporal, and that he comes from a long line of butchers. Yet, people pretend to believe him. Why not, if that makes him happy? He's really a dependable, loyal fellow, and a great help to me."

Both women finished their soup when the chimes of the front door became audible despite the gypsy melodies coming from the living room. Miklós, dressed in a gray summer suit, entered. He was carrying a black leather medical bag. Kati looked up in surprise and found it hard to hide her disappointment.

But Aunt Sári welcomed him with a sigh of relief, and her gaiety seemed more genuine than before.

"I'm sorry I'm late, Sárika, but something always comes up at the office. You know how it is." He glanced at Kati, mockery in his eyes. "You look better with your hair down, little girl. That sophisticated hairdo doesn't suit you at all."

Kati was appalled. How dare he say something like that?

Then Miklós turned to Aunt Sári. "But, you Sárika, you look absolutely ravishing, as always." He looked fondly at the older woman, although his customary cynical look did not leave his face.

To Kati's astonishment, something entirely unexpected happened. Aunt Sári stood up from the table and left the room through a small door in the far corner. Miklós followed, murmuring "excuse us for a minute," under his breath, as he glanced in Kati's direction.

Finding herself alone in the dining room she sat up straight, dumbfounded. She covered her face with her hands, putting her elbows on the table, a position *Anyuka* had forbidden her as a child. She may even have to face Walter again, she thought in panic. His sinister grin and colorless complexion made her feel insecure.

She sat motionless in the comfortable dining room chair, shivers running down her spine. Why did those two leave? Thoughts of mystery and intrigue ran through her mind, although she tried to dismiss them. "This cannot be happening to me," she told herself, as she recalled her ordinary life in Cleveland.

It took Kati a while to recover after Aunt Sári and Miklós returned. She was astounded that neither showed signs of embarrassment, and neither felt that Kati needed an explanation. Both acted as if nothing out of the ordinary had occurred. Aunt Sári returned to her place at the head of the table, and Miklós sat down across the table from Kati. Nonchalantly, he helped himself to the soup and made several enthusiastic remarks about Aunt Juli's cooking.

Walter entered again with an even larger and more elaborate silver tray, balanced carefully in his gloved hands. He placed several covered dishes with a large selection of the finest meats on the table.

"Please help yourselves, darlings," Aunt Sári said with the air of a good hostess. "Aunt Juli asked me what she should prepare for dinner. I told her any Hungarian dish would do. I was convinced that you would like them, Kati dear. Your mother probably cooked the same things." She touched her right eye, as if to wipe away a tear while she looked away from Kati.

"As for you, Miklós," she turned to him with a smile, "I know what *you* like."

Kati recognized dishes of *paprikás csirke*, chicken paprikash, and several varieties of grilled meat on the large tray, even *Wiener Schnitzel.* The customary garnishings of potatoes with parsley, *nokedli* or dumplings, and fresh cucumber salad with sour cream dressing sprinkled with red paprika completed the main course.

Despite the familiar aroma of the entrées being served, Kati's hunger had disappeared and only Aunt Sári's frequent prodding to help herself made her taste at least some of the dishes. She took a small helping of chicken paprikash and dumplings, and with blurry thoughts running through her head, she ate in silence.

Walter appeared again carrying a silver tray with several bottles of wine. Kati recognized a bottle of *Bordatello*, one of her favorite white wines. There was also a bottle of *Egri Bikavér* or *Bull's Blood*, a famous Hungarian red wine, and several French and Italian quality wines, whose names Kati did not recognize.

"I'll take some of that *Bordatello*," Kati said as Walter poured each of them their preference.

"To all of us," Aunt Sári raised her glass. "And welcome Kati darling, into our midst." Kati emptied half of her glass. It took several minutes before she began to feel more relaxed.

Meanwhile, Aunt Sári and Miklós took generous helpings from each dish and ate with great gusto. They talked about everyday topics such as the perfect weather and some of the guests who were expected at the reunion. Their names were completely unfamiliar to Kati, but when the name of László was mentioned, she looked up with interest. Although both acted as if nothing unusual had happened, and they made every effort to include Kati in the conversation, she felt a complete outsider, a fifth wheel.

What am I doing here, and what do I have in common with these two? Kati wondered as she listened to their conversation.

"You know, Miklós, our friend Sergio Lucca, wants to bring his new love, Bernadette to the reunion."

"You don't say?" Miklós asked with a sneer.

Aunt Sári turned to Kati. "Sergio is one of the wealthiest industrialists in this region. He has recently divorced his third wife, Maria. The couple had been good friends of mine," Aunt Sári explained as she shook her head. "There was an ugly scandal preceding their break-up."

"Really?" Kati asked, wide-eyed.

"I feel so bad about having to exclude Maria because of this nasty divorce. But then, I really don't care for this nineteen year-old starlet, either. I just hope I did the right thing..." Aunt Sári said. Kati detected remorse in her voice.

"You did," Miklós assured her. "You know how divorced wives are." Kati noted disdain in his voice.

In the meantime, ever since their return to the room, Walter had been silently standing behind Aunt Sári's chair, watching her every move, eager for instruction. But no one paid attention to him. Kati glanced up at him and noted the growing apprehension in his pale eyes. His expression turned more grim with every passing minute.

Suddenly she felt sorry for the man. So what if his father was a corporal? He seemed to be a decent enough man, working for a living. More than before, she understood his discomfort in the company of the idle rich, who appeared to have not a care in the world, and did strange and unexpected things they did not even bother to explain. For a moment she felt closer to him than to her aunt.

She was relieved when Aunt Sári and Miklós finally finished their meal and Walter left the room. He soon returned with one of Aunt Juli's famous desserts, a creamy chocolate rum cake.

Kati did not care for sweets, but now, just to have something to do, she helped herself to a thin slice.

"But Miklós darling, you know quite well that I don't travel anymore," she heard her aunt's voice. "I just don't feel up to it. Please go anyway... You need to get away too."

Kati was even more puzzled, wondering about these two. There was definitely something going on between them. One moment it seemed like a strong sexual attraction, while the next minute their relationship seemed Platonic, and much deeper, on a completely different level. At times, Aunt Sári's solicitous attention seemed more like that of a mother, concerned about the affairs of her grown son.

Aunt Sári suggested taking their coffee outside on the wide terrace, accessible through the French doors in the drawing room. Kati stood up and followed her aunt who had taken Miklós by the arm. Walter soon appeared with another tray stacked with a silver coffee pot, matching sugar bowl and creamer, and three small cups and saucers of exquisite Herend porcelain. Later, he placed a tray of beverages on a serving cart, including an unopened bottle of Napoleon brandy.

"László called this evening. He won't be arriving until tomorrow afternoon. He was held up by some unexpected events," Miklós began the conversation, taking a long penetrating look at Kati as they settled into the easy chairs on the terrace. He had hardly glanced in her direction since the incident on the stairs. His intense blue eyes glowed in the half-shadow of the evening as he glanced from one woman to the other. Kati wondered about the strange and distant look in his eyes.

"Yes, I know. He called me too. He was very upset by the reviews of the *London Times* and the *Frankfurter Allgemeine*. He thought both reviews quite unfair. But at least the article in *Time*...

László again, Kati thought. He must be the same László they mentioned before, the one Miklós talked about. He certainly appeared to be someone special, one of Aunt Sári's favorites.

Walter was standing in the dark shadow of the terrace, listening to their every word. When there was a pause, nothing but the soft tunes of the gypsy violin coming from the stereo inside were audible. Overwhelmed by the peace and calm of the evening, Kati felt as if all her troubles had faded into the night. Even Miklós failed to bother her anymore. She hoped and prayed that he would not try to make passes at her again, and that there would soon be an explanation for their mysterious disappearance during dinner.

Miklós gulped down his cup of *cappuccino* and stood up.

"I'll have to be going now, Sárika, dear." Kati heard his voice, surprised that his tone no longer had his customary derisive edge.

"We'll see you tomorrow then, Miklós darling," Aunt Sári answered.

"Good night, ladies." He bent down toward Aunt Sári and kissed her on both cheeks as he held her hands. Then he lifted her right hand to his lips with a well-rehearsed movement, revealing he was very much at home practicing this age-old custom that had its roots in centuries past when Hungary was part of the Habsburg Monarchy.

His expression changed as he shook hands with Kati. He looked her straight in the eye as if to say, "I'll get you yet, you little fortune hunter." It alarmed Kati to no end.

She watched his tall, impeccably dressed figure disappear in the dark. For the second time that day she was relieved that he was gone. She yearned to be alone with Aunt Sári, and wondered what had happened to the "cozy dinner" her aunt had promised. Who was Miklós to intrude upon them?

Aunt Sári rang the silver bell that Walter had left on the tray. It seemed strange to Kati that when the poor fellow was there, she ignored him completely, but once he was gone, she wanted something from him immediately.

"Pour me some *aqua minerale*," Aunt Sári said in a commanding tone when Walter appeared in front of her, waiting.

By this time he looked even more haggard and his resentment was more obvious. Now that Miklós had left, he probably would have liked to join their company, Kati thought. But Aunt Sári ignored him and smiled in disdain when he remarked with forced enthusiasm, "I must say, this was indeed a classic dinner."

A classic dinner? Kati had no idea what he meant. She sensed that Walter had finally realized that he was not to be included in their conversation, that his company was not wanted.

"Leave us alone," Aunt Sári soon motioned for him to leave as she leaned back in her chair. It was clear that she had no desire to retire for the night.

Kati sat still, and looked at her aunt with questioning eyes.

4

Meeting László

Villa Tokay, San Bartolomeo al Mare

"Let's stay out here a little longer, Kati darling. I love the peace and quiet of the evening. The tourists are gone and the neighboring bars and cafés are silent." Aunt Sári settled back in her chair and lit a cigarette. Kati watched her graceful fingers as she reached for the silver cigarette-case and stuck a Chesterfield into her gold cigarette-holder.

"It really upsets me to have to listen to that loud music. I prefer the soothing tunes of a gypsy orchestra and of course, the fiery *csárdás.*" She glanced toward the Mediterranean, a look of melancholy in her eyes.

"But then, this place was almost completely vacant, surrounded by palm trees and orchards when we first built this villa," she explained. Kati looked forward to finding out more about her aunt. She wondered what she meant by "we." She had no idea whether her aunt had ever married, nor whether she had any children.

"I know so little about you, Aunt Sári," Kati remarked quietly.

Aunt Sári took a long puff from her cigarette, blew a few smoke rings, and continued with a bitter smile. "I know. How would you? Your mother..." She shook her head and sighed deeply.

"I feel so bad that there wasn't much of a relationship between your mother and me," Aunt Sári remarked, her eyes becoming moist. She waved her right hand as if to dismiss the topic. "But let's not start on that right now. First, I'll tell you about my life. You see, I was living in Rome when I married Rodolfo. I was only twenty-one." Kati's eyes widened as she prepared to listen.

"I believed him when he promised to help with my acting career. But I found out later that he had no such intentions. All he wanted was a beautiful, radiant wife whom he could show off to his friends. And he did have many friends, influential and wealthy businessmen, politicians, industrialists, many titled aristocrats. I remember how delighted he was when he found out I was a countess from an old aristocratic family. He was a man of great ambition. We had an endless number of guests, and gave lavish parties and intimate dinners. We were living in Rome then, but often traveled to Sicily where we spent the time in our villa in Monreale, near Palermo. Many people came to see us. So many different kinds of people..." She sighed again and looked straight ahead.

Oh yes, Kati remembered. She didn't pay much attention to Miklós and Gino when they referred to her as the "*Contessa.*" Of course, *Anyuka* had been a countess too, but her parents never talked about it. And, anyway, in America, it didn't matter. They were immigrants, trying to make it in a totally alien world, without friends and connections, and most importantly, without money.

"Some of the men were suspicious-looking Sicilians," Aunt Sári took another puff as she continued. "They often came in the dark of the night and requested to see Rodolfo right away. I was too young and inexperienced to have the slightest suspicion. I trusted Rodolfo to the hilt. I also loved him, in my own way," she added, as if trying to convince her niece that she had married for love.

"Rodolfo kept promising that he would get me a part in a movie with one of the well-known directors in Rome. 'It just takes time,' he said." Aunt Sári's voice broke off. She looked into the night, inhaling the aroma of her cigarette, visibly lost in thought. Then she turned toward Kati and resumed her story.

"Well, five years passed, and there was still no offer for me to do a film. Then one evening at the Monreale villa, I heard muffled conversation from the front garden. I had been up late, waiting for Rodolfo's return. I listened through our bedroom window, but the talk was in rapid Italian dialect and I couldn't make out a thing. Then I heard two shots. I grabbed my robe, screaming for Aunt Juli who was asleep in her room next to the kitchen. Together we ran out, down the front steps and found Rodolfo lying next to one of the flower beds. There were blood stains on his sports jacket, right above his heart. I screamed." Aunt Sári took a deep breath before she continued.

"There was a bullet hole in his chest, and of course, there wasn't a soul in sight. Poor Rodolfo just lay there, murmuring inaudibly. A few last words." Her eyes filled with tears and she turned away from Kati to hide her face.

"This is how I lost my *first* husband."

The emphasis on the word "first" gave Kati additional food for thought.

"After the funeral people talked about his connections to the Mafia. It was rumored that they killed him out of revenge. But I never knew for sure. No one ever told me anything. I was young, a refugee and a stranger in a foreign land, and completely alone. I had no one but Aunt Juli. We had escaped together in '56. Just like your parents." She stopped and pursed her lips as if in pain.

"A few months later I found out that Rodolfo had accumulated tremendous wealth, and left me more money than I ever dreamed of." Her voice trailed off, and the two women gazed toward the sea, seemingly unaware of each other's presence.

"Did my parents know?" Kati inquired, almost in a whisper.

"A few weeks after the funeral I tried to get in touch with Anna, your mother. Oh, I tried so many times, but she never answered my letters. She didn't write me a single line! I even flew to Cleveland for a visit, you may remember. Your were about five then. I wanted us to be close again, just like when we were small children. But my trip didn't help at all. We just had a big argument, and then I was never to see her again."

Tears streamed down her cheeks, but this time she made no effort to hide them. She stood up slowly and walked to the far end of the terrace. Her slender figure was all but completely hidden from Kati by two large planters containing philodendron and luscious exotic palms.

"For some reason your mother never liked me," Kati heard her aunt's muffled voice coming from a distance. "For some reason, ever since we became teenagers," she repeated with a sigh. "Our personalities were so different."

That's probably true, Kati thought. *Anyuka* had been more down-to-earth and harbored few illusions about becoming a part of high society. Both her parents were diligent and hard-working and believed in the value of education. While Aunt Sári was much more temperamental and dreamed of becoming an actress. She even married for that reason...

"Your poor dear mother. She never liked the fact that the boys were always after me... I guess I was a flirt, while she was more withdrawn and quiet. A true introvert."

A few minutes later she emerged from behind the philodendron, with a look of pretended cheer. She sat down again.

"God rest her soul," She added almost as an afterthought.

Kati did not reply.

"Let bygones be bygones," Aunt Sári said pensively. For a moment she hesitated, and Kati knew that she had more to tell.

"Three years after Rodolfo's death I married Kálmán, Annie's father. We named our daughter after your mother." She broke off again, unable to continue. Kati noted the finality in her voice.

Kati sat stunned, fiddling with her napkin. She had no idea what to say, so she took another sip of *aqua minerale*.

"Let's go to bed now, darling. Suddenly I feel so tired. And I'm sure you must be exhausted after such a long flight. Don't forget we both have to look beautiful for Saturday evening," she added with a faint smile.

"Good night, Aunt Sári. Have a good night's sleep," Kati murmured and stood up to go. She bent down and gave her aunt a kiss on the cheek. She started to walk toward the French door, but could not help turning around to take a last look at the Mediterranean. It was completely dark and unfriendly; there were no lights from any of the boats, and Kati wondered what mysteries lurked behind the undulating waves that danced in perpetual motion, as did the waves of all oceans around the world.

I can't believe I'll be living here for a whole month, Kati thought with joyous anticipation. I never imagined that I would ever be part of luxury such as this. This must be a dream, such wealth and elegance! Yet, I feel so alone, so out of place. There are two people who seem to like me, Aunt Sári and Aunt Juli, but then, I hardly know them. And there's this Miklós. What a fresh and impertinent guy, grabbing me on the stairs. She had never heard of Hungarian men pinching girls and women. Miklós must have learned that from the Italians, she thought with a wry smile. Remembering him left a bad taste in her mouth, dampening her happy mood.

It took Kati hours to fall asleep. It wasn't only jet lag, although it was still afternoon on the other side of the Atlantic. She could have never imagined such strange events on her first day on the Riviera. She felt for Aunt Sári, who obviously had a tumultuous life, with two husbands, and maybe more. She wondered about her second husband and Annie, the cousin she had never heard about. Where were they now?

Then her thoughts turned to László, wondering who he was. Aunt Sári and Miklós mentioned him often enough. Was he a writer? Or a scholar whose books caught the attention of prestigious journals and newspapers around the world? She had great respect for writers; she had always loved to read. Reading serious books was a habit she had acquired from *Apuka*, she recalled fondly. They had spent many evenings discussing a book or a serious novel, and sometimes had heated arguments about the ideas the authors presented.

She found Miklós's sarcastic remarks about László puzzling. Was there envy or jealousy involved, she wondered. She recalled how Aunt Sári's eyes lit up when his name was mentioned. It made Kati even more curious, more anxious to meet him.

She thought about Michael and wondered what he was doing. Was he still angry with her for taking this trip? It was already two in the morning and she still lay awake. Her thoughts wandered about from Michael to this unknown László, like a pirate ship roaming the high seas. The more her thoughts dwelled on László the more ridiculous she felt. After all, she was engaged. Why was she so curious about a man she had only heard about? Could he have been the man at the airport? Finally she dozed off, with a vague image of László in her mind, the image of a debonair, intelligent, and intriguing fellow, someone she would love to meet. And the sooner the better.

*   *   *

The next morning when she opened her eyes Kati felt completely rested. I've never slept this late in my whole life, she thought to herself as she glanced at her watch. It was almost 12 o'clock noon.

After drawing the blinds she stepped outside on the terrace, and took a deep breath of the fresh salty air. Despite the noonday sun, it felt cool and refreshing. On her right lay the soft curve of the bay at Diano Marina. Palm trees, numerous orchards and olive trees, along with a multitude of condominiums and hotels, were clearly visible on the shore. Quaint villas lay tucked away on the mountain side, often accessible only by steep, narrowly winding roads. The sea was as calm as the night before, but seemed much friendlier. Its glittering expanse spread before her endlessly; its smooth surface changing color from blue-green to slate gray, then to a dark gray on the horizon. Its mirror-like, glossy surface was broken only by a few white sailboats and some colorfully dressed surfers who swayed gracefully in the gentle breeze.

Glancing to her left, she noted a great deal of activity at the *Hotel Stella Maris* next door, and at the long row of cafés, bars and restaurants that stretched out on the shore, in the direction of Cervo. She couldn't see the village with its tall church steeples from where she stood, but as they were leaving the *autostrada* the day before, she had made a mental note of wanting to visit there during her stay.

Her eyes swept the crowds of people in light summer clothes, wearing sunglasses and a variety of exotic hats, sitting leisurely in the comfortable chairs in the outdoor cafés, sipping a drink or enjoying a dish of Italian ice cream, *gelato*. A few bathers could be seen in all directions on the sandy beaches and on the corridors of huge rocks that stuck out from the sea. The wide quay, the *Passagiata al Mare* was crowded with tourists walking back and forth aimlessly, and like Kati, they seemed to be taking in the captivating holiday atmosphere.

After slipping into a light blue sun dress, Kati ran downstairs, eagerly awaiting the events of the day. Miklós's aggressive behavior, Aunt Sári's mysterious departure from last night's dinner and the story she told on the terrace seemed remote now, as if all the unpleasant episodes of yesterday had occurred many months, even years ago.

She wondered what Aunt Sári was doing now, whether she had slept as late as she. She recalled how emotional her aunt had become when she related stories of her turbulent life. But Kati dismissed unpleasant thoughts and concentrated on the reunion and the guests who were to arrive that day. Life seemed too exciting and full of promise on this sunny day on the beautiful Italian Riviera. Her Riviera holiday was just beginning.

She had breakfast in the dining area that adjoined the kitchen. The tray Aunt Juli had prepared for her had orange juice, crisp Italian *panini*, butter, jam and cheese, all of which she ate with a healthy appetite, remembering that she had hardly eaten the night before.

She was about ready to pour herself some freshly brewed coffee when she noticed a piece of paper tucked under the silver coffee pot. The note was scrawled in Hungarian, in a barely legible handwriting.

"Katika, little Kati, Your breakfast is on the tray. Had to go shopping before stores close at 12:30. Your Aunt Sári is still resting. Love, Aunt Juli."

Aunt Sári was always resting, both Aunt Juli and Gino kept reminding her. She thought about how her aunt had looked last night, recalling no signs of illness on her youthful face. It was only later that she seemed anxious, especially before Miklós arrived. And later, when she was telling Kati about her past, she looked so distressed and sad, although she probably cried because of the tragedies she had endured.

Kati thought of Michael. He is probably still asleep, or maybe tossing and turning in his bed, worrying about his fiancée. Yesterday she had thought that maybe he was right for opposing her trip. But today, as she inhaled the inviting aroma of freshly brewed coffee and took in the sights and sounds of the beautiful Italian Riviera, she felt different. Was he still upset with her for taking this trip? Suddenly, she felt apprehensive as she recalled his anger at her decision to visit her aunt. He has no right; he's too possessive, she thought. Since her parents' auto accident she had to fend for herself and made her own decisions. She hated to answer to anyone for her actions. At least not yet, not until they were married.

Her mind soon drifted toward the reunion. She'll meet some interesting people, that's for sure. Who will they be? Will there be someone closer to her own age? Maybe this intriguing, mysterious guy, László will be there. László again! Stop this nonsense, she told herself, you haven't even met him and have no idea what he's like. And after all, she reprimanded herself, Kati Mátrai, don't forget, you're engaged to be married.

She returned to her room after breakfast. Last night on the writing desk, she had noticed some postcards of San Bartolomeo and the two neighboring villages, Diano Marina and Cervo. She wanted to send a few postcards to her friends and co-workers back home, to let them know she had arrived safely. Then she remembered Uncle Tibor. She couldn't write to him any more; he was gone like *Anyuka* and *Apuka*. No negative thoughts, she told herself. Enjoy this beautiful place as long as you can.

She wrote a few cards, the first one to Michael, promising that she would write him a long letter soon. Kriszta was next on her list. She felt close to her old friend, although their lifestyles became very different since Kriszta's marriage to her childhood sweetheart. While in high school, they had often talked about their dream of a happy and satisfying life, and it seemed that Kriszta had already found it. Would Kati find happiness with Michael?

The truth was, ever since she had arrived, she had not given him that much thought. She was ashamed to admit it, but at times, it was almost as if he didn't exist. No doubt he was a nice fellow, but rather ordinary, lacking the least bit of imagination. Sometimes she even felt sorry for him because of his unconditional love, and she tried hard to return it. Yet, down deep she had doubts about the life he offered. The sense of excitement had disappeared from their relationship, although his patience and devotion assured Kati that he would be there for her always -- no matter what happened.

"You heard us mention László before," Aunt Sári continued the introduction. Then she turned toward László, the dazzling smile never leaving her face. "And this is my beautiful niece from America, Katalin Mátrai. You'll soon find that she is much more than pretty."

Kati blushed. She felt embarrassed by her aunt's words. She never knew how to react to compliments that were made directly to her face.

"Oh, really?" For a moment, László looked at her with interest.

"*Kezét csókolom,* I kiss your hand," he said in a formal tone that startled Kati.

Then, as she extended her hand for a handshake, he bent down with old-world gallantry and kissed it. The touch of his lips on her fingers sent pleasant shivers through her whole body. As he looked up she noticed his eyes, their color enhanced by the green of his silk tie. His manner was that of a man of the world coupled with a friendly demeanor that Kati found truly appealing. Puzzled, he looked at her closely, seemingly lost in thought.

"Didn't we just pass each other on the quay a few minutes ago?" He asked, smiling broadly.

"Yes, we did," Kati replied and blushed again. I guess I didn't make much of an impression on him, if he's not sure...

"You looked like you were in a great hurry..." She turned away, embarrassed.

"Well, no, not really. It's just that so many things were running through my mind. But I'm always happy to meet new people, especially beautiful girls and women." He smiled mischievously.

"Of course, I had no idea that the girl in blue happened to be your niece from America," he smiled again as he turned to Aunt Sári, displaying strong white teeth.

For a moment all three were at a loss for words. There was an uncomfortable silence in the room.

"I'm sorry to interrupt," Kati apologized, breaking the silence. She turned toward the stairway, and started to go up to her room.

"Oh, darling, don't go yet. Stay here and chat with us." Aunt Sári's words were cordial enough.

"Oh, please, don't go," László reassured her politely, avoiding her gaze. But Kati sensed that they had been engrossed in a deep discussion because they soon resumed the conversation about László's latest book. It must have created a stir in international circles, Kati concluded. But she found it hard to join the conversation.

She decided to stroll around the room to examine the photos, the statues, and artifacts in the display cases, sipping a glass of tonic her aunt had offered. She was still in shock about meeting László so unexpectedly. But we have nothing in common, nothing to talk about, she thought sadly. Face it, Kati, you don't belong here! For the second time since her arrival she felt out of place. It was hot and her hands began to perspire as she tried to calm herself by concentrating on the cool ice in her glass. She was about to excuse herself again, when she noticed that László and Aunt Sári had settled down on the sofa.

László's voice brought her back from her reverie.

"Maybe you're familiar with some of my books," he said in a loud voice, directing his comment toward Kati. There was a hint of sarcasm in his voice. "Or do only specialists and scholars read serious books in America?" He crossed his legs, spread his arms wide, and leaned far back on the sofa. His green eyes narrowed, and he didn't look directly at Kati.

"I heard almost everyone in America watches television day and night, and those who do read are only interested in books on crime, sex, and violence. And of course, books on business," he paused for a moment. "Oh yes, and they also love to read, how do you say, those 'how-to' books," he added.

Kati felt anger rising inside. László probably had never been to America. Or, if he had, like so many Europeans, he was prejudiced against Americans and drew his conclusions from Hollywood movies and short trips that only revealed American society's superficial side.

"That's not true at all. There are Americans who read and write serious books, on intellectual topics. You're thinking of the average person. They're the same everywhere." She added with a hint of scorn in her voice, "Even in Europe."

László seemed taken aback by her tone. He shifted his position on the sofa while Kati sat down in a comfortable chair close by. He looked at her with interest .

Suddenly, Kati remembered a college course that she had long forgotten.

"You may be interested in knowing that we used one of your books in an Economics class at the university," she said, recalling the name of László von Temessy as the author of a book on the reading list. At the time she never thought that she would ever meet him, nor did she have any desire to. Her image of authors of scholarly texts was that of old, scrawny-looking men wearing horn-rimmed glasses, who lived in an ivory tower, far removed from the real world.

"I'm happy to hear that," László smiled complacently, pleased with the news.

He apparently thinks a great deal of himself, Kati thought. Then his expression became serious, as he raised his eyebrows and shook his head. Kati sensed that something was bothering him.

"You know, I think young people today need to be better informed. They really should broaden their knowledge of the world. Especially today's American youth."

"Why, do you think Europeans are better informed?" Kati asked.

"Well... Yes, I do. I think Americans are completely unaware of the dangers of totalitarianism." László replied, frowning. He added derisively, "They are too caught up in today's world of materialism and self-gratification."

"And European young people aren't? I'm not so sure," Kati interjected, coming to the defense of "today's American youth."

"Materialism is a sign of our modern world," she retorted, "Moral and spiritual matters are not of much interest to anyone, no matter where they live."

László seemed intrigued by her reply, and Kati sensed that he wanted to continue the discussion.

But Aunt Sári looked bored. "All right, you two, you can continue your serious discussion some other time," she told them. "We have to think of the reunion tomorrow." She turned to Kati.

"László will drive you to my place in San Remo on Saturday evening. I'll be going there today with Aunt Juli and Walter. I have to supervise the preparations, you know." She turned to László. "You'll pick up Kati at seven, won't you?" Her question sounded more like a command.

"I'll be happy to oblige," László answered, but his tone failed to reveal whether or not he was pleased with the assignment.

"Kati darling," Aunt Sári faced Kati again, "don't forget to bring enough clothes. We'll be spending several days in San Remo. And from now on, take your meals at the hotel. Aunt Juli will not be here to feed you. You'll be all by yourself in the villa tomorrow. We all have to get things ready. Walter and Gino too. I'm sure you understand. I'm really sorry about not having time for you now, but we'll have plenty of time together later. We still have a month to ourselves."

Aunt Sári went on with her instructions and explanations, but finally turned to László again. Her eyes had a special gleam and it seemed to Kati that she had some more important things to discuss with him.

Kati excused herself and started to walk toward the staircase. This time they didn't protest; neither Aunt Sári nor László seemed to mind her departure as she took a last look at the two sitting cozily on the sofa.

Once in her room Kati stepped out on the terrace and took a deep breath of the salty air. She tried to calm her excitement by gazing toward the sea, losing herself in its vastness. No man she had ever met had such an effect on her before. Not even Michael who now seemed worlds away. She shut her eyes, and it was László's green eyes shaded by dark lashes that popped into her mind. She thought of the words they had exchanged, of the topics they had discussed. She should have asked him whether he had been at the Genoa airport yesterday. But then there had been no opportunity for that at all.

As she lay awake on her bed that night after a dinner of *Pizza Margherita*, delicious Italian fruit *torta,* and a bottle of coke, she thought of how Aunt Sári handled men. She manipulated them well. And it seemed that both Miklós and László simply adored her. They may be even in love with her, despite her age, she speculated.

The image of László was constantly in her mind. He wasn't really that old; she guessed him to be in his mid to late thirties. He looked about the same age as Miklós, but appeared to be quite a different type, cool and aloof, a bookish man. He also seemed self-assured, confident and... and... arrogant, Kati hated to admit. In that he was like Miklós. But he was more serious and restrained. He had barely glanced at Kati, not like Miklós who eyed her sheepishly from the first moment they met.

László seemed to live in a world of his own where thoughts and ideas prevailed. How could he feel at home in the world of the idle rich, Kati wondered. But maybe he was wealthy too. At first glance, he didn't seem to have much in common with them, yet there was an unmistakable air of worldliness about him. So unusual in an intellectual! He certainly didn't fit her image of some one who writes serious books. She had always imagined scholars to be mousy-looking men with hazy, faraway expressions and pale complexions, who wore baggy pants and dark-rimmed glasses.

She wondered where László would be staying the following two nights. Probably in San Remo, she reasoned, and he'll probably be having a great time with Aunt Sári and maybe some Italian women. Miklós did mention that many *signorinas* were out to catch him. Even that thought bothered her, and she was startled by the jealousy swelling in her heart.

And I am stuck here, she thought, almost resenting the place. She didn't really feel like spending tomorrow here, all alone. Then she heard a voice inside. What did she expect, anyway? Just a few days ago she was back in Cleveland, without any prospects for any kind of excitement. And now she was to spend a month in this beautiful place. She began to look forward to the reunion and a few days of thrilling events, meeting interesting and glamorous people, the jet-set. She had only a vague idea about who they were, but she imagined them to be rich and powerful, with that special look of accomplishment in their eyes. Miklós had mentioned that there will be over two hundred guests, and an orchestra had been invited from Budapest. The buffet dinner will be followed by dancing, he said. And Kati loved to dance. She soon fell asleep and dreamed that she was in László's arms, dancing to one of the popular romantic tunes.

The hours passed slowly on Friday. In the morning she took a swim in the indoor pool, and lay out in the sun for a while. After lunch she went for a leisurely stroll on the quay. She walked as far as the remains of the old bastion, almost to where she had seen László yesterday. A strange feeling of melancholy overtook her; she seemed to have lost her bearings. She felt lonely and alone, despite the lively crowd on the *Passagiata al Mare*.

What am I expecting from all this? She asked herself. A man like László would never give me a second thought. Compared to his world of success and glamour, mine is made up of ordinary people, working for a living, and battling the problems of everyday existence.

But by early afternoon her despondent mood changed. Her natural optimism took the better of her. Her feeling of anticipation returned, and she looked forward to Saturday evening. It felt almost like old times in Cleveland when she was a young girl, filled with excitement before one of the balls, sponsored by the Society of Hungarian Veterans or the Hungarian Scouts Association. She fondly recalled the flurry of activity that preceded each ball, the frantic shopping for that perfect gown, sitting for hours at the hairdresser's, wondering whether that special young man would be there. Life had been so pleasant then, so full of promise.

But I have nothing to worry about now, either, she cheered herself, and was glad she had packed her floor-length evening gown with the low scoop neck that had been one of her favorites. There were small bouquets of violets with green leaves woven into the white silk and a deep purple sash to match. Despite its girlish style, it made her feel elegant and sophisticated, at least in Cleveland.

She laid the gown and a pair of white silk pumps on one of the *fauteuils* in the corner of her room and prepared to go to sleep for the night.

5

Ball in San Remo

San Remo

Saturday evening, promptly at seven, Kati stood in the entrance hall, fully dressed and waiting for László. She turned left and right as she looked at herself in the cut-glass mirror. For once, she liked what she saw. She never really thought of herself as pretty, and envied girls who were born natural beauties. She always had to work on her looks, to make the best of her features. As she recalled Aunt Sári's words of introduction to László, "my beautiful niece from America," she felt warm inside.

The sound of the chimes at the front entrance brought her back to the present. She opened the door, her heart throbbing with excitement. László stood in the doorway, dressed in a blue-black tuxedo and a gleaming white shirt with dainty ruffles in the front. Overwhelmed by his presence, Kati felt ill at ease and could barely utter a word of greeting. As *Anyuka* used to say, the cat stole her tongue.

"I hope I'm on time," László broke the embarrassing silence. He stepped inside, bowed deeply, and reached for Kati's white gloved hand for a hand kiss. He looked her straight in the eye. The obvious admiration in his eyes caught Kati off guard.

"You look absolutely ravishing this evening," he observed. "Your aunt was right," he added sheepishly. This was the first time he had looked at her closely. Although such scrutiny by men always embarrassed her, his unexpected compliment made Kati feel more relaxed and comfortable. Her eyes shone with anticipation.

László led her to his red Porsche 944 and opened the front door with a gallant sweep of his left arm. She settled into the bucket seat, carefully gathering the folds of her gown. They soon entered the *autostrada*, and while Kati admired the countryside, László looked straight ahead and kept his eyes on the road.

It was a pleasant trip. They discussed life in Italy and Europe comparing it to life in America. This time László made no degrading remarks, and Kati felt relieved. Tonight he seemed less serious and reserved. Maybe he decided to leave his work behind, Kati thought, and she hoped that it would be so for the whole evening. He seemed more agreeable and pleasant, although when the conversation turned to Hungary, Kati detected deep apprehension in his voice.

"Don't tell me you've been visiting Hungary. And your parents too. I can't believe it. After all what they had done to your family. You've heard of Recsk, the forced labor camp where your great uncle spent five years of misery, haven't you?" His eyes flashed and he looked at Kati as if to reprimand her.

"Recsk?" Kati repeated. Miklós had also mentioned Recsk.

"Yes, I've heard something from *Apuka* about a place called Recsk. He said it was a terrible place, a work camp for those who opposed the communist regime. But I never bothered to find out more."

"Well, you should." He sounded adamant.

"I'll make it a point to read about it," Kati replied in a light tone. She was taken aback by László's harsh tone.

"You won't find much literature about it, I can tell you that. You'll have to talk to people who were interned there and had to endure the horrors of that camp. People refer to it as the 'Hungarian Gulag.'" László's voice was filled with anger.

"Oh, please, don't talk about suffering, pain, and deprivation," Kati begged. "Not when we're on our way to a fabulous ball on the enchanting Italian Riviera."

"I guess you're right," László forced a smile. "Let's just forget our native land for tonight. At least the bad parts."

"There's nothing we can do about what's going on in Hungary," Kati observed solemnly.

They were traveling on a winding narrow road, driving toward the city and the sea, passing fashionable villas on the way. Not all were visible from the road; most were enclosed by high wrought iron fences with trees and shrubbery inside, to keep out inquisitive eyes. They reached the lower part of the incline when László stopped in front of the highest gate Kati had ever seen. A pleasant, well-tanned young Italian in uniform opened it, welcoming them with a salute. He motioned them to pass.

Kati's eyes opened wide. Although she was growing accustomed to Aunt Sári's luxurious lifestyle, she had never dreamed of anything like this. She never expected to be a guest at a palazzo. Aunt Sári's "San Remo Place" was truly a palatial structure, a residence fit for royalty.

A wide paved road led to the huge, impressive building, made almost entirely of white marble. The road was flanked by palm trees and perfectly kept flower beds were planted with a profusion of red geraniums and white petunias. There were rose bushes close to the fence on all sides. A large circular flower bed with red and white roses graced the area right in front of the building. As Kati remembered the garden at the Villa Tokay in San Bartolomeo, she noted several similarities between the two, although this one was much larger, and its opulence more pronounced.

Several automobiles were already parked in the large area to the right of the building. Most were luxury cars, Mercedes's,

BMW's, Porsche's and several Rolls Royce's. Kati noticed Miklós's gold Mercedes among them.

László pulled up next to a white BMW four-door sedan. It's not such a big car at all, Kati thought, as her parents' one-time plan to purchase a BMW flashed through her mind. But they had given up on it, for such foreign cars were beyond their means. Here, everyone drove luxury cars, she reflected, as she watched László walk up to her side. He opened the door and as she stepped outside, she tried to conceal her astonishment behind a cheerful smile.

László led her toward the wide marble steps, offering his arm for support. Kati tried to look nonchalant as she surveyed the palazzo, trying to look as if she were accustomed to entering such a magnificent place.

She had never seen anything so dazzling, not even in the movies. There were four high ornate columns that supported the portico, while a wrought iron handrail enclosed the terrace above. That was the main entrance. Tall windows opened up to private balconies on each of the three floors on both sides. On reaching the landing of the marble steps, Kati noted that the main entrance consisted of a large double door with cut crystal windows and two smaller doors in similar style. Two giant planters with perfectly manicured shrubs stood on each side, enhancing the extraordinary elegance of the building.

After passing through the main entrance guarded by two doormen, they took the red-carpeted flight of stairs that led to the central hall. Ornate columns of reddish beige marble supported an unusually high ceiling decorated with colorful frescoes. The marble of the floor matched those of the columns, and Kati noticed several oil paintings in large gold frames on the walls covered with exquisite silk wallpaper of deep beige.

At the entry to the ballroom that opened directly from the entrance hall, Kati saw Aunt Sári standing outside the French doors, with Miklós at her side. Miklós again, Kati thought in alarm as she remembered the incident on the stairs. Why is he always at her side?

"My little Kati, darling," Kati heard her aunt's voice, barely audible above the sound of conversation and the vibrant tunes of the gypsy orchestra. There were several guests inside, standing around in groups, sipping champagne that the liveried stewards offered on silver trays.

"*Katikám*, László, welcome to the reunion," Aunt Sári called to them with great enthusiasm. All traces of tension were gone from her face, and tonight she seemed especially beautiful in her bright green full-length gown with a low décolleté. Probably a Gucci, Kati thought.

"Please stay here with me, Kati darling. Help me greet our guests," she said with a welcoming smile. She motioned to Kati who was more than happy to oblige, although she looked wistfully after László who had quietly disappeared from her side. She was just beginning to feel comfortable and at ease in his company.

"This is my beautiful niece from America, Katalin Mátrai," her aunt's words of introduction seemed as endless as the line of guests they had to greet. With a smile permanently glued to her face, Kati dutifully shook hands with everyone and tried her best to appear friendly, radiant, and hospitable.

The guests were an international set. Although the majority were native Italians and Hungarians who lived in various western countries, there were several Germans, Austrians, and even a few Spaniards. Most were men and women of position and wealth: politicians, industrialists, and some highly successful physicians and military men, along with members of the aristocracy, counts and barons. Kati noted that even those who were less accomplished put on such airs that it was difficult to distinguish them from the rest. They were all elegantly dressed and Kati saw that the women were unusually attractive, well-rested, and put on a glamorous air.

She couldn't say that about the men. Most were wiry little fellows, some of them bald with an unattractive face, while others were fat with huge protruding bellies. So far, she had met only a few distinguished-looking gentlemen, regardless of age. Men of position and wealth did not need good looks to attract beautiful women. It would be a great misfortune, Kati mused, if the daughters of these men resembled their fathers instead of their stunning mothers.

Although she made a special effort to remember the names of the guests, making a mental note of their identities, Kati gave up after a while. Later, she could recall only those who attracted attention by their strange looks, unique behavior, or something odd that they said.

"I am Marquis Angel Yordanos," she heard a short, middle-aged man explain loudly. He wore a white military uniform with gold braids and buttons. A long shiny sword was dangling at his side, and he sported numerous fancy decorations on his chest.

Aunt Sári hardly had time to whisper to Kati that he was Spanish royalty when she heard Yordanos again. "It's *passé* for us aristocrats. I say, *passé*." His bearing made Kati wince, and she was glad that "it was *passé*" for such men. She hated conceited, high-handed people, and Marquis Yordanos seemed a perfect example of haughtiness and vanity.

An insignificant-looking, short man followed the Marquis. His tall attractive wife was at his side. He kept his eyes to the floor, as if asking pardon for his existence.

"Baron Lodi," he muttered as he raised his eyes to Kati and tried to smile. He looked so awkward and out of place that Kati felt like getting a hold of him and shaking him up a bit.

"I'll pass on, I'll pass on," he murmured under his breath, as he moved to the front of the ballroom, his wife following him like a puppy.

"Dr. von Dorog, Physician and Professor of Medicine," she heard the dauntless voice of a short, fat man whose bulging belly made him look more like a cook or a butcher. He wore a white tuxedo and the black sash around his waist was getting dangerously loose. Kati was afraid it would slide down to his knees at any moment.

"I am the Director of the Cancer Research Institute of America," he declared in a boisterous voice. Kati was taken aback for there was no research institute by that name. Anyone living in America knew that, but some Europeans seemed to have believed him, while others smiled cynically, and moved away from him as quickly as they could. But some guests hurried to meet him, thinking he was an important personage.

"Forgive my language, Kati dear, but he's a pompous ass," Aunt Sári whispered under her breath. That's all she could say, for there were other guests in line. Kati began to feel tired. The flood of guests seemed never to end.

A distinguished looking Italian couple, accompanied by a striking girl in her mid- twenties came next.

"My beautiful niece from America," Aunt Sári introduced Kati, as she had done countless times before.

"Darling, these are the Ruggieros. Count Ruggiero, his wife, Countess Elena and their daughter, Angela," Kati was impressed and felt immediately drawn to the family. The parents exuded an air of cordiality, rare among the guests she had met so far. She took a good look at Angela. Kati had never seen such perfect features in a girl. Her voluptuous, yet graceful figure, her dark eyes shaded by black lashes and her black wavy hair framing her classic features made for a stunning appearance.

"Angela is the oldest daughter in the family," Aunt Sári explained. "You two will have to get together," she smiled brightly, looking from one girl to the other.

Kati immediately noticed that Angela paid little attention to those around her. Her dark furtive eyes swept the crowd and she hardly acknowledged Kati's presence.

"Where's László?" she asked in a demanding voice, looking straight at Aunt Sári.

"I haven't seen him for a while, although he was around a half hour ago," Aunt Sári answered absentmindedly.

Kati's heart fell. Ah, Angela must be one of the *signorinas* who is out to catch László. I would never be able to complete with the likes of such Italian beauties. Never!

The Ruggieros moved on and the line of guests finally subsided. Kati was looking for an excuse to leave Aunt Sári's side, but thought better of it. The only two men she knew were not in the vicinity, and she hated walking around without an escort. Yet, she wanted to get a feel for the place. She opened her eyes wide and took a deep breath. When she saw that Aunt Sári was deeply engrossed in a conversation with a blonde man in a German military uniform, she excused herself and slipped away from her aunt's side.

She stepped inside the ballroom. The whole place was lit up by crystal chandeliers, and three buffet tables stood along the left wall. Hot and cold dishes, trays of delicious meats, a variety of cheeses, various types of salads and vegetables and an array of fruits and pastry were arranged on the snow-white linen tablecloths. Kati guessed that the main entrees had been prepared under the supervision of Aunt Juli. She and her helpers must have spent days getting ready for this special feast.

A separate, large table held an incredible variety of beverages, including the best wines of Italy and France. Kati noticed that some of the guests were already beginning to help themselves to the delicious food, and she hoped that she could soon do the same. She did not care for today's lunch of *frutti di mare* which the pushy waiter at the *Hotel Stella Maris* persuaded her to try. She never really liked seafood, except shrimp. She was famished since she had not eaten anything since lunch.

She spotted Miklós who had left Aunt Sári's side when Kati joined them, almost an hour earlier. He was standing in the front of the ballroom by the Hungarian gypsy orchestra, engaged in animated conversation with the first violinist, the *prímás*.

He's probably suggesting tunes they should play, Kati thought and recalled that he had mentioned making the arrangements for the music. The Gypsy band looked familiar, and reminded her of the musicians at the Gypsy Cellar on Buckeye Road on Cleveland's East Side. The seven Gypsy musicians were dressed in white, wide-sleeved shirts and wore red vests decorated with gold braids and buttons. Their fiery black eyes gleamed with a special light, and their engaging smile lit up their dark faces. Most were young, and Kati thought that the one who played the *cimbalom*, a special Hungarian string instrument, was especially good-looking.

She hesitated about her next step. She did not feel comfortable with any of the guests in the ballroom, and she would never seek out Miklós after the way he acted. I hope I won't have to go through that again, she told herself and shivered with fear and contempt.

She thought of László, who was at the back of her mind even during the flurry of greeting guests. Now that she had a little time to herself, she looked around, hoping to spot him in the crowd . But he was nowhere in sight, and for a moment, she even worried that he had disappeared for good. But, he would never do that to Aunt Sári, she consoled herself. Bewildered, she searched the ballroom again and decided to walk back to her aunt, who was still at the entrance door, surrounded by guests.

"*Katikám,* darling, I was looking for you. Where were you?" Aunt Sári glanced nervously toward the entrance at the top of the stairs, her dark eyes filled with anxiety, as if expecting someone.

She did not have to wait long. A moment later László appeared at the top of the white marble steps, accompanied by a tall, distinguished looking gentleman at his side. Kati judged him to be in his late sixties. Both had wide grins on their faces.

Aunt Sári's eyes lit up and she quickly excused herself. She ran to meet them.

"*Sándor bácsi,* Uncle Sándor! At last. It's absolutely marvelous that they finally gave you a visa for a visit. I worried so much."

The two embraced with such gusto that guests stopped to watch them. Uncle Sándor looked around, his eyes wide with amazement. "*Sárikám,* my darling Sári, this must be a dream, it cannot be true!" He shook his head and the furrows on his forehead deepened as he surveyed the hall.

"Oh, I'm so happy to be here. It means so much to me." He looked around furtively. "But where is my little niece, Kati? I can hardly wait to meet her. Is she here?" Uncle Sándor asked.

"Of course she's here," Aunt Sári replied and motioned to Kati who hurried to join them. Kati's questioning glance flew back and forth between Aunt Sári and the new guest.

"This is your great uncle, darling, Count Sándor Miskolczy de Baranya," Aunt Sári explained proudly.

Kati was speechless. This was a surprise indeed! She remembered her parents mentioning an Uncle Sándor, but she had not expected to see him here.

"Let me look at you, *Katika,* little Kati. You have Anna's eyes..." Uncle Sándor said. Kati felt immediately drawn to her great uncle as they hugged each other and he kissed her warmly on both cheeks.

"Don't mind me, I am an old man now." He turned to Aunt Sári, "Please forget about the 'count.' I haven't been one for almost forty years. Although, God knows, I have suffered enough for it." He smoothed his forehead, trying to forget the past. Then he took Kati's hand and eyed her closely.

"Little Kati, you remind me so much of Anna. How I wanted to see your mother once more." Fighting his tears, he made a valiant attempt to appear jubilant. "Please don't mind me," he excused himself, "I'm just a sentimental old fool from another age, a time that is no more."

His eyes moved from Kati to Aunt Sári. "But at least for now, I have both of you here," he said, glowing with happiness. He looked fondly at both women.

Uncle Sándor's aristocratic background was evident in his every move. He never lost his elegant bearing, although he had made a living doing physical labor for years.

Apuka had told Kati once, she remembered now, that they had some relatives who still lived in Hungary, an Uncle Sándor and his wife Irén. They were forced to vacate their large country home in Szabolcs County in Eastern Hungary. The communists confiscated their land and their mansion was designated as the party headquarters of their town. He was arrested and imprisoned for conspiracy and sentenced without a trial. He spent five years in a labor camp in Northern Hungary. Years later, they settled in Transdanubia where he worked on a collective farm. With time they managed to buy a small two-room apartment in Buda, his present place of residence. From there he traveled by train to the outskirts of Budapest working as a stable boy until his retirement. The communists thought he was "good with horses" anyway, so that was a perfect job to suit his talents. But Uncle Sándor remained a true *cavalier* and gentleman. He took both women gallantly by the arm as he prepared to accompany them into the ballroom.

"I hope to be your escort for the evening," Uncle Sándor's eyes twinkled mischievously as he looked at his grand niece. Then he turned to László who stood somewhat apart, watching the family reunion from a discreet distance.

"I'm just joking, of course. I'm sure there are many eager young men here tonight, waiting to enjoy your company." He looked meaningfully at László, who pursed his lips and turned away. He soon excused himself and left while Uncle Sándor escorted the two women into the ballroom.

"I can't believe that anything like this still exists in the world today. Ease, wealth, and elegance," Uncle Sándor observed, overcome by the spectacle of the ballroom, the orchestra, and the distinguished group of guests. His approving glance went everywhere.

"We used to have such balls too, but that was so many years ago," he said. For a moment his expression darkened, although he made every effort to appear in high spirits.

Aunt Sári suggested tasting the delicious food and led the way to the buffet table. After taking generous helpings of the most appealing dishes, they sat down at one of the small tables that had been set up along the opposite wall of the ballroom.

Shortly after they began their meal, a corpulent, bald man stepped up to their table. He appeared out of nowhere, bringing a wry smile to Aunt Sári's face. Kati did not remember meeting him at the entrance.

"I was hoping he wouldn't show up tonight. His name is William Fábry," her aunt murmured.

"I kiss your hand, Sárika, my respects to you, Uncle Sándor, Sir," the man exclaimed with great gusto and touched Uncle Sándor's shoulders, wanting to embrace him. His bulging belly shook under his second-hand tuxedo and his shirt sleeves were frayed.

Kati wondered where he had met her great uncle, since he was addressing him with such familiarity. He chatted for a few minutes but seeing that he was not welcome, he finally took his leave. Aunt Sári was visibly relieved; finally the three of them could enjoy their dinner in peace.

"He is a frequent phenomenon in the West," she explained, noticing that both Kati and Uncle Sándor looked puzzled at the presence of the man.

"He passes himself off as a prominent businessman from Calgary, but everyone knows that he barely ekes out a living as a small contractor. It's his naive little Canadian wife who supports him, while he travels around the world, under the pretense of 'business trips.' He shows up everywhere and finds a way to get an invitation to every Hungarian event."

"But he is a harmless fellow, and rather nice," Aunt Sári
added, smiling apologetically as she shrugged her shoulders. She
apparently felt she needed to explain the presence of such a man
at her elegant ball.

"I certainly have never seen him before," Uncle Sándor
noted. "Although from what he said, he must be a frequent
visitor to Hungary."

Kati began to wonder about László, hoping that he would
join them for dinner. He had disappeared for the second time this
evening. Several guests stopped at their table, but no one joined
them, knowing well that the three preferred to spend those
precious first moments of their reunion together as a family.

Then a tall, youthful looking, gray-haired man came up to
them. He was clutching a small paperback in his hand.

"Sárika, this is my latest poetry book. I autographed a copy
especially for you. It's my fifth volume in Hungarian. I've
already published seven in French."

Kati was startled by the sense of urgency in his voice. She
knew well that Hungarian poetry books had very limited reader-
ship in the West, to say the least. She watched as the man turned
earnestly toward Uncle Sándor, and continued in a fervent voice.
"They are even publishing some of my poems in Budapest
journals," he said proudly. Then he handed the slim volume to
Aunt Sári, who accepted it gracefully.

Kati gazed after him as he disappeared in the crowd,
wondering which one of the numerous "poets in exile" he
happened to be. There were plenty of them around.

Soon after the guests had finished their dinner while
listening to the soft strings of the gypsy band, the tables were
cleared and only the ashtrays and bouquets of red roses in
slender crystal vases were left.

It seemed to Kati that for a moment she had seen Walter,
wearing his customary white gloves, waiting politely on the table
where guests were entertained by the boisterous voice of a
German general. Walter was looking very solemn and superior

as he gave instructions to the waiters who were offering after-dinner drinks.

Then the ball began.

The orchestra started to play "Tales of the Vienna Woods," and Kati felt at home, recalling those memorable balls in Cleveland which she had enjoyed so much as a young girl. Soon Uncle Sándor stood up, and made a deep courtly bow toward Aunt Sári, asking her for the first dance.

Kati watched in awe as she followed the movements of the distinguished couple as they whirled around the vacant dance floor, in the midst of the admiring glances of the guests. A few minutes later, she noticed László standing directly in front of her.

"May I?" He asked with a faint smile. Kati's eyes lit up, although he seemed so serious and aloof.

"Yes," Kati whispered and blushed. They made their way to the dance floor, joining Aunt Sári and Uncle Sándor and other couples who had already begun to dance.

Kati was soon caught up in the whirl of her first waltz with László, hoping that the music would never stop. His strong embrace made her feel secure. They spoke very little as they moved in perfect harmony, swaying gracefully to the melodious tunes of several Viennese waltzes.

It seemed as if they had danced together all their lives.

What an excellent dancer, Kati thought, and as if reading her thoughts, László remarked, "You dance very well, little Kati." He pulled her close, and she felt his right arm tightening around her waist.

This cannot be happening to me... Kati recalled the sleepless nights when as a young girl, she had lain awake, dreaming of the man she could truly love, the one with whom she could share her life, its joys and tears. She fondly recalled the slumber parties with her high school friends Eva and Judy, when the main topic of conversation had been love and boys, as they giggled through the night, making fun of every boy they knew. They broke into fits of hysterical laughter as they searched for names of animals each boy resembled. They gave them such names as "Bull," "Rabbit," "Goat," "Squirrel," and "Mouse," and made fun of their real names by exchanging the beginning letters of their first and last names, so someone with the name "Sanyi Farkas" became "Fanyi Sarkas." They would spend half the night laughing at these funny sounding names, as if life were a basket filled with laughter, mirth, and joy.

Kati and her friends knew that "true love" could only be found in fairy tales and romance novels, yet, like so many young girls, she hoped that her life would be an exception. Later, when she had to face one tragedy after another, Michael was already on the horizon, and she had little time for such romantic fantasies.

Several other waltzes followed. Then came Kati's favorite tango, "La Paloma," so full of passion and fiery temperament.

"We'll dance this tango yet," László said unexpectedly and smiled. "Then I have to ask some of the other ladies to dance. Out of sheer politeness, you understand," he added with a twinkle..

Both gave themselves up to the rhythm of the dance. Their eyes met several times, but Kati could not return László's searching gaze. She found it difficult to look into his eyes in fear of revealing how she felt. She looked away, fixing her eyes on the movements of other couples on the dance floor. But they could not finish the tango because Miklós suddenly appeared at their side.

"May I?" Miklós asked as he gave Kati a penetrating look. There was a hint of mockery in his voice. The frown on László's face signaled that he was not pleased, but he removed his arms from Kati's waist, freeing her up for her next partner. All this happened so quickly that Kati could not even put in a word.

"You won't find a better dancer than little Kati," Kati heard László's voice, as she watched him disappear into the crowd. Why do these men keep calling me "little Kati," she wondered. I am a grown woman!

Kati had the feeling that Miklós had asked her to dance only to annoy her.

"You're not angry with me, little Kati, are you?" he asked as she found herself in his arms. "You're just acting hard to get. I know your kind," he added and squeezed her hand.

How dare he talk to me this way? Kati was livid. She was hoping someone else would cut in and rescue her. "How about meeting me after the reunion?" He asked. "*Hotel Diano Marina* would be the perfect place, in San Bartolomeo. Sometime in the evening."

Kati's face flushed. "I don't want to make a scene," she said, her eyes flashing. "But I am not dancing with you any more." She pulled away, and dashed from the dance floor toward Aunt Sári and Uncle Sándor sitting at their table.

"You look flustered and unhappy, darling. What's the matter?" Aunt Sári asked.

"Oh nothing," Kati replied and sat down. She took a sip of Perrier and tried to relax and forget Miklós's insinuations. He was ruining her evening.

But soon she was swept up by the mood of the ball. Young men she had barely met asked her to dance. She moved from one man's arms into another's, completely absorbed in the music and dance.

Meanwhile, she began to feel light-headed. Between dances when her partners escorted her back to the table, they offered her wine, and she drank freely, without thinking of its effect.

Once, on her way to the powder room, she noticed two middle-aged men looking in her direction, eyeing her every move. Although she was getting used to being watched, for the guests were naturally curious about Aunt Sári's "beautiful American niece," she found the blatant stares of these two highly annoying. Their eyes shone with pure impudence, and as she walked past them, she could hear snippets of their conversation.

"Do you think Sári will leave her anything? I heard she's planning to change her will," the stodgy man in the white tuxedo asked his companion. "Maybe we should get to know her... She's a pretty girl, one of a kind, and the aunt is quite..." But Kati could not hear the rest because he lowered his voice as she passed them.

Kati's heartbeat quickened. The thought of an inheritance had never once crossed her mind. Before her arrival, she had no idea her aunt was so wealthy. But what was the man saying about Aunt Sári? That she was quite what? She wondered again, worried that something may be seriously wrong. Not another tragedy, she prayed. There had been too many for one family to bear.

She made an effort to dismiss all unpleasant thoughts. After all, this was a once in a lifetime experience. She was determined not to let it be spoiled by idle gossip.

Kati was totally engrossed in dancing all evening, yet ever since Miklós had cut in, she often thought of László. She spotted him several times on the dance floor, once with Aunt Sári, but most often with Angela who seemed to cling to him like a grapevine. Once when the orchestra was playing a slow foxtrot, Kati saw them dancing very close, and Angela's eyes were closed dreamily as she lost herself in the rhythm of the melody. Kati had the feeling they had known each other for a long time; there was an air of familiarity between them. Her thoughts were quickly interrupted, for just as another foxtrot began, the fat man from Calgary asked her to dance.

"I was a good friend of your father's, back in Cleveland," he began the conversation. But Kati did not remember him at all.

"Your father was such a nice man, and your mother a beautiful lady," he continued his remarks in a zealous voice.

"Yes, yes, they were," Kati replied, but could not recall ever having seen the man. Anyway, it was inappropriate to remind her that they were gone, to bring to mind her family's tragedy. Apparently, the fat man failed to realize that he was being tactless as he continued his idle chatter.

"I remember how some Cleveland people thought there was something between you and your Uncle Tibor," the fat man continued. "But I always defended you against such malicious talk."

Kati's face flushed. Defended me? The audacity of this man! "I also remember well how people in the Hungarian community disapproved of your family's visits to Hungary. Some even said that your father supported the communists and accused him of being a two-timer, even a traitor."

"I know," Kati replied, unwilling to get into further conversation with the man.

She was relieved when the orchestra took a pause and she could return to the table to chat with Aunt Sári and Uncle Sándor. Both seemed to enjoy themselves, and her aunt appeared more radiant than ever. Not even the slightest sign of fatigue was visible on her face. Just looking at her made Kati forget the unpleasant things she had heard, and she dismissed the stodgy man's remarks from her mind.

This was Aunt Sári's night, one that she had planned for years. She wanted to show off what she had accomplished, who she had become, and that her life had been a good one. Many of her old friends from Budapest were here, and Kati overheard their lavishing praise on the magnificence of the palazzo and Aunt Sári's superb entertaining. But behind her back they made snide remarks.

Kati watched Uncle Sándor as he looked around the ballroom in awe. Only once did she notice sadness in his eyes. "If only your Aunt Irén could see all this..." he remarked wistfully, "She would really enjoy it." The two were sitting alone at the table when he turned to his niece.

"My dear Kati, tell me, what are you going to do now that you are completely alone in that big country, America? Your Aunt Sári and I..."

"Oh, I can take care of myself. I've managed pretty well during the past few years." Kati explained to him that she had a great future ahead of her. International trade was expanding, and with her knowledge of languages, her background, her degree, and her strong determination, she would surely succeed.

"And... I hope you don't mind my asking," Uncle Sándor hesitated as he took a deep breath, "Is there a young man on the horizon? You don't mind my being curious?"

"Uncle Sándor, I'm already engaged. To a nice American," Kati replied in a solemn voice.

Uncle Sándor swallowed hard, obviously surprised by the news. "An American? Engaged to an American?" he repeated. He paused, then added, "If you're engaged it must be serious."

Kati did not reply. She saw no reason why she should defend her decision. A long silence followed, and Uncle Sándor decided to change the subject.

"Katika, I wanted to see you so much when you visited Hungary during those summers. Your Aunt Sári just told me that your mother was upset with me because she thought I favored your aunt over her. At least that's the impression she had of me."

"I could never figure out what went wrong between them, why they lost contact. They should have been glad to have a sister," Kati said sadly. "I don't have anyone."

"I know. I know you're all alone. But I can tell you one thing. Your mother and Sári had always been so different. They were not like sisters at all. Your mother thought I approved of Sári's, let's put it this way, "lively character," and her desire to become an actress. She just didn't think it was proper for someone from our family to engage in such frivolous activity as the theater." He sighed deeply and his expression darkened. "That's probably why she never came to visit your Aunt Irén and me."

Her parents had been mentioned for the second time this evening. Kati became very conscious of their absence, and she felt more lonely than ever before.

She remembered how they had loved to chaperone her to the balls, and how proud *Apuka* had looked as he introduced his debutante daughter at her first formal ball sponsored by the Association of Hungarian Veterans. They had always been pleased with their daughter's popularity, for she was always surrounded by young men asking her to dance.

"Are you really in love with that American, Katika dear?" Uncle Sándor's unexpected question brought her back to the present.

Kati hesitated for a moment. "Well..." She quickly corrected herself. "My fiancé Michael Keller, is a wonderful person and I'm sure we'll be happy together," Kati added, trying to ease her uncle's concern.

"But do you love him? Do you love him enough to spend your whole life with him?" Uncle Sándor insisted.

László's sudden appearance at their table saved her from having to give an answer.

"Come and sit down with us," Uncle Sándor offered, "but I can see that you would rather dance."

"Well, yes." László turned to Kati. "I finally found you, little Kati. It's almost impossible to dance with you. There are so many men to compete with," he said with apprehension in his voice.

Kati thought of the way he danced with Angela. You never even tried to ask me, all evening, she thought to herself.

"I've been here all evening..." she replied.

Despite the advances of women's liberation, this age-old custom had not been put aside and Kati was grateful. She would have felt awkward if the roles had been changed, and she would have had to ask a man to dance. If László had wanted to dance with her, he could have. This male prerogative was among the many advantages men had over women.

"You were pretty busy yourself," she said, making sure that he understood what she meant. Although László ignored her remark and shrugged his shoulders, a slight movement of his upper lip signaled that he knew what she was hinting at. His self-assurance, bordering on arrogance revealed that he felt free to do whatever he pleased, and his actions were no one else's business. "Well, may I have the next dance, then?" His question sounded more like a command.

"All right," Kati said reluctantly. She was annoyed by his demeanor, for she too liked to be in control of the situation at hand. The hardships she had endured in the past few years taught her that.

László took her in his arms again and she was surprised at herself that her apprehension melted with each dancing step. The touch of his hands sent shivers down her spine, and as he held her by the waist and pulled her close, she felt immune to future misfortunes. Her heart leaped in excitement as they danced to the tune of a romantic melody that seemed to have been played only for them. Her forehead touched his cheeks and as she glanced up, she noted a glint of passion in his eyes.

I should probably tell him I'm engaged, Kati thought. She looked straight into his emerald eyes, and made an effort to pull away. But he tightened his grip on her waist and squeezed her fingers with his left hand. If Michael would see us now, he would be horrified, Kati thought in panic. He would immediately break off our engagement.

László probably never looked at my hands when we first met, and tonight my engagement ring lies hidden under my elbow-length white gloves, she reasoned.

"You're acting like you're afraid of me," László said. "As if your heart belonged to someone else. Yet, when I watched you..." László insisted, referring to her being on the dance floor all evening, "You definitely had a good time dancing with everyone all night." He pulled her even closer and she felt more and more vulnerable in his embrace.

This is not right, her good sense whispered inside. But the feeling of elation was so new and so irresistible that it totally knocked her off her feet. Live for the moment, another voice prodded her on, pulling her in the opposite direction. She felt as light as a feather, and was soon swept up by the exhilarating mood of the dance, and by her partner, the intriguing and mysterious László von Temessy, the darling of all the girls and women who knew him.

Then the music stopped. László did not let go of her arm. He guided her out to the terrace, accessible through wide French doors on both sides of the orchestra. The city of San Remo lay at their feet in all its splendor. It was a starry night. The full moon, the lights of the city, along with the shimmering lights of distant fishing boats hinted at mystery and expectation Kati had never felt before.

She welcomed the faint chill blowing from the sea, cooling her body and calming her spirit.

"I'll be back in a minute," László beamed and soon returned with two slender glasses of champagne. They stood by the rail, drinks in hand, taking in every detail of the view.

"To us and to the magic of the night," László raised his glass and clinked it to Kati's. "Chin-chin," he said, "Or better yet, *'egészségünkre,'* to our health."

"To our health," Kati replied.

"Have you ever seen anything so beautiful?" László asked as he moved closer to Kati, almost touching her arms.

"No, never. This whole evening is more like a dream. I never imagined that anything like this even existed, at least not in real life. And that I can be part of it."

"At times like these one even forgets that there is another world outside. A world of cruelty, suffering, and pain." László's voice was somber.

Suddenly, Kati recalled a poem by Matthew Arnold. She slowly began to recite the words, switching from Hungarian to English:

The sea is calm tonight,
The tide is full, the moon lies fair
Upon the straits; -- on the French coast the light

Gleams and is gone; the cliffs of England stand,
Glimmering and vast, out in the tranquil bay.

For a moment, she hesitated, searching for the next line in "Dover Beach." László came to her rescue:

Come to the window, sweet is the night-air!
Only, from the long line of spray
Where the sea meets the moon-blanched land,
Listen! you hear the grating roar
Of pebbles which the waves draw back, and fling,
At their return, up the high strand,
Begin, and cease, and then again begin,
With tremulous cadence slow, and bring
The eternal note of sadness in.

László stopped after the first stanza.

"So you know this poem? It's one of my favorites," Kati was surprised that he knew the poem by heart.

"Mine too."

She felt an unexpected warmth running through her whole body, as if the poem had brought them closer together. For a while they stood in silence, overawed by the magnificent view. László placed his empty glass on a small table nearby and reached for Kati's glass, even though she had not finished her champagne.

"Let's go over to the far end," he suggested and took her by the arm. "It's way too noisy here." They walked toward the far corner of the terrace, part of which was hidden by large containers of exotic plants.

"These guests are too annoying and boisterous," László said.

Then he did something that caught Kati completely off guard. He reached out and pulled her close, searching for her lips. Kati was so surprised that she didn't have time to draw back. Not that she really wanted to. I shouldn't be doing this, she thought in alarm. I am engaged... Michael... But she couldn't help clinging to him, losing herself in his embrace, returning his kiss.

Thoughts of fear whirled in her mind. He's just using me, she thought, ashamed of her weakness. This is a perfectly romantic moment, and I happen to be the one close by...

She pulled back with a jerk. László let her go. She straightened her dress and hair with a few self-conscious movements.

"I hope you don't mind, little Kati. I got carried away. But I simply cannot resist such moments. And, you are a beautiful girl, you know. Although rather inexperienced..." László added with a meaningful gleam in his eyes.

Kati stood motionless, trying to hide her embarrassment behind a smile. She had always dreamed of a moment like this and now that László had kissed her she should have been overwhelmed with happiness. In spite of Michael...

"I'm not in the habit of kissing strange men," she said in a defiant tone.

"I know you're not." László's reassurance calmed her.

Then he pulled her close again, and for the second time, the touch of his lips and his passionate embrace made her forget where she was, that anything outside their world even existed.

László let her go slowly, and his self-assured manner told Kati that he knew exactly what he was doing. He turned his back on her and walked to the small table to pick up Kati's unfinished glass of champagne.

"Finish your drink, little Kati," he whispered as he placed the glass in her hand. His eyes searched hers, but he said nothing more.

One minute he treats me like a woman, and in the other as if I were a mere child, Kati thought with scorn. Then she looked straight into his eyes that seemed a much deeper green than before, and returned his gaze. I am not afraid of you, her look said. She imagined a multitude of thoughts hidden behind those eyes. She would have been happy to know just a few.

They soon noticed Aunt Sári and Uncle Sándor walking toward them.

"Oh, you're here! Kati darling, we have been looking for you." Aunt Sári burst out. Kati blushed, embarrassed for the second time this evening. But László seemed calm and composed, as if nothing had happened between them.

"Your niece and I were just admiring the view. What a wonderful evening this is! Little Kati is not used to such surroundings."

"I'm not either, believe me. Not anymore." Uncle Sándor said in an effort to make Kati feel more at ease.

"Let's go back to our guests," Aunt Sári suggested.

As the four of them entered the ballroom, Kati noted that some guests had already left. Several approached Aunt Sári to bid farewell, showering her with enthusiastic comments about the marvelous time they had.

Aunt Sári glowed with pleasure and pride. "Yes, it turned out to be a pretty nice affair," she acknowledged.

"It's an evening I'll never forget," Kati assured her enthusiastically. László smiled at her, his eyes gleaming with satisfaction.

"We'll see you tomorrow, Kati darling. Walter will pick up both of you at 11:00 in the morning." Aunt Sári turned to Uncle Sándor. "He'll drive you to the seaport. We'll continue the reunion on the yacht."

Kati was surprised by this new bit of information since no one had told her of plans for the next day. But it wasn't really Aunt Sári's fault. She was too busy seeing that everything went smoothly. She could not be expected to inform Kati about everything.

Suddenly, as if out of nowhere, Walter appeared in their midst, waiting to carry out Aunt Sári's orders. "Darlings, Walter will see you up to your rooms," she said.

"Good night," Kati turned to László, her voice shaking a little as she extended her hand. He took her hand and held it to his lips. He looked into her eyes. What was he trying to tell her? But Kati could not return his gaze. She looked away, confused and embarrassed.

Then the moment was gone, and she was following Walter as they left the virtually empty ballroom, with Uncle Sándor at her side.

"Did you have a good time?" Uncle Sándor asked as they were walking up the luxuriously carpeted stairway. "You were the *belle of the ball.* There wasn't a single dance that you sat out. I kept an eye on you."

"Yes, it was a wonderful evening. I still don't believe that I'm here, and all this is happening to me."

"I know what you mean. Believe me, I feel the same way," Uncle Sándor assured her. He kissed her on the forehead when they reached her room.

"Good night, sweet dreams," he said with a twinkle in his kind eyes.

The guest suites were furnished with great luxury, just as Kati had expected. She was a little surprised at herself and the ease with which she adapted to such extravagant surroundings.

Lying in bed after a refreshing bath, the events of the evening raced through her mind. She recalled the multitude of peculiar guests and wondered whether she would see them tomorrow. Then she recalled Uncle Sándor's reaction to her engagement to Michael. He was apparently not happy about the news. But I'm going to marry whomever I choose, she resolved. No one is going to tell me what to do. Not even Aunt Sári or Uncle Sándor.

Then her thoughts turned to László as she recalled the way he had danced with Angela. Are they planning to get engaged? Or maybe they are already engaged, she thought with alarm. That's impossible! She recalled his unexpected kisses; I should feel guilty about them, she reminded herself. After all, I have a ring on my finger... But Michael seems so far away from where I am now. It's like he's living on another planet, a pretty drab one at that, she mused.

Kati could still see in her mind's eye the way László looked at her when they parted. But I'm just a gray little mouse, compared to his world of glamour. And I know so little about him, she reflected. He certainly has power over women, and he knows it. She could see all the women falling in love with him, as Miklós had suggested.

A terrible thought flashed through he mind. What did the man in the white tuxedo say? His words still rang in her ears. Was there something seriously wrong with Aunt Sári? What could it be?

After pondering that possibility, she finally fell asleep, but not before an array of confused emotions swelled in her heart: emotions of hope, doubt, and fear.

6

Cruising on the Mediterranean

At sea

The next morning Kati woke up to the bright sun shining through the cream-colored silk curtains of the magnificent window of her bedroom. It was an especially sunny day with clear blue skies. Just perfect for a cruise, she thought, as she remembered the plans for the day. She looked forward to it with anticipation not only because she had never been on a cruise, but because she was eager to meet more of Aunt Sári's friends. And then, there was László...

She had breakfast in her room from a tray that had been placed by her bedside. She did not even notice when it had been put there, she thought ruefully, hoping that it wasn't Walter who crept into her room while she was sound asleep. She felt uncomfortable about the man. There was something disturbing about his manner and the way he stared blankly at her with blatant suspicion in his pale blue eyes.

She had a few hours before he would be picking her up along with Uncle Sándor. It was only 9:00 o'clock. She was thankful Uncle Sándor would be there in the Mercedes with her. She looked around wondering how she could spend the time when she remembered the copy of the European edition of *Time* magazine she had bought in San Bartolomeo. She had stuck it in her purse at the last minute.

Kati had the odd habit of starting to read a magazine from the back, so she quickly came to the book review section. As she turned the pages, she became conscious of a familiar face staring straight at her.

Oh my God, it's László's photo! Not a strand of his black hair was out of place, and his mustache was perfectly groomed. Although his over-all expression was serious, there was the hint of a smile on his face and a special gleam in his eyes. Kati's heartbeat quickened as she looked at the photo, recalling the events of the previous evening, his kisses and his embrace. She could still sense the warmth of his breath as he had whispered "little Kati" into her ears.

I should have known that his newest book would be reviewed here, she told herself, as she remembered Aunt Sári's comments during her first dinner at the Villa Tokay. A whole page was devoted to László's book, *The Economic System of the Socialist States.* As Kati quickly read the critic's words, her heart skipped a few beats. She was only conscious of the overall ideas, not the specific details. Aunt Sári had been right. The critic made several favorable comments, praising the work as a milestone in the assessment of contemporary East-Central European economic affairs. At the end, however, he mentioned that in this day and age it is not exactly to an author's advantage not to have visited for over a decade the part of the world he was writing about.

"In spite of this," the critic concluded, "Professor László von Temessy seems to know exactly what he is talking about, and his analysis of the situation is quite realistic and often brilliant."

Kati looked anxiously for information regarding László's private life. She found very little, but she did learn that he was also Professor of Political Economy at the Sapiensa University of Rome, and had been recently nominated by the Italians to the European Parliament in Strassbourg. Kati had no doubt for a moment that his lectures were well-attended. The female students must be flocking to his classes, she thought with a hint of jealousy, as she recalled his magnetic charm. The article also mentioned that he had been educated at the University of Budapest and did some post-doctoral work at the University of Vienna. He left his native land right after earning his doctorate. According to the article, he had already made a name for himself at the age of thirty-two when he brought new insights into the economic structure of socialist states.

An unusual career, Kati noted, because she had heard from *Apuka* that most scholars start getting recognition in their forties and fifties. But László's case was different, and his books had been well-received, the latest one having merited international attention.

Kati was pleased with the *Time* magazine review. An unexplainable pride rose in her heart, as if she had something to do with László, his book, and his success. Then, having grown tired of reading serious articles, she glanced over to a small table nearby that had several colorful magazines strewn on top. A cover with three shapely girls, slightly clad in tiny bikinis, strolling down the beach caught her attention. It was one of many magazines she had seen at the news stands on the quay in San Bartolomeo, published in French, German, and Italian. Such magazines specialized in the intimate affairs of the rich, the famous, and the powerful. The articles were about European royalty, TV and movie stars, producers and directors, starlets and singers, whose every move became a sensation at the stroke of a pen of eager journalists, and devoured by readers hungry for scandalous details. Although aware that these magazines had a wide appeal, Kati herself rarely read them. This time she broke her habit of not perusing such publications and decided to take a look.

A moment later she was trying to decipher a well-illustrated article whose title she made out despite her scant knowledge of Italian, "Famous Men and the Women in their Lives." She was in shock when she read László's name among the interviewees, and as she turned the page, a half-page photo of László stared her in the face.

He looked debonair in a navy leisure suit, flanked by two scantily dressed girls in mini skirts who pretended to listen to what he had to say. In another, smaller photo, he wore swim trunks, and had his arms around a dark-haired beauty clad in a hot pink bikini. Kati immediately recognized Angela Ruggiero. The caption under the photo said something about an engagement and a wedding, at least that's what Kati was able to make out.

She stared at the photos in shock. László was a kind of celebrity in Italy, and he was certainly good-looking. Yet, she considered it below the dignity of an intellectual to be featured in such magazines. He was supposed to be a serious scholar who scorned frivolity, but then, what was he doing in a magazine such as this one? Did he have anything to do with it? He had said he was concerned with the dangers of totalitarianism and Kati recalled his scorn for young people who were "caught up in a world of materialism and self-gratification." Those were his exact words.

These photos gave the opposite impression of his convictions. Kati stared at the photo with Angela, and her heart sank. Why had he kissed me? What kind of a man was he anyway? I don't want to see him again, she told herself, and wished she didn't have to go on the cruise where she might have to face him again.

She put on a pair of white linen slacks and a top to match, having no idea what people wore on a cruise. At the moment she didn't care. Her outfit revealed her shapely figure, displayed to advantage in close-fitting Capri pants. She wore her hair down, and the tan she had acquired in San Bartolomeo set off the whiteness of her blouse decorated with tiny red sailboats and anchors at the neckline and at the sleeves. She decided to wear one of those fashionable hairpins in red to match the red in her blouse, as she pulled back her hair with it on one side. Many girls were wearing these, and Kati thought they were both attractive and practical.

Put László out of your mind, she kept telling herself as she took her time walking down the grandiose staircase. She stood in admiration in front of each exquisite piece of art, looking closely at every detail. She found Aunt Sári's San Remo residence even more magnificent in daylight, delighting in the fine pieces of sculpture and paintings along the walls as she made her way holding on to the dark mahogany bannisters.

Uncle Sándor was already waiting at the bottom of the marble steps. His back was to Kati as he stood lost in thought in front of a large still life painted in pale hues of blue, green, and orange. He turned to Kati and smiled, looking distinguished in a navy sports coat, white slacks, and a light blue sport shirt open at the collar.

They stepped outside. Walter, dressed for the occasion in a black chauffeur's uniform, whisked them into the navy-blue Mercedes that was parked in front. They reached the San Remo seaport in ten minutes, and Kati was surprised to see a crowd of about fifty people standing around in small groups, laughing and talking. She recognized some guests from the ball, but most were total strangers she had never met before.

Uncle Sándor led the way toward Aunt Sári who stood at the center of a group on the left, dressed in a stunning white outfit of slacks and a blouse with sleeves that covered her elbows. She wore a wide-brimmed hat with a navy blue ribbon. Looking radiant and without the slightest sign of fatigue, she carried on a lively conversation with a fragile-looking young woman who stood next to Miklós. The sullen, lifeless expression on the woman's face seemed out of place. Two children, a little girl of four and a boy of six, dressed in sailor suits, were running around them, playing tag. Both had Miklós's vibrant good looks. He gazed at them fondly, paternal pride replacing the customary mocking expression in his eyes.

My God, Kati thought, that must be Miklós's wife. She wondered why she hadn't seen her at the ball the night before. "I'm Inge. So glad to meet you, Kati," the woman extended her hand. It was fragile and cold. "You know, I only came along for the sake of the children. They wanted so much to ride on a boat," she explained in a nasal tone. "I simply loathe crowds," she continued."But then, I also wanted to meet you. Miklós told me all about you. You're Aunt Sári's 'beautiful niece from America,' he said."

Inge's face lit up for a moment, and Kati noted that she said this in earnest, without a hint of malice in her voice. She was glad to hear that someone was eager to meet her. But a moment later, Inge became solemn again and showed no interest in her at all. She turned away to reprimand her children who were causing a commotion, running around undisciplined in the crowd of adults.

Kati could not help but wonder why Miklós had married such a woman. They were total opposites. Inge seemed plain and unassuming, so spiritless and dull. Why do such totally opposite personalities ever get married?

Miklós stepped up to Kati and surveyed her with the same ironic glint in his eye that Kati knew well from the days before.

"Looks like the *belle of the ball* is dressed for the occasion," he remarked, and his approving glance signaled that he meant that as a compliment. Inge's expression turned more dispirited than before. She sported a sour look, as she touched her forehead with nervous hands. An embarrassing silence followed.

"I better go and meet some of the other guests," Kati said, looking for an excuse to move on.

Soon she became conscious of loud, boisterous laughter behind her. She turned around, curious to know what language was spoken, Italian or Hungarian. Often, from a distance, Italian sounded like Hungarian, she thought. There was something similar in the intonation and the sound of the vowels, so that for a moment she mistook their *lingua bella* for her native Hungarian.

When she turned around she saw that the group spoke Italian and included the Ruggieros, Angela, and László. The two were standing side by side, the center of attention and laughter. Kati's heart sank. She remembered the interview and the photos in the gossip magazine, and her premonition that this was not going to be a pleasant day strengthened. Pull yourself together, she told herself, as she tried to conceal her disappointment by stepping over to the group and starting a conversation.

"This is Sárika's niece from America, Kati Mátrai," László introduced her to the two ladies in the group, using English as the common language. Kati greeted them and the Ruggieros with a friendly smile, shaking hands with everyone.

A look of disdain appeared on Angela's face as she extended her hand to Kati.

"This whole place must be so new to you. You probably feel utterly out of place here," she remarked in broken English, with unmistakable scorn in her voice.

"She'll get used to it, I'm sure. Most people do. In fact, some are very reluctant to leave...." László looked at Angela, beautiful as usual in light blue Capri pants and a top of the newest design. Kati threw him a grateful look. But László failed to acknowledge it, and Kati felt uncomfortable as she forced herself to participate in the idle chatter. László seemed entirely at ease, very much enjoying the company and being the center of attention.

One by one, they boarded the magnificent yacht amid cheerful chatter. Kati felt neglected and forlorn, and to cheer herself, she took a deep breath of the clean air as she gazed into the far distance, surveying the incredible blue-green of the Mediterranean. A few shimmering white sailboats broke the monotony of the blue horizon. The sunny weather soon cheered her mood, and the deep azure sky reminded her of the family vacations of years ago, on Florida's Longboat Key.

Kati caught László looking in her direction several times as they were standing in line. But he stayed with the Ruggieros. When she noticed that László was holding Angela by the arm as he helped her board the yacht, her heart sank. Why doesn't he help me? Angela was right, I am out of place here. For the sake of appearance, I must pretend to be enjoying myself, even though I feel miserable. How can I keep this up for the whole day? For a whole month?

The weather was perfect. There was not a cloud on the horizon, and the gentle breeze made the bright sun bearable. Everyone around her was in a buoyant mood. If my friends in Cleveland could see me now.... They'd die of envy, she thought, suppressing a smile. And Michael, he would certainly feel totally out of place here...

After boarding the yacht, Kati watched the Gypsy band settle down on the main deck, ready to set the mood with their music. She waved to them as she searched for her aunt and uncle, but they were nowhere to be found. Lost in the crowd, she got up enough nerve to join the company of an attractive couple from Germany.

"I'm so glad to meet Sárika's niece," the man said, smiling. He was a Professor of Economics at the University of Cologne. "So nice to have you along on the cruise," he added in a friendly voice. "We're sorry we arrived too late for the ball last night."

"It was a magical evening," Kati said wistfully.

The professor's wife was a lively blonde woman, very articulate, who asked questions about life in America. They found topics of mutual interest and their company had a calming effect on Kati as she tried hard to dismiss László from her thoughts.

The couple introduced her to several of their Hungarian friends from Switzerland and Germany. Kati found the short, wiry-looking man who worked for Radio Free Europe in Munich rather obnoxious. He had already drunk too much and was constantly alluding to Kati being so young and beautiful and tried to make passes at her, right in front of his stern-faced wife who was taller than he and wore over-sized, black-rimmed sun glasses.

"The only thing I don't like about you is that you keep going back to communist Hungary. How do I know? Well, well, you see, Miklós told me," the little man repeated several times as he wagged his finger at her. "You shouldn't do that. You're a bad little girl..." he warned, as if he had any authority over Kati's actions.

Kati wanted to break away from them as quickly as possible, so she looked around, searching for someone she knew. She finally spotted Uncle Sándor at the opposite end of the yacht, but he seemed engrossed in deep conversation with a lady near his age. Kati did not want to disturb them.

She saw that Aunt Sári was occupied with making her guests feel comfortable, while Aunt Juli supervised the preparations for the buffet lunch. She was running up and down between the main deck and cabins below, with Gino and Walter close behind.

Kati found no one to talk to.

I should have stayed in Cleveland, where I belong, she told herself. This world is so different from mine. This is so embarrassing... I have no idea how to relate to these people... I wish Michael were here... Oh Michael, you're so far away... You wouldn't feel at ease here either; I'm sure of that. Neither would Kriszta, or any of my friends in Cleveland.

Her melancholic mood grew deeper by the minute. She walked up to the nearest guard rail where there were no guests standing by. She stood mesmerized by the vast beauty of the sea, and leaned on the rail looking beyond the horizon. She tried to make sense of her life, her future. Aunt Sári's lifestyle turned out to be so different from hers, so much beyond her reach. Yet, at times, she felt quite at home in it, if only she had a chance...

We live in two completely different worlds. I don't even know anymore what I want out of life, what I should do with my life. Is marrying Michael the right thing to do? He is so down to earth, so average. There is such a lack of flamboyance in his personality. No spirit, no passion, just steadfastness and dependability. But at least he's stable and together we could have a safe and secure life...

Lost in thought, she felt a gentle touch on her shoulder, almost as if someone were stroking her. Who could this be? She turned around slowly.

László stood behind her, a faint smile on his lips, looking his usual handsome self in his impeccable white pair of slacks, white shirt and a navy sports coat. Kati tried to hide her surprise.

"You're acting as if you don't know me," he remarked, and she felt charmed yet alarmed by his presence.

"Why do you say that? Of course I know you." Then she added with an unmistakable apprehension in her voice: "I also know you from magazine articles, *Time* for instance, and some others..." Then she added cynically, "You're so well-known, world famous."

László smiled, unruffled.

"Well, I'm really pleased with the *Time* review. I can't say that for the others though..."

"You really must be leading a fast life here. Professors in America don't have their pictures taken with girls in bikinis, and they are rarely featured in trashy magazines." Kati looked him straight in the eye. "You know, I find this totally undignified, to say the least."

Then she added in a shaking voice that she was unable to control. "By the way, congratulations on your engagement."

László looked puzzled as he returned Kati's penetrating gaze.

"Engagement? What engagement?" He looked long and hard at Kati, visibly aware of her foul mood. Then he smiled mischievously. "This may be just idle gossip, but aren't you the one who is supposed to be engaged? I heard it at the ball last night."

Kati blushed, but said nothing.

"Well, anyway, your Italian needs some brushing up, little Kati. We were at a beach party and some *paparazzi* got a hold of us. Now that I've become an overnight celebrity..." he laughed again as Kati's blush deepened.

"Well, it doesn't really matter," she muttered.

"You're not upset with me, are you?" For a moment he touched her hand, and his green eyes had that "deep as the ocean" look. "But then, you're pretty even when you're angry!"

"I'm not angry. Why should I be?" Kati retorted, and looked away. She tried to disguise the jealousy she felt as she remembered László accompanying Angela to the yacht. He had paid no attention to Kati at all ever since the yacht had left the port at San Remo.

"You're a strange girl. I have no idea what you think, and what you're like," László shook his head. "And I don't even know whether you're engaged or not..." He paused for a moment. "It's hard to figure you out," he added.

"I'm not the only one who's hard to figure out," Kati snapped, unsmiling. It was welcome news that László was not engaged to Angela, but she didn't dare to show her relief. Her foul mood was like a thick November fog settling on the Ohio countryside.

She turned her back on László and continued gazing out toward the sea, hoping that László would join her. The sea always had a calming effect on her nerves.

But when she turned around, László was gone. His spirited laughter resounded on the other side of the yacht as he was welcomed by another group of ebullient guests.

A buffet lunch was served on board and Kati drank white wine mixed with *aqua minerale*, a popular drink Hungarians call "fröccs," for she was afraid too much alcohol would go to her head. Her despondent mood slowly disappeared, and she made an effort to feel at ease, to enjoy the luxurious surroundings. Back in Cleveland, it would have been out of this world even to think about a cruise on the Mediterranean, let alone experience it. Everything will be OK, she reassured herself. Aunt Sári looks healthy and fit, and who could ever figure out László? Then a sudden, inexplicable fear took hold of her. What if Aunt Sári was really ill? Kati would lose her only relative in the West, a relative she was just beginning to know and to love. Most of the guests were helping themselves from the buffet table. Kati sat alone at one of the corner tables when Uncle Sándor walked up to her and sat down. "May I join you?" he asked as he scrutinized Kati. A worried look appeared on his face as he placed his plate next to Kati's.

"Is anything wrong, my child?" His voice was full of concern. "What happened? You look so pale and lifeless."

"No, nothing happened and nothing is wrong," Kati answered, forcing herself to smile. She was silent for a moment, then added, hesitating, "Uncle Sándor, I ... I feel so lost among these people. I really shouldn't have come here in the first place. This is such a different world from mine. You see, I've already made a place for myself in America. There is my career... and I'll be married soon, to a nice American fellow. I just don't belong here. I feel so out of place."

Uncle Sándor put down his knife and fork, reached across the table and stroked her hand.

"I know how you feel, little Kati," he whispered. "I understand. I'm not used to being in places like this any more either. There were times before the war when your Aunt Irén and I used to travel here. We could afford it then. But now... So much has happened. The horrors of communism, the constant fear and misery has dampened my spirit too. There is such a great difference between our lives at home and this..." He motioned toward the guests.

Kati ate in silence.

Uncle Sándor continued. "I know you have it good in America, but this here is utter luxury. Most of these people are so superficial and selfish, and ah, so materialistic. Always putting on airs, trying to appear more important and wealthier than they really are. I can see right through them. And most don't care about how people live back in Hungary. They only care about themselves and their position in the world. I can see how lonely and out of place you feel among them."

"Uncle Sándor, some of them are such fakes. I have a hard time warming up to them. This guy from Munich, for instance. He's pestering me, and I don't want to make a scene..."

"Don't worry so much, Kati dear. Everything will be all right. You'll see," Uncle Sándor patted her hand affectionately. "And I'll take care of the guy from Munich," he added.

Kati reached for her purse, took out a Kleenex and wiped her tears. She tried to smile as she gazed into her uncle's eyes. "Thank you, Uncle Sándor. I'll be all right. Please forget what I just said." The conversation soon turned to more cheerful topics. A few minutes later they became aware of a lively discussion at one of the nearby tables.

"Conditions in Hungary are still pretty bleak," Kati heard the boisterous voice of the radio announcer from Munich. "Nothing has really changed. They're just trying to make things look good for tourists from the West. This 'goulash communism' is completely ridiculous and misleading. The whole country is overloaded with debt. People still live in fear and endless restrictions are put on their lives. And economically, well, they are the pitts."

Uncle Sándor stood up slowly. He surveyed the guests, one by one. Kati watched her uncle wringing his hands and looking unusually solemn. People at the nearby tables turned toward him. "I would like to know what he has to say," a lady in blue whispered. "After all, he has first-hand experience."

Uncle Sándor cleared his throat.

"Dear friends, it's easy to criticize Hungary and the people from a luxury yacht in the Mediterranean. You can enjoy the opportunities the West has to offer. But it's quite different to live in your native land and to try to do something for the country."

An uneasy silence followed. Only a few people chattered on; the majority prepared to listen.

"We are making the best of an unfortunate situation," Uncle Sándor continued in an earnest voice. "You all know quite well that aggressive nations from the East have always wished to rule our country. First came the Tatars, the Turks, then the Habsburgs, and now the Russians. It's part of our thousand-year old history." His tone was bitter.

The eerie silence continued. No one denied the truth of what Uncle Sándor had said. Kati felt like voicing support for his views. She had wanted to tell these people who had countless gripes and found so many faults with their native land, that in spite of everything, Hungary was still the home of Hungarian language and culture, regardless of the government.

"I think it's important to go back for visits," she heard herself speak as she stood up next to her uncle. Her voice was strong and emphatic. "I think young people should get to know the country of their ancestors. To experience its unique culture first hand. We only have one life to live, and anyway, nothing lasts forever... Who knows, maybe in the near future..." She looked meaningfully at László who stood close by, looking at Kati with curiosity in his eyes.

Kati continued. "Of course, there is no easy solution to all this. But, how can we feel attached to a country if we refuse to set foot on it? If we refuse to have anything to do with those who live there, those who stayed behind?" Even she was surprised at her own bold tone, but she felt strongly about this, and at this moment she didn't care on whose toes she had just stepped. She was aware that visiting communist Hungary was a major issue among Hungarians in the West, and those who set foot on Hungarian soil under the present government were labeled as "fellow travelers," "communist sympathizers," or even traitors. Kati and her parents were among them.

Then a tall, middle-aged man with sandy hair that matched his mustache spoke up, obviously trying to relieve the tension created by the mention of the motherland.

"I agree with the young lady. The new generation is in a different situation. They don't have bitter experiences from the past like we do. How can we expect them to have an attachment to their parents' homeland, if they have never been there? Of course, there are Hungarian communities in the West where they can participate in Hungarian activities, but that cannot replace the experience of a real visit. And anyway, most families live scattered throughout Europe and North America, and most don't have the money to send their kids to Hungary."

"You're right." The man from Calgary who said he knew Kati's parents agreed. "But you know what, all of us heard of all the bickering that's going on in these communities, and a lot of young people get fed up and resist learning the language, and leave their culture. But a visit home often gives them an incentive to find out more about the land of their ancestors."

"Yes, everyone knows if there are two Hungarians together, they form three political parties," a lady observed in a somber tone. Her voice was harsh.

"That's not true," the radio announcer from Radio Free Europe shouted from the back. "I'll never set foot on Hungarian soil until those damn Russians leave," he continued. "It's not my country as long as those commies are there."

"But what about the people who live there? Don't you think our visits give them hope?" Kati asked.

"Ah, you're so naive," the radio announcer shouted back. "No decent Hungarian wants to support the commies." His face turned so red, that Kati was afraid he would have a heart attack.

"Let's leave such serious discussions for another time." Uncle Sándor interrupted, forcing a smile. "I'm sorry I started this topic." His gentle voice had a calming effect. "The day is just too magnificent, the food and wine too delicious and the women too beautiful to think of such serious matters."

Kati was grateful to her uncle for having saved the day with his wit and charm, like a well-versed diplomat. Thank God, a nasty confrontation had been avoided.

A man in his early forties soon caught her attention, someone she had not seen before. He was sitting at the far end of the deck with some other guests. Kati watched him stand up, his gaze focused on her. He walked straight up to Kati.

"Let's dance the *csárdás,* little girl, I hope you learned to dance in America," He motioned to the Gypsy band, and they began to play a familiar lively tune.

Kati was reluctant to accept, for she was in no mood for dancing. She glanced at László with pleading eyes, but he only smiled and shrugged his shoulders, signaling to go ahead. When Kati nodded her consent, he did not take his eyes off the two as they began to dance, first slowly, then with increasing temperament.

Kati decided that she would show the man what she had learned in America. Giving herself up completely to the rhythm of the dance, she remembered her Girl Scout days in Cleveland when she had been a member of the folk dance ensemble and had learned the intricate steps of this most popular dance of her parents' homeland. Soon a whole crowd of guests gathered around them. The admiration in their eyes matched László's look of approval, giving her added incentive. Her partner turned out to be an excellent dancer. The music finally stopped, and they sat down, both totally exhausted.

There was more dancing, pleasant conversation and the question of the proper attitude toward present-day Hungary did not come up again. The afternoon passed quickly, and soon it was time for another meal. Delicious food was served again, and Aunt Juli, Gino, and Walter kept busy catering to the needs of the guests. Aunt Sári still looked bright-eyed and lovely, although Kati noticed that when she was alone for a moment, signs of weariness appeared on her face. She saw Miklós glancing in her aunt's direction several times, and once the two of them disappeared in the cabins below.

Kati hoped that no one had noticed their departure, for she felt embarrassed by their strange behavior.

It was already getting dark when the guests settled comfortably into the deck chairs, continuing their chatter, telling jokes, and laughing exuberantly.

Then a few of the guests began to sing some Hungarian folk melodies and Kati watched as the others slowly gathered around the singing group. Even the Italians stopped their animated conversations, and prepared to listen. Like Hungarians, they too enjoyed singing together. As was the custom, they first began with lively tunes, but gradually turned to those sad, melancholic songs that are the closest to the heart of every Hungarian. Soon everyone joined in, and as Kati recognized the songs she had learned in Cleveland, she marveled at the strange fate of her ancestors: The same melodies were sung in the tranquil mountains and forests of Transylvania, the Great Hungarian Plain in Hungary, the Hungarian Scout camps in North America, and on a luxury yacht in the Mediterranean. Singing these songs always brought a peculiar feeling of camaraderie and togetherness. Kati noted the same sad and melancholic expression on the faces of singers and listeners alike, as they gazed straight ahead into the darkness of the sea, or with glazed eyes stared at the floor of the yacht.

Kati's gloomy mood had all but disappeared. Yet she found herself dwelling pensively on her own life, pondering her future. She thought of Michael, their different background and culture. He would never feel comfortable listening to these songs of her heritage, never would he be able to understand her deep attachment to everything Hungarian. There were a little over three weeks left of her Italian holiday. These fabulous surroundings, the seaside Villa Tokay, the San Remo palazzo, last night's magnificent ball, and this cruise would soon be nothing but a memory she would fondly remember in her old age. She thought of last night, László's kisses and his embrace, and she felt a great emptiness in her heart. They had not talked since early afternoon when he disappeared so suddenly, leaving her alone with her melancholia. She had seen him a few times since, and he never took his eyes off of her when she danced the *csárdás*. But he spent most of the day in the company of Angela and other women, where he was always the center of attention, laughing and talking gaily. Kati had the feeling that he had been avoiding her on purpose.

The man who had occupied the chair next to her had just stood up, promising to return with a refreshing drink. She happened to sit down next to him right after the *csárdás*, and he had stayed close to her ever since, following her with annoying determination. His wife, a frivolous and flirtatious blonde, was occupied with several other men, so she didn't mind at all. But his racy stories about his affairs with women, and his constant bragging about his prominence in the steel industry bored Kati. She was glad when he left, and decided to leave the table by the time he returned.

As she stood up and looked around for a place of refuge, she saw László walking in her direction. Surprised, and as if mesmerized by seeing him again, she sat down, almost mechanically, in the nearest chair.

László walked straight up to her and settled casually in the empty seat next to hers. Kati blushed when she realized that László saw that she had stayed around because of him. She avoided his glance, and the very thought of his knowing why she stayed made her feel uncomfortable. The more she tried to hide her embarrassment, the redder her face became.

"How's the *'csárdás'* girl' doing?" László asked with unmistakable irony. "I thought you only liked waltzes, tangos, and those slow romantic tunes."

"As you could see, I like other things too..."

"You're a strange girl, little Kati. Shy and withdrawn in one moment, full of fire in the next."

Kati did not reply. What could she say to that? She searched for a new topic.

"You didn't speak up when we talked about serious subjects," she remarked.

"You know how I feel."

"Well, I think it's outrageous to write books about countries one has not visited for years," she said vehemently. "I happen to know some other people like that, besides you." The next moment she wanted to take back what she had said. László was probably one of those people who stuck to his views, and would not change them, no matter what.

But he gave no sign of disapproval, and did not seem to mind her comment.

Kati felt emboldened. "You know, I think you should go and visit Hungary. Just to look around. My father always told me to have an open mind, to examine the situation and then form an opinion."

László seemed lost in thought, but did not reply.

"Things do change, you know."

"We'll see little Kati, we'll see," he said in a calm voice. It was clear he did not wish to pursue the subject. "Anyway, did you know that we are related? Sort of," he asked in a conciliatory tone.

"Related? How?" Kati could not imagine how this could be.

"Well, my half-brother, Kálmán, married your Aunt Sári. It was a great love affair. You mean, you didn't know?"

Kati suddenly remembered that on their way from the Genoa airport, Miklós had alluded to Aunt Sári and László being related. But the information had completely slipped her mind and she never gave it a second thought.

So that was the second marriage Aunt Sári had mentioned.

"Oh, and they had a daughter, Annie," Kati added eagerly. "Aunt Sári told me. But where are they now? What in the world happened to them?"

László's face darkened. He lowered his voice. "Kálmán became a successful politician here in Italy. But as it always happens, he had many rivals. One day when he and Annie were driving to Rome to visit me, they simply vanished. There was one inquiry after another. Some people even speculated that the Mafia was responsible. That was five years ago. We haven't heard from them since." László's voice quivered.

"They both disappeared without a trace. You can imagine how devastated we were, especially your Aunt Sári. But I miss them too. I miss my brother terribly. He was much older than I, but he was such a great guy, a good person, and a caring brother."

"You mean they both just disappeared? Just like that?" Kati thought more about Aunt Sári's grief than anything else. For a moment her own problems dwarfed in comparison.

László continued, looking straight at Kati.

"As you can imagine, your aunt took it very hard. The endless investigations, many from high places, brought no clues. For years after the tragedy she wouldn't see anyone except a few close friends. She still tries hard to hide her pain. She adored Kálmán. It was a great love affair and their marriage one of perfect harmony, very rare these days."

Both were silent for a moment. "I remember how upset our parents were at the time. They were very much against Sári, the wealthy young woman who had gotten rich by marrying into the Mafia. They didn't think she was the appropriate wife for a von Temessy, even though she had the proper pedigree."

Kati listened intently. All this was news she had never heard before.

"But your aunt is a great lady, Kati, a wonderful, warm person. She is also very..."

László did not finish, yet his look revealed that there was something wrong.

"Oh, László, is... is Aunt Sári ill?" Kati stammered. "I heard a man at the ball mention something. But I couldn't hear clearly..."

"Yes, little Kati, your aunt is very ill. She has SBE, subacute bacterial endocarditis. Miklós has been treating her."

"I've never heard of the disease."

"Well, it's not very common. They had a hard time diagnosing it. The symptoms vary greatly, such as fever, fatigue, headache, and at times chills, nausea and vomiting... If she's not operated on soon, she won't have much time left..."

He paused, avoiding Kati's eyes."And there is little hope, even with surgery." Although he tried to control his emotions, László's voice was shaking.

Two big tears rolled down Kati's cheeks. She made no attempt to hide them.

László continued quietly.

"She didn't want to tell you. She just wanted to see you once more. She told me how she always liked you when you were a little girl. The reunion was a good excuse to invite you."

László turned his head from Kati. Both looked pensively into the darkness of the sea. The perpetual rhythm of the waves was ringing in their ears, enhancing their melancholic mood. Kati thought about the strangeness of life, the peculiar things that happen to people. Here was Aunt Sári, so beautiful and wealthy, yet laden with so much grief and misfortune.

"I know life had not been too kind to you, either." She heard László's hushed voice, sounding as if he were far away. She was touched by his concern.

"I managed." she said and forced a smile. But when she thought of Aunt Sári she had a hard time controlling her tears.

"I'm glad you told me," she said. At least now she would be more attentive to her aunt and would try harder to bring some happiness to the days she had left.

László reached out to touch her hand and squeezed it gently.

"Everything will turn out all right, you'll see. It's just so hard sometimes." His voice broke, and for a while they sat in silence. Then, as if to drive away all pain and sadness, he stood up and stroked Kati's head like a father.

"Chin up, little Kati," he said with forced cheerfulness. He motioned to some guests to join them and the conversation took a different turn.

The cruise continued into the night and it was past midnight when they arrived back at the San Remo port. Kati watched the lively crowd as they left the yacht, laughing and talking, amid vigorous gesticulations, a habit that Italians and Hungarians share.

As Kati watched Aunt Sári saying good-bye to her guests, she scrutinized her aunt's face and her movements. She noticed no trace of any illness, although she remembered her strange disappearances with Miklós. His frequent presence at her side was finally cleared up by László when he told her that Miklós was a physician, and had been treating Aunt Sári for several months.

László said good-bye and left with the Ruggieros. Kati felt empty inside, yet she knew that there was nothing she could do to change his relationship with the beautiful Angela. Her own problems were pushed to the back of her mind when she thought of Aunt Sári's illness. At least she was in good health, and would soon be returning to a secure and comfortable life with Michael, while Aunt Sári's very existence was at stake.

"The Ruggieros hope that László will marry Angela," a young woman remarked in a loud squeaky voice. She was standing next to Kati as they watched the four of them disappear behind the olive trees.

"László is an exceptional fellow, quite intriguing, don't you think?" She turned to Kati with a sly smile. "We're all out to catch him," she laughed excitedly, but we haven't been successful yet." She paused with a knowing smile. "Although, he is not immune to the charms of attractive women..." She looked meaningfully at Kati again, obviously trying to give the impression that she knew from first-hand experience.

The guests were finally gone, and Kati settled into the backseat of the Mercedes with Aunt Sári, when she noticed a tall figure approaching them in the dark. It was László. Her heart skipped a beat. She did not expect to see him again so soon.

"I just wanted to see the three of you again," he said with a mysterious air, as he leaned on the back window where Aunt Sári sat. "You know, I have to fly back to Rome tomorrow..." Kati's heart sank. He is leaving already. I'll probably never see him again, she thought. What an unpleasant day this turned out to be! How long, will he be gone, she wondered. She knew that he had business to attend to, but secretly hoped that he would spend one more day at the palazzo. There was still another day left of the reunion.

"I'll take Kati home. Do you mind?" She heard László's deep baritone as he looked at Aunt Sári.

"Not at all. Go ahead." Aunt Sári gave László an approving nod. "Young people always have so much to talk about."

Kati felt anger swelling inside. Why didn't he ask her? She was an adult! If László felt like doing something, he just went ahead, disregarding everyone else. He must have always had his way, she reflected, and wondered how anyone could put up with that for long. One minute he seemed so understanding and kind, yet the next moment he was a tyrant, demanding total control.

She did not want to make a scene. After all, she was a guest here. She planted a quick kiss on the cheeks of her aunt and great uncle and walked over to László's Porsche.

"You're angry with me again," László remarked as he opened the door.

"Everyone is treating me like a child," Kati said. "No one asked me what I wanted." She knew she should be flattered at the prospect of spending more time with László, as she recalled the words of the squeaky-voiced woman.

László ignored her remark. "I have an idea. Let's stop at a café on our way back to the palazzo," he suggested as he started the motor. Kati did not reply. She felt overwhelmed by his presence. The seats were close in the small car, and she was beginning to feel very vulnerable, having to sit so close to him.

In a few minutes her anger and frustration subsided, and a feeling of coziness enveloped her whole being. As they were driving up on the winding road, Kati noticed a well-lit café at the top of the hill with soft music filtering from the same direction.

"This is it," László said, and pulled up in front of the quaint building appropriately named Café Eldorado. To Kati's surprise there was still a large crowd inside. All but a few parking spaces were left. An all-night café, Kati thought as she recognized the soothing voice of Julio Iglesias on the stereo, singing his popular romantic tunes of love. The feeling of romance was in the air.

László led the way inside. The head waiter must have known him, for he hurried toward the door as they stepped inside.

"*Dottore Professore! Salute!*" Kati was surprised by his boisterous enthusiasm. He quickly led them to a small table in the back as he took a long, approving glance at Kati. She had the distinct feeling she was not the first woman the kind "*dottore"* had brought to this place. And how could it be? There was Angela... And who knows how many more...

They sat down, and Kati found herself face to face with László. It was hard to avoid each other's eyes, for the table was small and Kati had to shift in her chair several times to avoid touching László's knees.

"It must be a wonderful feeling to be rich and famous," Kati began, just to break the silence, although there was a hint of sarcasm in her voice. A moment later, she was embarrassed for having made such a stupid, everyday remark.

But László showed no signs of disapproval. He looked her straight in the eye.

"You know, I worked very hard to get where I am. And it wasn't that easy for a foreigner to work his way up. There is a lot of competition, and people are often at each other's throats. They watch each other like hawks, hoping that the other person will make a mistake." He paused for a moment. "There is so much politics everywhere. Not to mention the world of academe. You really have to play your cards right."

"My father told me about that. He was Head Librarian at Cleveland State University."

"Then you know what people are like and how they behave."

"You're not going to believe this," Kati said, animated by the topic. "But the President of the University even received a letter from a Hungarian emigré, urging him to fire my father from his position because he dared to visit Hungary in the 1970's. He insinuated that *Apuka* was an agent, working for the communists."

"Really?" Now it was László's turn to be surprised. "Someone would actually do something like that? A fellow Hungarian?"

Kati nodded. They stopped talking for a while, pondering about the state of affairs in the world, a world so clearly divided by differing ideologies and diverse political convictions.

"Everyone who disagrees with mainstream beliefs is under suspicion," Kati added in a serious voice.

"Let's not get carried away by such tedious information." László remarked playfully, taking a sip from his glass as he eyed Kati closely.

They listened to the romantic tunes in silence, searching for a new topic.

"Let's dance," László finally suggested. "May I?"

"All right," Kati replied as she emptied her glass of *Frascati* while László motioned the waiter for another bottle. "The same," he whispered.

They squeezed their way from behind the small table and László took her in his arms. Immersing themselves into the rhythm of Julio's newest hit "Natalie," they barely noticed when another of his melodies filled the air.

I feel completely out of this world in his arms, Kati admitted. Her anger and frustration disappeared. László pulled her closer while they danced in such harmony that it felt like they had practiced together for years. "A kiss on the forehead won't hurt you, will it, little Kati?" he whispered.

They kept on dancing. Then László pulled her even closer, so that her forehead touched his chin. She could hardly breathe as he squeezed her against his muscular torso. He bent down slowly, searching for her lips. He began kissing her as she felt all her resistance melting into thin air. The excitement of his touch brought feelings Kati had not experienced with such intensity before. Another passionate kiss followed and Kati was beginning to feel embarrassed. She was sober enough to realize that his touch was becoming too intimate.

"Please don't," she whispered and pulled away.

Kati knew that László felt offended. He has probably always gotten what he wanted from women, and apparently, he believed she was no exception. They squeezed through the dancing crowd, back to their table.

"You've already heard that I'm engaged to be married." Kati blurted out, looking across the small table, straight into his eyes.

"Are you really?" He looked at her in surprise. "I thought it was just a piece of gossip circulated by those who felt threatened by Aunt Sári's 'beautiful niece from America.'" Kati noted a shadow crossing his face. For a moment he sat motionless, his expression solemn. Then he leaned closer to Kati.

"Who is the lucky fellow?"

"An American. His name is Michael Keller."

"I see. An American? You mean you're going to spend your life with an American?" He sounded incredulous.

Kati nodded. "Why not? Michael is someone I can always depend on. He's helped me through so much when I needed help. He was always there for me." Then she looked straight into László's eyes. "And I love him."

"Really?"

Kati did not reply. The shadow of doubt passed through her heart.

For a while they sat in silence listening to Julio's soothing voice. Then László leaned back in his chair and the intimate aura between them vanished. Kati watched in alarm as his expression turned distant. The romantic tunes of the handsome Spaniard no longer seemed to matter.

"Tell me about life in America, little Kati," László tried to make the best of the situation. Again this "little Kati business," she thought, as if I were a child.

"What is it like to live in the best and greatest country in the world?"

"It's nice, very pleasant," Kati stammered still under the influence of his kiss and his embrace. "But I really don't know American society that well. At least from close up, from my own experience. I grew up in a Hungarian neighborhood, and our lives revolved around Hungarian churches and organizations, especially the Scouts." Furrows appeared on her forehead, as she became thoughtful. "You know, our customs were so mixed. A strange world, I have to admit. Neither Hungarian, nor American."

"How fascinating," László leaned closer.

"I have to admit one thing. Americans are very friendly and open, and not as biased as some Europeans," Kati observed.

"Well, if you say so," László did not seem convinced. "But I've heard about those ethnic neighborhoods. There is this new interest in ethnicity. I wonder if it will last."

"I don't know, László. The fact is those neighborhoods still exist, although many are dying a slow death. The younger generation is moving out. But I know one thing, I am glad I grew up in two cultures. It made my life more interesting, more meaningful." Kati's voice had the ring of certainty.

László eyed her with interest. He reached over the table and touched her hand.

"Can't we just forget that you're engaged? He asked in a spirited voice. "Let's just forget it while you're in Italy."

"No, I can't forget," Kati replied. "It's like a brick wall surrounding me, keeping me in check." But she did not withdraw her hand. A peculiar feeling of calm coupled with excitement overwhelmed her. She wished this unexplainable feeling would last forever. They emptied the second bottle of *Frascati,* but they talked only about everyday things. Then László looked at his watch and a worried look crossed his face.

"Let's go, Kati. It's getting very late. Your aunt and uncle are probably worrying about us," he added with a gleam in his eyes that shone cat-like in the dimly lit room.

They soon arrived at the tall gate of the palazzo, and László walked her to the top of the marble steps. As Kati extended her hand to say good-bye, he took both her hands and whispered.

"You know, I will be gone for a while. Actually, I don't know how long." His eyes sparkled. "You can spare an old book-worm a farewell kiss, can't you?"

Then he kissed her so hard and so long that Kati lost track of time completely. She felt herself yielding more and more to his embrace. He is leaving, maybe I'll never see him again, she thought wildly.

Then he let her go, planting a last kiss on her forehead.

"Sleep tight, little Kati. Good night, and good-bye."

"Good night," Kati whispered. She watched his tall figure disappear in the darkness. For a while she just stood there, unable to move.

Why did he say "good-bye," she pondered.

When László's spell was finally broken, she pushed the massive front door open and entered. For a moment she stood in the great hall, mesmerized. Then she walked up the staircase and stepped into her room. She threw herself on the bed, and her thoughts flew to Cleveland and to Michael who seemed farther away than ever before. She had never felt this way about him; she hardly dared to admit this, even to herself.

She had felt so vulnerable with László, as if from now on she were completely in his power, without a will of her own. Yet, she felt perfectly at ease in his company and his entire being filled her with expectation, of exciting things to come. The feeling was entirely new.

This cannot be happening to me, she kept telling herself, as she lay on top of the comfortable bed, relishing those new sensations of infatuation and maybe... maybe... love...

The next moment she tried to dismiss László from her thoughts; after all, she had already committed herself to someone else. But all her attempts were in vain.

Kati hoped and prayed that he would come back soon. Where was he going, she wondered. She could not imagine her stay on the Riviera without him anymore.

7

Aunt Sári's Illness

San Remo

The third day of the reunion turned out to be uneventful. László was gone, and although Kati was determined to forget him, she could not put him out of her mind. Even at the garden party held on the palazzo grounds, in the midst of a large crowd of guests, her thoughts turned to him as she recalled for the hundredth time every small detail of their conversation on the yacht and during the few hours they had spent together at the Café Eldorado the night before.

She smiled politely at the guests, but her mind was like a soaring falcon in the blue sky, oblivious to what was going on down below. Some eyed her with curiosity, and even whispered behind her back, but she was determined not to take anything to heart.

"She'll inherit Sári's wealth for sure," the awkward Baron Lódi remarked to his wife when Kati walked past them. "She's nothing but a fortune hunter," Baroness Lódi added with a frown. "That little bitch is so lucky. She didn't do anything to deserve it. Look at us, we hardly have anything, although we both worked hard all our lives..." She made a face at her husband, and it was apparent that she felt bitter about her own circumstances, blaming him for their misfortunes and lack of prosperity.

Kati tried to act as if she did not hear them, and made an effort to chat with everyone, just trying to get through the day. She even endured the arrogant speech of Marquis Yordanos, but she did all this with her mind not being there at all. Late afternoon, when she noticed that the couple from Cologne were saying their final good-bye to Aunt Sári, she hurried to join them.

"We are delighted to have met you," the professor's wife smiled as she gave Kati a kiss on both cheeks. "Don't forget to look us up if you travel our way..."

"I won't be going to Germany. But I'll be back in Cleveland soon. I'll write to you from there," Kati promised.

Besides her aunt and uncle, they were the only guests she felt close to, and she sensed that the feeling was mutual. She sighed in relief when all the guests had finally gone and only Aunt Sári and Uncle Sándor remained. She sat down at their table in the spacious garden while Walter brought out a large tray with hors d'oeuvres and lemonade. Kati was put off by his toothy smile as she noted the perpetual suspicion in his cool blue eyes as he glared at her slyly. This fellow can't stand me, she thought for a fleeting moment while she concentrated on what her aunt and uncle were saying.

"My dream has finally come true. I had all my friends here. And of course, I'm so happy that both of you came," Aunt Sári settled back in her chair. She was glowing with satisfaction as she looked at Uncle Sándor and Kati.

"Everything went so well, didn't it? Just as I had planned." But she became misty-eyed for a moment, and Kati felt certain that she was thinking of her loved ones, her husband Kálmán and daughter Annie. Uncle Sándor and Kati tried to cheer her.

"Did you see how your old friend William was flirting with the Countess Ruggiero?" Uncle Sándor asked. "She must have felt pretty offended by his advances."

"I actually think she enjoyed all the attention. William is a great flatterer and a charmer," Aunt Sári smiled. "And he acts like he knows everyone who's supposed to be important. A typical name-dropper, and a sleek one at that."

They related unusual and funny incidents that took place during the three days.

"Did you notice how that crazy poet pursued Angela all afternoon, reciting some of his verses to her?" Aunt Sári asked, "Good thing László wasn't there." Then she added as an afterthought, "He would have told him to lay off."

Kati bit her lips, registering Aunt Sári's remark with alarm. There must be something to their relationship after all, she thought darkly. I don't have a chance...

From then on, she sat in silence, not knowing what to say next. Hopeless thoughts raced through her mind. I am just an outsider here, so far removed from this world of wealth and glamour... László would never take me seriously. But then, I am the one who's engaged to be married, she reminded herself.

Although Aunt Sári and Uncle Sándor joked about the strange antics of the peculiar guests, Kati could not let up, and her mood changed from bad to worse.

"I have such a headache," she complained to her aunt. "I'll just lie down a little."

She ran up the magnificent staircase, not even bothering to glance at the splendid paintings on the walls. She threw herself on her bed and began to sob. What am I doing here? Why did I come? I should have listened to Michael... She thought of making up a story about her having to return immediately, but when she thought of Aunt Sári's illness, she could not bring herself to go through with it.

Kati spent the next several days at the San Remo palazzo, almost exclusively in the company of her aunt and uncle, admiring the magnificence of the building, the exquisite period furniture in every room, and the exotic flowers, plants, and trees on the surrounding grounds, delighting in every newly discovered detail.

Aunt Sári and Uncle Sándor usually slept late and had breakfast in their rooms from a tray expertly prepared by Aunt Juli, while Kati slipped into the kitchen very early, eager for an hour's chat with the cheerful housekeeper. Aunt Juli was always in good spirits, going about her household chores with an air of importance, and Kati was touched by her common sense philosophy and her ability to see the bright side of things. "Always look at the sunny side of life," she kept telling Kati. Her words restored Kati's mental balance, and she soon regained her former sense of well-being and optimism. The depression and loneliness she felt so acutely on the cruise and after the reunion gradually disappeared, and she became her old self again, determined to make a life with Michael, and to succeed in her career back home in Cleveland.

Aunt Juli was eager to share small bits of information about her own life, her childhood in the village of Buják in northern Hungary, her escape from the country in 1956, and her marriage to the good-natured Gino. "I've been with your aunt ever since she married Rodolfo Pugliese, her first husband," she told Kati. "I enjoy working for her. She is such a great lady."

It seemed to Kati that through the years Aunt Juli had become more like a loving and concerned relative than a housekeeper. She loved Aunt Sári to the point of adoration, satisfying at the same time her own frustrated maternal instincts. She displayed the same affection toward Kati from the first day they had met, and Kati was thankful for the genuine friendship that had developed between them.

One morning as they were chatting in the sunny breakfast room just off the kitchen, Aunt Juli sat down across the table from Kati and lowered her voice. The deep lines on her face showed more than ever before, and Kati wondered why she looked so upset.

"*Katikám,* my dear little Kati, you know your aunt is very ill," Aunt Juli smoothed her forehead with her right hand and adjusted her red polka-dot scarf which had become her trademark. "Yes, I know. László told me. Oh, Aunt Juli, I am so worried." Kati had not discussed her aunt's illness with anyone before, not even with Uncle Sándor. The subject never came up, and it seemed to her that everyone was avoiding it, as if their silence would make Aunt Sári's illness disappear. Aunt Juli went on, as Kati listened eagerly.

"Miklós was here last night and told me that in a week or ten days she will have to leave for Baltimore, in America, to the Johns Hopkins University Medical Center. Maybe they can help her there, he said. He had already made arrangements." Aunt Juli's voice wavered, and for a while she sat still, struggling to keep her composure.

It was Kati who finally broke the silence. "I was hoping it wouldn't come so soon."

"Me too. Actually, your aunt waited too long with the reunion. And your invitation. She should've asked you to come a long time ago."

She fought her tears as she leaned both elbows on the table and looked Kati straight in the eye. "Your aunt is such a wonderful person. How I hate to see her so sick! I can't imagine life without her..."

"I love her dearly too. I'm so sorry I didn't get to know her sooner. But there was nothing I could do."

"What's going to happen to you, dear? She may have to go to America before the month is over. What will you do here, all alone?"

"I can always go back to Cleveland sooner."

"I'm going to miss her so much," Aunt Juli burst into tears. "And you know little Kati, I'll miss you too." It was apparent she was no longer able to control herself. Feeling totally helpless, Kati stood up and walked over to her side of the table. She began stroking her head, at times touching the gray strands of hair that peeked out from under her red polka dot scarf.

"We must be strong," Kati whispered, trying to console her.

"I know. I know. But what's going to happen to all this? To all of us?" Aunt Juli stood up and made a sweeping gesture with her arm. She looked around helplessly, as if waiting for Kati to offer a solution.

"I don't know. I have no idea," Kati said. I just got here ten days ago, how should I know what to do, she thought to herself. Then she said outloud, "Aunt Juli, I'm sure everything will be all right. There's always hope. Medicine is well-advanced in America, and the Johns Hopkins University Hospital is a good place to be..."

Reluctantly, Aunt Juli wiped her tears. She took a deep breath and crossed herself. Her expression gradually changed to one of determination.

"God will help us. God *must* help us," she said as she wiped her eyes repeatedly, and looked straight ahead. "You're right, little Kati. Maybe they'll be able to cure her. Maybe things won't be so bad. Things have a way of turning out all right in the end. After all I have been through, I should know..."

She looked closely at Kati, as her deep brown eyes glowed through her tears.

"Sometimes I worry more about you than about your aunt. You are still so young. What are you going to do in Cleveland, married to that American, without your family?" Then, as if she just had a brilliant idea, she exclaimed enthusiastically, "Why don't you just stay here until your Aunt Sári gets back? There are many young people around to keep you company."

She stopped for a moment. "For example, there's László." Her eyes twinkled as she added, "He's not married yet." She put a special emphasis on the word "yet."

Kati blushed and whispered, "László?" Hearing his name took her by surprise. For a moment, she felt immobilized, and hid her face behind her hands. "Don't mention *him* to me, Aunt

Juli," she burst out. "I don't want to see *him* again, and it would be better if we never meet again!"

Aunt Juli was taken aback. "You don't mean..."

Having vowed not to let anyone know her feelings toward László, Kati forced herself to calm down, afraid that she would betray herself. "He's a nice fellow, but... but I am not his type. And as you well know, Aunt Juli, I have plans, I am engaged, even our wedding date..."

Kati could not finish her sentence, for Gino appeared in the doorway, and after planting a quick kiss on his wife's cheeks, he asked her something very urgent, in rapid Italian. Kati had the feeling it had to do with Aunt Sári's illness, yet she was thankful, for the interruption had put an end to their conversation about László.

Aunt Juli got up quickly from the table and hurried out with Gino. "I'll see you later, little Kati," she whispered. Kati sat stunned, wondering what had happened. She had no choice but to return to her room. She spent the rest of the day there reading.

Each day, she was more and more plagued with the idea of Aunt Sári's illness. The uncertainty was beginning to wear her out. Yet, since neither her aunt, nor her uncle revealed the slightest sign of concern, she thought it best to remain silent. Since they never mentioned it, nor alluded to it in any way, she considered it improper to ask questions.

There were days when she even felt that it wasn't at all true, that her aunt enjoyed perfect health. Aunt Sári's looks and demeanor were certainly deceiving. She appeared cheerful and seemed to be in good humor, and Kati detected no tell-tale signs of illness on her face. She had even taken Kati on several shopping trips in San Remo. They went in and out of the fashionable boutiques, while Walter waited for them on the corner of the Via Andrea Dorea in the *Café Danilo*. Kati thoroughly enjoyed these excursions, and she was delighted by the shopping district, the orange and lemon trees lining the narrow streets, and the crowds of people walking leisurely, savoring delicious Italian *gelato* or simply sitting at one of the sidewalk cafés, sipping a cup of *cappuccino* or a glass of refreshing beer.

Kati noted that the salesgirls were especially attentive to Aunt Sári. Most of them seemed to know her, addressing her as *"Contessa."* The two of them bought some of the most beautiful outfits that Kati had ever dreamed of, all highly fashionable and of the finest material. Kati trusted Aunt Sári's taste, and although reluctantly at first, she accepted the clothes they had chosen together. Once, as she was trying on a pretty summer dress, László flashed through her mind and she wondered whether he would ever see her wearing it. Would he notice how flattering it was to her slender waist and tanned good looks?

After dinner in the evenings, they would take long walks in the palazzo garden that seemed to Kati more like a paradise every day, and Aunt Sári and Uncle Sándor would talk about old times and family affairs.

"Do you know how upset I was when you and Anna left Hungary in '56?" Uncle Sándor remarked one evening. "I wondered what would happen to you in a strange country. I felt better about Anna," he confided, "At least she was married. But you, you were alone. When both of you left, we were heartbroken. It took your Aunt Irén a long time to recover..."

Uncle Sándor looked away, avoiding Aunt Sári's eyes.

They were strolling along lush flower beds studded with red geraniums and white petunias. The walkways were lined with flowering magnolias, olive trees, and a wide variety of palms. Tell-tale signs of Gino's gardening expertise were visible everywhere, for he kept the garden in perfect order, yet it seemed to Kati that he was rarely visible. He must be working during the night, she thought. As she looked around, savoring the wealth, comfort, and ease evident everywhere, she thought that if people were to see them now, walking together, impeccably dressed, at ease, and conversing quietly, they would not believe the tumultuous life each of them had. How could they guess what the three of them had been through? And now, there was Aunt Sári's illness, the impending doom hanging over their family.

"You shouldn't have worried," Kati heard Aunt Sári's voice, as she reflected on what Uncle Sándor just said. "Look at me now. I have a more than comfortable life, you know that. Of course, Kálmán and Annie..." She suddenly lost her composure and a big tear appeared in her dark eyes, flowing down her cheeks. She no longer tried to hide her sorrow from her uncle and niece, and Kati was grateful that the three of them got along so well, and enjoyed each other's company. Kati was convinced that the feeling of closeness, the idea of belonging together as a family became stronger with each passing day.

"And now, what's going to happen to all this? If only Annie were alive," Aunt Sári sighed and looked at Kati as if embarrassed by her presence. This was the first time that she had even alluded to her illness. Kati listened closely.

"Look at it another way, Sári dear." Uncle Sándor attempted to console her. "At least you had several years of uninterrupted happiness. Even I can say that, despite all the misfortune that came my way."

Then he went on in a husky voice, without the slightest tone of bitterness.

"Of course, you know quite well that we were filled with terror and fear when we had to leave our home and were transported to Transdanubia, to Enying. Even your Aunt Irén had to work out in the fields. Then came Recsk for me and your father." He sighed deeply. "First Kistárcsa, then Recsk. Those utterly demeaning and inhuman conditions in the prison, and the forced labor camps... The uncertainty and the fear of death..."

He took a deep breath. "The communists were determined to annihilate the upper classes. And they succeeded. Your Aunt Irén took it very hard. I think that's what killed her," he added sadly.

"My parents too. They couldn't bear the shock of it all." Aunt Sári said with emotion.

"The worst thing was when the Hungarian Secret Police, the AVH came to take me. Your father and I had no idea why we were arrested."

Each day, Kati was learning more about her family. Her grandmother, Aunt Sári's mother, had also been deported to Transdanubia. They lived in a one-room peasant hut. She just could not imagine her own mother living there as a teenager, let alone Aunt Sári, who looked as if she had lived in luxury all her life, without interruption.

"When you are on the losing side of two devastating wars," Uncle Sándor explained in a low voice, "then you can expect a lot of calamity for the nation. It's always the people who suffer. Everyone. Regardless of class."

After a while Kati grew tired of listening to depressing stories about the past. She was curious about the future. It was true that she had been in low spirits just a week ago, but those days of melancholy and gloom were behind her. She saw clearly that it was László, the way he treated her, and his relationship with Angela that had caused her bad mood. The thought of him still sent shivers down her spine, but she tried hard to concentrate on her own life, and, of course, she could not avoid thinking of Aunt Sári's impending trip to America. It was now her aunt's fate that worried her most. Everything else seemed trivial.

"László called this afternoon," Aunt Sári remarked unexpectedly, waking Kati up to the reality of the present.

László's name had not been mentioned since he had left, except for that brief incident with Aunt Juli when Gino put an end to their conversation. Yet, no matter how she fought it, even the mention of his name sparked her interest and she looked eagerly at Aunt Sári.

"He's coming by before his trip," Aunt Sári continued, seemingly unaware of the effect the announcement had on Kati.

Kati tried to act nonchalant, and was determined to be satisfied with the information her aunt supplied willingly. *I don't dare ask more about him, but it would be nice to know when he's* coming, and what trip he was planning, she thought. But then the conversation turned to other subjects and László was not mentioned again.

Soon after the reunion Aunt Sári had made arrangements for Kati to spend some time at the Tennis Club every afternoon while she took her customary nap. Kati went, rather reluctantly at first, although she was a seasoned player, and had already beaten several women at the club. She had even won most of the mixed doubles when she teamed up with Antonio, who became especially attentive to her. Antonio, a dark, curly-haired, cherub-faced Italian student of 24, was always at her side. He entertained his friends by telling them how he enjoyed "running around" with American girls, especially those who were as beautiful and intelligent as Kati, and had grown up in two cultures. "They're especially good at tennis," he would say. "And of course, so unique and intriguing. They have the best of two worlds."

Kati found his jokes ridiculous. He and his friends seemed so childish and naive. One afternoon, however, she gave into their coaxing, and agreed to say a little longer to enjoy some refreshments after a game of tennis and a swim in the large outdoor pool. On earlier occasions, she had always excused herself, saying she had to be back on time when her aunt ended her siesta.

That afternoon, Angela appeared at the club accompanied by her two teenage sisters who were just as lovely as she. All three looked ravishing in their white tennis outfits, their olive skin, black eyes and dark lustrous hair providing a striking contrast. Angela's eyes flashed when she noticed Kati.

"Oh, you're here too," she said loudly, acting very surprised, as if Kati had no business being at the club. Kati did not reply.

"László will be coming soon," she continued casually, giving Kati a meaningful glance. But Angela didn't say when, just as Aunt Sári had kept László's time of arrival a secret.

"Oh, you mean the mysterious Hungarian professor?" the Italian boys teased her. "Are you carrying a torch for him, like so many others?"

Everyone at the club knew that Angela was in love with the handsome Hungarian and many of the girls envied her because László spent so much time with her.

"She's so stuck up and spoiled," Kati overheard one of the girls in the locker room, "but it looks like she got László..." The men admired her beauty and would have been delighted to get some of her father's wealth by marrying her. But she would not have anything to do with Italians. She had set her eyes on László. She even persuaded her parents to use their friendship with Aunt Sári, so that she could get closer to him. Before Kati's arrival everything had gone smoothly. When he was around, László spent a lot of time with her, and seemed to enjoy her company.

But now, with the unexpected visit of Aunt Sári's "beautiful American niece," Angela had noted a certain coolness in his behavior.

"When are you going back to the States?" Angela regarded Kati quizzically. She used British pronunciation in her English, which mixed with her Italian accent, seemed peculiar to Kati, and she had to strain her ears to understand. Kati had heard that Angela had spent a year in London in an exclusive finishing school where she was consistently caught in the act of "getting acquainted" with Swedish and Norwegian boys.

Once Kati overheard some of the girls discussing that Angela had acquired such a taste for foreign men that she vowed never to marry an Italian. She found foreign men more fascinating, she said, and had set her eyes on László.

"She even said that this László had more charm, good looks, and brains than all the Italians put together," one of the girls related. To the annoyance of the Italian girls at the club, Angela often bragged about the photos in the gossip magazines, showing them to everyone in sight. Today she was waving the latest edition of *Cronaca Martina* which Kati had seen several days ago.

"I'll be leaving in about two weeks. I only came for a month." Kati answered Angela's question, as she noted the Italian girl's complacent smile when she turned away with satisfaction.

From her point of view, the sooner I leave the better, Kati thought, for it was clear that Angela considered her a rival. Angela doesn't need to worry, Kati reflected, László is not in the least interested in me. I have not heard from him since he left, and that was almost two weeks ago.

*   *   *

The next day Aunt Sári told Kati and Uncle Sándor that they would soon be returning to San Bartolomeo al Mare. She said she felt more comfortable and more at peace in the seashore villa and anyway, it was time for a change.

"I spent many happy years there with Kálmán and Annie," she reminded her niece and uncle.

Walter drove them to San Bartolomeo in the navy-blue Mercedes, and as Kati settled into the back seat between her aunt and uncle, she had to admit that she was happy about the change. She could never warm up to the opulence of the San Remo palazzo. It simply overwhelmed her, and although she appreciated its beauty and magnificence, she had always felt more out of place there than at the Villa Tokay.

It was still early morning when they arrived in the village and Kati took her time unpacking the fabulous clothes Aunt Sári had bought her in San Remo. She was glad to be back in the blue and white room that she had immediately loved, but could enjoy only for a short time. After a light lunch of cold cuts and cheese with her aunt and uncle, she decided to take a walk on the *Passagiata al Mare*.

She put on one of her new summer dresses, the one with the red flowers that she liked so much. It fit her mood perfectly, for she was in bright spirits, enjoying the closeness of the sea, the bright sun, and the brilliant blue sky.

She walked very slowly, looking in at a few cafés and shops, remembering where she had bought the copy of *Time* magazine that contained the article about László's book. She watched the carefree tourists looking gleefully around, and noted the presence of many more now than two weeks ago. So many were Italians, and she was surprised at the number of babies and toddlers that young couples, as well as doting grandparents pushed around in baby carriages. She had never seen so many grandfathers holding their grandchildren, running around and playing with them, and so many grandmothers singing to the little ones.

Kati continued her stroll in the direction of Cervo toward the remains of the old tower, and when she passed Via Sicilia, her attention was caught by a group of elderly Italians who stood in front of the *Lido Bar*, singing. Most were women of the working class, their faces weathered by years of life and labor. Their faces were lit up by an inner light of camaraderie, a sense of well-being and contentment that comes from the joy of singing together. They seemed totally unconcerned by the increasing number of curious onlookers who gathered around them, and as Kati moved closer, her own fascination with the melodious Italian songs made her stop and listen. She was not in a hurry at all. She had the whole afternoon to herself, since Aunt Sári and Uncle Sándor were busy with some business affairs.

As she stood there, lost in the power of the songs, watching the expressions on the faces of both singers and bystanders, she had an eerie feeling that someone was watching her. She felt self-conscious so she decided to change her position, moving to the other end of the group.

She was on her way when she happened to glance in the direction of the *Lido Bar* that was now packed with people who sat at the small, cozy tables, laughing and talking, and enjoying the impromptu concert. In the front right-hand corner she became conscious of a man sitting alone. His head was bent down, and with pen in hand, he was perusing a pack of manuscripts neatly stacked on the table in front of him. Several books were scattered on the small table top, and a small cup and saucer were sandwiched in between.

Kati could hardly believe her eyes.

It was László.

She stopped for a moment, and as if hypnotized, her feet were glued to the ground. Her heart beat so fast that she could hardly breathe. All this happened in a flash, and as she was about to move on, László looked up, smiling.

"Hello, little Kati. Don't you even recognize your old friends?"

"László, I didn't expect to see you here."

"I am just looking over some manuscripts. I like to do some work here. At least there are people around, and I don't feel so isolated."

"Oh." Kati stood still, mesmerized by his presence.

"May I invite you to join me? Have a seat. What would you like to drink?" László stood up and pulled up a chair.

"A coke, please," Kati answered, as if in a daze.

"*Una coca, per favore,*" László said to the waiter who just happened to pass by. Kati sat down, trying desperately to conceal her joy at seeing him again, so unexpectedly.

László smiled broadly.

"You know, little Kati, you are even prettier than I remembered."

"Oh."

"It's probably the dress," Kati blushed. "Aunt Sári bought me some beautiful clothes in San Remo."

"Oh, it's not the dress, although it's pretty and very becoming."

Kati felt self-conscious. She never knew how to react to a compliment. *Anyuka's* words rang in her ears when she told Kati, "You know, European men have a charming way of paying compliments to ladies, not like Americans. American men just don't dare to...But European men... oh, they are experts at flattery..."

"I wondered where you were, László. Aunt Sári did say that you would be coming back soon, but she didn't say when."

"I have been incredibly busy during the last several days. Exams at the university, several interviews with the press and radio. I even appeared on a few Italian and German television shows. I still can't believe that my book attracted this much attention. It's probably because it's so controversial."

Kati was beginning to relax as she took a few sips of the coke the waiter placed in front of her. She was surprised by the slice of lemon in her glass, but she didn't mind, finding that it gave the familiar drink an additional tangy taste.

She finally felt at ease enough so that she dared to look at László. He seemed more handsome than ever. His dark wavy hair was perfectly combed, and she noted that he had trimmed his mustache since they had seen each other. He had an air of well-being, and looked completely relaxed, the feeling of success evident in his every move. There was, however, that hint of conceit and arrogance that had bothered Kati before, and she felt put off by his self-assured manner. He gave the impression that he thought himself infallible, someone who could do no wrong, and whose wishes must be carried out without any questions asked.

"And what have *you* been doing? He pronounced the words very slowly, putting a great deal of emphasis on the word "you." He looked at her long and hard, and Kati found herself unable to meet his gaze. She looked in the other direction.

"Not that much. Just resting, reading, and playing tennis at the club. Walking around in the garden with Aunt Sári and Uncle Sándor who talked about old times..."

"Not very exciting for a young lady, is it?" László asked and Kati knew he was referring to those more "exciting times" they had together.

"This is such a beautiful place, and I'll miss it very much when my holiday is over. Cleveland is not exactly the *Riviera dei Fiori.* Especially in winter."

"I know what you mean. I hate winter weather myself, although I enjoy skiing in the Austrian Alps."

Kati had always wanted to learn to ski and she remembered Uncle Tibor who had often invited her to join him, even on his last ski trip to Colorado, which to Kati's great sorrow, turned out to be his last.

"It's a dangerous sport," Kati said. "Last winter in America was terribly harsh with lots of bad weather, and my uncle Tibor, with two other skiers, lost his life in an avalanche."

"Yes, I know, your Aunt Sári told me about it."

"But life is dangerous everywhere... Yet, one has to live, to do things," Kati said thoughtfully.

"I agree," László said. "I believe in living dangerously. One should make full use of one's opportunities and then be prepared to take the good with the bad. One must have courage to dare..."

"I hate inaction and indecision, especially in men," Kati agreed and saw that László had similar views, for he could not have been successful otherwise.

He had cleared the table and put his books and manuscripts back into his briefcase. They sat enjoying the exuberance of the holiday atmosphere and the view of the sea. In the meantime, the singers slowly dispersed and the curious onlookers went with them. The quay was virtually deserted, and Kati welcomed the peace and quiet. There were times when she felt almost strangled by the wall to wall people on the *Passagiata al Mare,* and if one really wanted to enjoy its quaint atmosphere, it was better to go there when the Italians and tourists were taking their siestas.

Suddenly they became conscious of the sound of old-fashioned dance music coming from the direction of the *Hotel*

Ondina. The rhythm of the waltzes, polkas, and tangos broke the lazy silence of the afternoon, and it seemed to Kati that although the music seemed out of place, it was just perfect to complement the special atmosphere.

"Let's go and listen from close by," László suggested, "I know you like that type of music."

He took care of the bill and they walked out of the *Lido Bar*. Once, Kati felt László's hand touching her arm, as he guided her past the small tables and chairs. A feeling of pleasure surged through every nerve of her body, and for a moment she felt as if they belonged together, as if their ways would never part.

It took a few minutes to reach the *Hotel Ondina.* They looked inside, past the wall of plants and flowers that separated the outdoor restaurant from the quay. Kati was touched by what she saw. Couples of elderly Italian ladies were dancing in the shade provided by the canvas top above, while others, both men and women, sat at the tables, watching the dancers with great interest. It was 1:30 in the afternoon and broad daylight.

"You would never find anything like this in America," Kati exclaimed, overawed by the spectacle. Women dancing in early afternoon with their men looking on..."

"This is Italy, and the Italian Riviera," László remarked, as they sat down on one of the benches, close to the sea. There was no room in the restaurant. "Aren't they absolutely delightful?" László continued and moved closer to Kati, touching her right shoulder with his outstretched hand.

The dancers enjoyed the afternoon, oblivious to everything and everyone around them. A sense of contentment exuded from their every move as they gave themselves up to the rhythm of the melodies, leaving their everyday cares behind. Tourists were entranced by what they saw, and stopped to watch the couples as they whirled about. Kati even had the feeling that some were as envious as she, for she marveled at the old people's ability to shed their inhibitions completely. Dancing on the street at 1:30

in the afternoon, in broad daylight, was not exactly something one did every day. Not even in a resort town in Italy. Then the tune of a popular tango resounded in the air. Kati remembered the words well, in Hungarian.

"Never leave the one who adores you from the bottom of his heart..."

Kati began singing the words aloud, when she heard László's voice, "May I?' He stood up from the bench, and made a courtly bow. She was taken aback by his gesture. She just could not imagine the two of them dancing in broad daylight, right on the street. A moment later she replied, "Why not?" By then, she was determined to shed all her inhibitions. "If László and the little old ladies can, so can I," she told herself.

László reached for her hand, and they moved closer to the small platform that was over-crowded by the dancers. "There is no room for us," Kati whispered, secretly hoping they would not start dancing.

"Oh, yes there is," László replied forcefully.

Then he drew Kati close, and she found herself yielding to his embrace. She felt ridiculous, dancing in the street, with the sun shining above.

"If my friends in Cleveland saw me now, they would think I'm crazy," she said, yet found that a few steps of the fiery tango in László's arms was not such a bad idea. It felt great to be so close to him again, to be held in his strong arms. A feeling of security overcame her and her former resolve to forget him disappeared.

László squeezed her hand as he quietly hummed the words, "Never leave the one who adores you from the bottom of his heart..."

Kati looked up with reproach in her eyes.

"László, you could have at least sent me a postcard."

"I didn't really have time."

"You wrote to Angela. She knew you were coming."

"I called her father about some business. He is giving me some advice about investments. Now that my income has tripled recently..." He smiled with a look of pride and a sense of accomplishment in his eyes.

What happened to his mission of "educating today's youth," and his indictment of "materialism and self-gratification?" Those were his exact words; he had definitely scorned materialistic values. But how could she begrudge anyone who was successful and earned money? That would be silly! Kati thought it wiser not to bring up sensitive topics that would destroy the joy of being together again. They danced a few more tangos and some romantic fox-trots, but sat down when they heard a polka.

László ordered a bottle of *Chianti Melini*. The waiter quickly filled their glasses.

"I never drink in the afternoon," Kati protested. "It goes to my head very quickly."

"I won't mind. I won't mind that at all. At least you'll feel a little more at ease with me," László answered.

All of a sudden, Kati realized that the older and wiser László could see right through her. He had a great deal of experience with women, and was aware that they found his charm and good looks irresistible. She remembered the people at the Tennis Club gossip about how married and unmarried women carried a torch for the bewitching Hungarian. Although he was known to shrug off his conquests, and showed no serious interest in anyone, he paid the most attention to Angela. Now that he had become an overnight celebrity, Kati thought, his self-esteem will grow with his prospects.

"I feel quite at ease. I don't need alcohol to relax me," Kati's eyes flashed in anger. "Please order me another coke."

"Come on, don't be so childish. Drink wine, little Kati! You're old enough," László commanded. Kati detected a hint of mockery in his voice.

"I said I will not drink wine in the afternoon," Kati's eyes flashed in anger.

László looked at her in surprise and his expression turned severe. He was not used to women disobeying his orders. "You still didn't tell me whether you wrote to Angela or not. You just said that you called her father," Kati brought up the topic that was bothering her. But the moment she uttered those words, she felt foolish. Now he knows that I am jealous of that Italian girl, she thought.

László's eyes narrowed. He would not answer her question. Then his expression changed as he broke into an all-knowing smile.

Kati pursed her lips and turned her head. She just couldn't bear to look at him.

"And I thought we would have a pleasant afternoon, meeting so unexpectedly. We could even dance some more," László suggested. Kati detected a slight regret in his voice.

"Those ladies over there are still having a lot of fun," he continued as he gestured toward them. "We could too. We could have some more fun, if only you would drink..."

By now Kati's thoughts were blurred with anger and frustration. I will not be one of the women who fall for him, and then be cast aside, she told herself. László watched her closely, and caught the fire in her eyes. He smiled complacently, shook his head, and looked even more amused.

Kati could not take him anymore. I'll show him what I think of him, she thought, determined to teach him a thing or two. She stood up quickly, reached for her purse, and shouted "Good-bye" in his direction. With deliberate and quick steps, she marched out from the terrace of the *Hotel Ondina*.

László looked after her as if to say, women, who can understand women?

After passing a few shops and café's in the direction of the Villa Tokay, she was sorry she had lost her temper. It wasn't exactly polite to walk out on someone like that, especially in a public place. Yet, down deep, Kati felt her action served him right. Her final good-bye should send the message that she did not want to see him again. She was not going to join the ranks of women who fall hopelessly in love with him.

She reached the villa and ran up the front steps. She hesitated, still breathless, before she entered the front door. She found the French doors that led to the drawing room wide open. Aunt Sári and Uncle Sándor were sitting quietly on the sofa, engaged in intense, but muffled conversation. Their faces looked troubled and Kati sensed an air of gloom in the room. Aunt Sári looked very tired. There were lines on her cheeks and deep circles under her eyes. Uncle Sándor sat close to her, stroking her hand. Both looked up when Kati entered, and Aunt Sári forced a smile.

"Kati, darling, where have you been? You look disheveled. What happened?" Aunt Sári searched Kati's eyes, puzzled.

"Oh, I ran."

"Why in the world did you do that?"

Kati did not feel like telling them the truth. She did not want them to know that she had quarreled with László. Yet, she could not bear to lie to them either. She knew that Aunt Sári had enough problems of her own, and troubling her with her own trivial affairs was simply bad form.

"I'm sorry. I'm just in a bad mood this afternoon." Her brows were knitted in a frown.

"Sit down, Kati dear. You need a rest." She heard Aunt Sári's voice, and she was thankful that she understood and did not wish to pry into her private affairs.

Kati looked at her aunt and uncle and thought how ridiculous her own behavior had been. There are serious problems of life and death in the family, and she was furious because László had wanted her to drink wine. How juvenile!

"I'll be all right," she said quietly, as she sat down.

Aunt Sári looked at Uncle Sándor, as if expecting his approval. Then she took a deep breath, and turned to Kati with a mixture of sorrow and fear in her eyes.

"Kati, darling, I'll be leaving for America very soon. For the operation. You know of my illness. The time has come, much sooner than I expected..." Her voice wavered. "Miklós is coming with me."

Kati looked up, tears gathering in her eyes. Should she go with Aunt Sári too? She did not dare to bring up that possibility.

"I'm so sorry, Aunt Sári. I'm sure you'll be all right. American medical care is the best in the world. I'm convinced the operation will be a success." Kati tried to sound encouraging, in spite of her own dread.

"I'll be leaving soon too, then, Aunt Sári. There is no point in my staying here while you're gone."

"No, we would like you to stay, Kati dear," Uncle Sándor said earnestly. "Your aunt will be gone for a few weeks only."

"But they are expecting me at the office. And Michael is waiting for me. There is no way I can stay longer."

Kati saw no point in her staying. She was fed up with the situation. Her visit turned out to be unpleasant, not what she had expected. Three weeks of it was enough, and she certainly did not want to lose her job in Cleveland. Good jobs were not easily come by these days.

"I have to go back. I can't afford to lose my job. I'll call Uncle Sándor every day to find out how things are going for you, Aunt Sári," Kati insisted. These two don't have the vaguest idea about my situation, she thought.

"I have to support myself, you know," she added in an earnest tone.

Aunt Sári and Uncle Sándor exchanged glances.

"Kati darling, I wanted to wait until tonight at dinner to tell you, but I might as well tell you now." She paused. "I have changed my will. If something happens to me..." her voice wavered and her eyes became moist, "if something happens to me, I want you and Uncle Sándor to inherit what I own."

Kati turned pale and glanced uneasily at the floor. Her aunt's announcement was totally unexpected.

"Oh no, you shouldn't do that," she murmured. "I don't know what to say, Aunt Sári," she continued. "But I know one thing. I want to be independent, to stand on my own two feet. To make it on my own."

She felt awkward, and was relieved that her aunt and uncle looked at her kindly.

"All I want to ask you, dear, is that maybe you could postpone your return to America. Then, when I come back you could help me get back on my feet."

"I'm staying too," Uncle Sándor interjected. "Of course, it's easy for me. The government will be glad that they won't have to pay my pension since I won't be in Hungary for a while. Not that it's a large sum, but I can live on it."

"Couldn't you write your employer that you'll stay another month? We'll know how things stand by then," Aunt Sári added quietly.

"Please stay, Kati dear. It will be easier for me too," Uncle Sándor pleaded.

Kati's eyes filled with tears. "I'll think about it, Aunt Sári. I really don't know what to say... and that inheritance... but I hope it won't come to that... not for a long long time. Just come back completely cured, Aunt Sári, please."

Aunt Sári was touched by Kati's concern. It was she who was ill, yet at the moment she was the stronger of the two.

"You and I can stay here together until Sárika returns," Uncle Sándor coaxed. "Please stay. That would be the best for all three of us."

"I really don't know...," Kati said in a shaking voice.

At that moment Kati raised her eyes and saw László standing in the doorway. He looked quite pleased with himself. He smiled broadly and not a trace of anger was visible on his face.

"László, how glad I am to see you!" Aunt Sári cried as she ran to greet him. "You're right on time!" She glanced in Kati's direction. "We're just trying to persuade Kati to stay another month," she said with a twinkle in her eyes. For a moment, traces of all anxiety disappeared from her face. "Maybe *you* can help."

Still grinning, László turned to Kati. "Your beloved niece already said good-bye to me, and it sounded like it's forever," László laughed under his breath. "How can *I* persuade her to stay?"

"I can decide for myself," Kati retorted. "I don't need anyone's advice, especially yours." Her eyes flashed with fury as she turned toward László, but only for a moment.

Aunt Sári and Uncle Sándor looked puzzled, and gazed at both of them. Then their eyes met, and suddenly they understood. "Lovers' quarrel," their look said.

Kati felt completely superfluous.

"I'm going upstairs. I'll think about what you both said," she told her aunt and uncle.

She excused herself, and without even looking in László's direction, she stormed out of the room.

8

Visit to the French Riviera

Nice

K ati was still upset by the events of the previous afternoon, and didn't feel rested at all when she woke up the next morning. Her head ached, her thoughts were fuzzy and confused, and there was a constant throbbing in her brain. Every detail of the day before was vivid in her mind as she recalled her happiness at being able to spend more time in the Villa Tokay. She remembered her delight when she unexpectedly ran into László on the quay, and the disappointment afterwards.

The day that started out well ended in a catastrophe. It was really László's arrogant air that made her lose her temper. He thinks he can count me among his flock of admirers, she thought, still upset. I'm not going to be one of them! I'll forget him soon, and won't even think of him again. There must be some truth to the old cliché, "time cures all."

She felt uncomfortable about the way she took Aunt Sári's announcement of the inheritance, and wondered how she should have reacted. But she couldn't come up with an answer. Should she have jumped up and down with joy and kissed her aunt in gratitude? When the whole thing depended on her death? That would have been out of place. She concluded that she had done the best she could under the circumstances. At least she was sincere, and Aunt Sári must have realized that the idea of an inheritance had never entered her mind.

Kati felt no pangs of conscience about László. She could still picture his self-satisfied air when he came into the drawing room. He acted as if nothing had happened between them. The whole incident didn't even touch him. He doesn't care what I think or how I feel, Kati concluded.

She wondered what she should do. One moment she felt she ought to comply with her aunt's wishes; after all, Aunt Sári needed her after her operation. And Kati did feel an obligation toward her. She couldn't have been nicer to Kati, not to mention the inheritance. Yet, at another moment, she was convinced her presence was superfluous. It should be enough if Uncle Sándor stayed around to wait for her, she reasoned.

Still undecided, Kati ran downstairs for breakfast. As usual, Aunt Juli was waiting for her in the breakfast room. She sat with her elbows on the table, her head buried in her hands.

"What happened, Aunt Juli? Are you sick?" As Kati entered, the housekeeper glanced toward her, an inquisitive look in her tear-stained eyes. Her red polka dot scarf looked disheveled on her head. Her customary cheerful self was gone, and the deep circles under her eyes were tell-tale signs of lack of sleep. She must have been up all night, Kati asserted.

"Oh nothing happened... And I am not sick." Aunt Juli paused. "It's just that... that...Tell me, Katika, what's going to happen if Aunt Sári... Heaven forbid," she sighed deeply and continued, "doesn't make it back... What will happen to all this?" She made a sweeping gesture with her right arm as if indicating all of her employer's wealth.

"Well..." Kati didn't know what to say.

"Katika, you have to stay... as the heir to all this, with you taking over, things could go on as before... if...if something terrible were to happen ..."

She's thinking of her job and Gino's, Kati thought in panic. Are people that selfish? Aunt Juli must have realized that she had made the wrong impression. She tried another angle. She sat up and tried to appear composed.

"Katika, your aunt would be so relieved if you would stay a few more months. At least two," she pleaded.

"And your uncle too," Aunt Juli went on, "at least the two of you would be here together. That would make your aunt feel better in the hospital, so far away across the ocean. Think of her, Kati dear. She loves you very much, and you two are the only relatives she has left."

Kati was at a loss. How can she tell her boss she's not returning as planned? What will happen to her job? What will Michael think? He would probably be very upset and threaten to break off with her if she didn't return on time.

Aunt Juli wiped her tears. "Katika, think about your Aunt Sári," she repeated. "She needs you. She needs you so much."

Yes, and you need her too, Kati thought. Or even me. You and Gino need us. And Walter. Kati had not seen him for a while and wondered where he was. Where else could they earn such good wages and be treated like family?

She sat down and stared into space as she drank her orange juice. She could not bring herself to eat some of the delicious rolls and strawberry jam. If I stay, she thought, I'll ruin everything for myself in Cleveland, and if I don't, everyone here will be upset with me.

Aunt Juli began to sob, looking even more anguished than before. I'm making the whole household miserable, Kati thought. She hated to make people feel wretched. I'll have to make up my mind pretty soon, she told herself.

She sat quietly, looking out the window, musing about her dilemma. I really got myself into a lot of trouble by coming here, she thought. What would *Anyuka* or *Apuka* advise me to do? But then, if they were alive I wouldn't be in this situation...

She did not want to hurt Aunt Sári's feelings, nor Michael's. She yearned for the security and stability he gave her. She thought about his last letter. It was a short, one page handwritten one with few details. After all, he was an engineer, and they're usually not very good with words. But he mentioned again and again that he was counting the days until her return, and he could hardly wait until he would have to drive to the airport to pick her up. Good old Michael, the faithful one, Kati thought. I should be happy that he loves me... But, most of all, Kati could not afford to lose her job. Maybe there was room for a compromise. As the Hungarian saying goes, "The goat's hunger should be satisfied, yet there should be cabbage left over." How will I accomplish that, she pondered.

"I honestly don't know what to do," she told Aunt Juli as she stood up and walked over to the large picture window. It was open and the gentle morning breeze caressed her cheeks. Lost in thought, she stood there for a long time. Sometimes the color of the sea is one that has no name, she mused as she gazed at the Mediterranean in all its splendor. How I love the sound of water, and how I'll miss everything here... And... and... if I stay, I may even see László again, she thought, surprised at her own line of thought. A minute ago I was convinced he meant nothing to me and now... now... I'm thinking of him again. She stood motionless for a while as confusion and indecision dominated her thoughts. Then she turned around and looked at Aunt Juli who was still sitting at the table wiping her eyes with her handkerchief.

"You know what, Aunt Juli," Kati paused, and took a deep breath, "I'll stay," she finally blurted out. "If that would make Aunt Sári happy, maybe I owe her that. She has been so good to me." Her eyes filled with tears.

The sense of relief on Aunt Juli's face was immediate. She jumped up and spread her arms wide. She ran over to Kati and hugged her with great gusto.

"But I can only stay an extra month. That's still about five weeks. I don't want to lose my job. I'll write to my boss today. I can just see his face," Kati added, knowing full well how upset he will be.

"Katika, God bless you... Thank God...I'm so happy...Thank God you're staying a while."

Aunt Juli quickly resumed her activities in the kitchen. She began humming her favorite tune, a sure sign that her heart and mind were set at rest.

"Thanks for the breakfast," Kati called after finishing her coffee. She ran up to her room. Now that she had made up her mind, she felt relieved.

I'll be able to spend more time with Uncle Sándor. He can tell me more about the past and our family. There's so little I know, even now. I can swim every day, in the sea or in the pool, and I can read some good books. She remembered Aunt Sári's library and was sure she would find books to her liking.

Then her thoughts turned to her aunt's illness and she prayed that her operation at Johns Hopkins would be a success. Actually, Kati reasoned, if that goes well, Aunt Sári has nothing to worry about. She had so many crises in her life already; she'll manage this one too.

I'll help Aunt Sári recuperate, and then I'll be on my way back to my life in Cleveland, and marry Michael as planned, she consoled herself. Oh, Michael, I do miss you, no matter what, she sighed. She remembered how well they got along, how they hardly ever quarreled. But there was one thing that always came up. Her heritage. She wanted to know as much as possible about her family and the Hungarian past, while he kept saying that she was American-born and should feel totally at home in the country of her birth.

She sat down at her desk and began composing a letter to David Johnson, her boss. She wrote the truth, that her aunt was very ill, and she had asked her to stay longer to help out after her surgery. Kati hoped that he would understand, although he was ill-humored at times, and had been somewhat reluctant about giving her a month's leave in the first place. But he knew about her situation, and understood her plight. He does have a good heart, and Kati hoped he would approve of her staying another month.

Writing to Michael was much more difficult.

He'll be so upset and may even suspect that I found someone else; he had always been the jealous type. Maybe he won't even believe the story about Aunt Sári's illness. Poor fellow, I know he doesn't deserve this, but then, I hope he'll understand. He had always been so patient with all the things I wanted to do. He'll get over my staying longer...

She finished both letters, and walked over to the post office. She had to stand in line for what seemed like ages. Most of the customers were Italians, and Kati watched the four clerks stamp each letter and document with an air of great importance. The tourists bought stamps and were quickly waited on, but the shopkeepers carried large books of accounts and stood for endless minutes until the clerks filled out each receipt and stamped every piece of paper three or four times. Kati finally mailed her own letters. She was irritated with the system and upset with the bureaucracy and the time and energy wasted to comply with its many rules.

When she returned to the villa she found Miklós's gold Mercedes parked in the back, on Via Europa. A bad omen, Kati thought. She remembered Aunt Sári saying that he would accompany her to Baltimore, but she didn't say when they were leaving. It may even be today, she thought with a sense of impending doom.

She ran up the steps at the front entrance. Two large suitcases stood in the front hall, sure signs of her aunt's imminent departure. She went straight to the drawing room. Aunt Sári and Uncle Sándor were sitting on the couch. Miklós stood by the French doors, looking out toward the sea.

She ran to Aunt Sári first, looking at her in disbelief. Kati gave her aunt a kiss on both cheeks. "I didn't think you would be leaving so soon," she whispered.

"Oh, Kati darling, I'm so glad you're staying, Aunt Juli told me." Aunt Sári's voice was cheerful. "We have to leave on such short notice. I'm so relieved the two of you will be here together," she looked fondly at Uncle Sándor. "At least it will be worthwhile to come back. You'll be waiting for me."

Kati turned toward Miklós, and for the sake of Aunt Sári, she greeted him warmly. After all, he was taking care of her aunt. But he eyed her with his customary sarcastic look. Kati watched him turn to Aunt Sári with a smirk on his face.

"Of course she's staying! Of course! Why shouldn't she?" He asked with indignation.

Kati heard him mumble under his breath, "I would too."

She knew Miklós was referring to the inheritance. What an unfair insinuation! She couldn't stand the man. How dare he make such accusations! She found him obnoxious and thought he deserved that scrawny, nagging wife of his. It served him right.

"I'm staying because Aunt Sári asked me to," she said, and looked sharply at Miklós. "For no other reason." Her feelings were evident in her tone. The atmosphere was thick with tension, and Kati felt as if the air could be easily cut with a knife.

Kati was surprised that Aunt Sári did not seem to notice. She was glad when Uncle Sándor came to the rescue, trying to dispel the ill-will between them. He smiled at all three of them.

"We'll be all right here, Sári dear. Katika and I," he said in his relaxed manner as he took Aunt Sári's hand. "It's you we're concerned about. Take care of yourself, follow the doctors' orders, and don't worry about us." Kati was glad the former tension had eased somewhat.

"Everything will turn out all right, you'll see," he continued as Aunt Sári stood up, and took a last look at the drawing room. Suddenly she looked sad and weary. "I hope this is not the last time I'm seeing all this," she observed. It was clear she tried to hide her fears, and wished to appear courageous in facing the operation. She smiled wanly.

Kati noticed Walter standing in the doorway. His presence signaled it was time to drive to the airport. He eyed Kati with more suspicion than ever, and she detected contempt in his watery eyes. Why does he hate me so much, she wondered. His mere presence made her feel uncomfortable. She stepped closer to Uncle Sándor, as if seeking his protection.

Uncle Sándor and Kati accompanied Aunt Sári to the car, with Miklós and Walter following close behind. Kati looked at her aunt with admiration, noting that she looked composed again and in control of her emotions.

"Good-bye, Uncle Sándor. Take care of little Kati while I'm gone." She gave both of them a big hug and patted Kati on the head. She settled into the back seat with such nonchalance, that an outsider would have never guessed that she was on her way to a serious operation, a matter of life or death.

"I'm so happy you're staying, Kati darling," were her last words as she waved good-bye and the three of them sped away in Aunt Sári's navy-blue Mercedes. Miklós left his own car behind, having parked his gold Mercedes in the garage.

Kati felt Uncle Sándor's hand gently touching her shoulder as they stood in silence, waving until Walter turned the corner and they could no longer see the car.

"May God be with her," he said softly.

"She's a brave lady," Kati added.

They fought their tears as they walked back to the villa which seemed empty and forlorn without Aunt Sári's radiant personality and natural kindness.

"This reminds me of the time my parents had that accident," Kati remarked, taking Uncle Sándor by the arm. "I feel the same loneliness and doom inside."

It seemed to Kati that the rest of the day would never end. Both she and Uncle Sándor made every effort to dispel the air of sadness that settled on the Villa Tokay. They had a quiet dinner together, and even Aunt Juli, whose optimism always shed a bright light on those near her, was unable to alter their mood. They went to bed earlier than usual. I hope we'll see things differently after a good night's rest, Kati thought and fell asleep.

*   *   *

The next morning, Kati felt more at ease than the day before. A good night's sleep made her see the bright side of her own situation and her optimism regarding Aunt Sári's chance for recovery returned. Miklós had promised to telephone as soon as they arrived in Baltimore, and Kati and Uncle Sándor spent the morning in the drawing room, waiting for the telephone to ring.

She searched the book cases in the drawing room, looking for books that she could read, although at the moment she could not bring herself to concentrate. She was anxious and tense, but knew that later she would have a great deal of time to immerse herself in her readings.

Aunt Sári's collection included books by British and American authors, as well as volumes in their native Hungarian, works of both classical and modern poets and novelists from Sándor Petöfi, Mór Jókai to Endre Ady, Attila József and András Sütö. Kati chose two volumes from the more recent works by Gyula Illyés, the poet laureate of contemporary Hungarian literature.

"Two of László's books are on the shelf," Uncle Sándor noted, as he looked up from his own reading.

"Oh really?" Kati's eyes brightened when she saw the books by László von Temessy. She didn't want to take them off the shelf, afraid that Uncle Sándor would ask questions about the two of them.

She found it peculiar that neither her aunt nor uncle had said a word about László since that afternoon of their quarrel. He must have returned to Rome since there was no trace of him the next day. He had come by to say good-bye to Aunt Sári before her trip to America. After all, he was her brother-in-law, and Kati saw that he loved her dearly. Then she remembered that László was to take a trip too, but she never found out where, and she really did not want to ask, fearing that she may arouse suspicion.

Maybe I shouldn't have lost my temper with him. For a moment she questioned her own behavior. Maybe he was right; I acted like a child...

Yet, she refused to admit that she had treated him unfairly when she walked out on him in anger. He deserved it, she kept telling herself. No matter how hard she tried to avoid it, László always popped into her mind. One minute she lost herself in the memory of their encounters, wondering whether she would ever see him again. The next moment she resolved to forget him completely.

It's Aunt Sári I should be thinking about, she reminded herself.

She took a good look around her. Two oil portraits at the far end of the room caught her attention. Funny, how I didn't notice those before, she thought. Then she remembered that she had spent only a short time in the the drawing room, and she began to recount those occasions.

She recalled the first evening of her arrival when she entered the room for the first time and had dinner with Aunt Sári and Miklós. Her first meeting with László came to mind as she remembered her exhilaration when he kissed her hand in greeting and she ran upstairs, her heart almost jumping out of her chest. She thought of the afternoon of the quarrel and her refusal to look in his direction when she stomped out of the room. This is a fateful room, she concluded, as she tried to convince herself that László was no longer part of her life.

She surveyed the two oil portraits from close and noticed that Uncle Sándor was following her with his eyes.

"Both your mother and your aunt were very beautiful. We had those portraits done when they were young girls. They were certainly two different types."

"Which type am I, Uncle Sándor?" Kati asked, remembering what Miklós had said the first day on their way from the airport.

"You are yet another type, dear. You didn't take after either of them," Uncle Sándor answered. "And I am glad of it."

Kati didn't have the faintest idea what he meant, and she couldn't ask, for at that moment the phone rang and both jumped to pick up the receiver. Uncle Sándor got there first and Kati could see from the expression on his face that Miklós was at the other end. He held the receiver with trembling hands.

"Oh, they'll have to wait, you say. How long? You don't know? Please call again soon. We are so worried. Tell Sárika we love her very much." He stopped for a moment.

"Kati is here. Do you want to talk to her?" But it was obvious that Miklós did not, for Uncle Sándor replaced the receiver and looked at Kati with concern.

"They're doing some additional tests. It will be a few days before they'll know more about her condition and then they can decide on the proper treatment."

"Oh," Kati could not say more.

"So the uncertainty continues," Uncle Sándor remarked in a hollow voice. He looked so depressed that Kati felt she had to be the stronger of the two.

"Don't worry, Uncle Sándor. We can wait it out. We have to be patient and hope for the best. Imagine how Aunt Sári feels. Her life is at stake."

"I guess you're right, little Kati. At least you and I are healthy. So far, anyway," he added. Her words had eased his concern as he tried to look upbeat again. He attempted to dismiss his gloom and said with forced enthusiasm:

"I was just reading a travel book on France. You know that Nice is just an hour's drive from here. Why don't we take a trip there tomorrow? It would take our minds off this constant worry."

"That's a great idea. There is really nothing we can do but wait." Kati agreed immediately. She had read about a quaint medieval village in the vicinity and had hoped that she would get there some day. She remembered that Friedrich Nietsche had spent some time there. In fact, he wrote his most important work, *Also sprach Zarathustra* in that village.

"There's the village of Eze nearby, built in the Middle Ages. We could stop there on our way back," she added enthusiastically.

"All right. I'm glad you agree. I'll talk to Walter and ask him to drive us." Uncle Sándor stood up and left the room.

Kati felt a sense of relief. She was glad they would do more than just sit around. She took one of László's books off the shelf, and began to leaf through the table of contents. Soon Uncle Sándor returned, so she quickly put it back. He had a troubled look on his face.

"Kati, did you notice how strange Walter has been acting lately?"

"Not only lately, Uncle Sándor. He had been eyeing me with suspicion ever since I arrived. Somehow I never liked the man. And he certainly doesn't like me."

"I almost mentioned him to Sárika," Uncle Sándor continued, "but I didn't want her to worry. When I told him of our plans to drive to Nice he almost said that he didn't have time. Yet Sárika told him to be at our disposal while she was gone. And Gino is staying at the palazzo until she comes home. So Walter doesn't have any work there."

They soon dismissed Walter from their minds, and the next day, exactly at eight o'clock, they were sitting in the navy-blue Mercedes, looking forward to a pleasant day of sightseeing. They traveled past Italian cities before reaching the French border. Kati read the exit signs: *"Imperia," "San Remo,"* and finally the last stop on the Italian Riviera, *"Ventimiglia."* San

Remo brought László to mind, the fabulous ball at the palazzo, the cruise on the Mediterranean, as well as the few hours they had spent dancing in the *Café Eldorado.*

There is always something that reminds me of him, Kati reflected. The more I try to forget him, the more I am reminded of him, she mused, as the memory of his embrace overwhelmed her and brought a slight blush to her face.

When they reached the French border Walter joined one of the long line of vehicles. Confusion was everywhere. Tourist buses from several European countries, huge noisy trucks and cars of all sizes were trying to out-maneuver each other. Kati noticed a white Fiat whose driver was especially pushy, and almost ran into the other cars in the front. His aggressiveness irritated the other drivers. A woman stepped out of her car and began arguing with him in a loud voice.

All this happened while a group of French border guards stood around, engaged in a lively chat, obviously unmoved by the mood of the agitated travelers. Kati was especially annoyed when, as they inched closer, she saw that only one line was open, and that at the height of morning traffic.

Walter held their passports in hand, placing Kati's on top, and when the border guard saw the US document, he simply motioned them to pass. After driving through several tunnels Kati noted the exit sign for the tiny fairy-tale principality of Monaco. They soon reached the Nice exit, and since Walter was already familiar with the city he easily found his way, driving on a narrow, and very busy street that had several different names. Uncle Sándor suggested driving straight to the bay area, and Walter parked the Mercedes right on the *Promenade des Anglais,* close to the opera house.

"Why don't we meet at one o'clock at the *Acapulco Restaurant?*" Uncle Sándor suggested.

Walter looked at them darkly.

"All right, if you say so," he replied.

As they watched him disappear in the direction of the old city, they sighed in relief.

"There's something about the man that I don't like," Uncle Sándor remarked, "But Sárika seems to cling to him, and I have no idea why."

Uncle Sándor looked around with anticipation as they crossed the busy boulevard lined with palm trees.

"I didn't tell you this, Kati dear, but I've been here many times before."

Kati was taken aback.

"Really? When?"

"Before the war. We spent our honeymoon here, your Aunt Irén and I, and we returned several times afterwards. Many of our friends chose Grado or Jesolo, but we always came back to Nice."

"How happy we were then," he continued, misty-eyed. Your grandparents, my brother and his wife spent many vacations here. We stayed in the *Grand Hotel* where the great novelist Jókai used to stay with his second wife, Bella. A plaque commemorates their stay on *Promenade des Anglais No. 67.*"

Kati enjoyed hearing about her grandparents and the past, and looked forward to learning more from Uncle Sándor.

Having reached the quay, Kati was struck by the fascinating view of the bay. The sandy beaches and the crystal clear water glistened in the hot sun. She had never seen the sea in such varied colors, and for a while she stood awestruck, watching the foamy waves as they danced on top of the sparkling water. The colors were in constant flux, playing in shades of purple, blue, and green. The place had a holiday atmosphere since the wide, gently curving beach was already crowded with bathers who shielded their semi-naked bodies with umbrellas of red and blue. Others lay motionless absorbing the direct rays of the sun, challenging the sun god Apollo to imbue their pale bodies with a healthy tan.

Tourists strolled leisurely on the quay, mostly in groups, their shoulders weighted down with expensive camera gear. To complete the scene, a large crowd of French youngsters raced around on roller skates. A few carried radios and their movements were accompanied by the loud noise of the newest American hits they were able to get a hold of.

"Things haven't really changed that much since we were here last," Uncle Sándor remarked thoughtfully. "The color of the Mediterranean is as changeable as ever, the sun is just as bright, and the beaches just as crowded. People come here to forget and to escape, and to gather strength to solve their problems at home."

"Except, of course, the sun worshipers. They changed, to say the least," he added, alluding to the many women who were prancing around in topless bikinis without the slightest sign of embarrassment.

Kati felt uncomfortable. She was not used to such display of human flesh, and was surprised when women, especially mothers, went topless in front of their sons and daughters. It was something that was not done on American beaches, unless it was a nudist camp.

"Of course, there are other changes too," Uncle Sándor chuckled as he noticed Kati's embarrassed look. "Look at the new buildings and hotels. Most grand hotels have been torn down and replaced by modern and more efficient ones."

After inspecting a plaque on an old, dilapidated hotel informing visitors of the Russian writer Anton Chekhov's visit in 1891, they took the long walk on the quay in the direction of the castle on the mountain top, toward the eastern part of the bay.

They took the elevator up, planning to walk down on the narrow stone stairway that runs along the *Bellada Tower*. When they reached the top, Kati felt completely overwhelmed. She stood in awe of the stunning view of the city bathed in the bright morning sun.

"I have never seen anything so beautiful before," she said, turning to Uncle Sándor. She consciously made an effort to imprint the view into her memory for as long as she lived. The soft curve of the bay lay before them, enclosed by lush vegetation, and the splendid luxury apartments and hotels presented a sight that she wanted to preserve forever. When things go wrong in my life, she told herself, I'll try to envision this view to cheer me up, to remind me of the incredible beauty present in the world.

They took a short rest and drank *cappuccino* in the café at the top, appreciating the cleanliness that was everywhere. On their way down they inspected the Roman ruins and enjoyed the view from another angle. They made a right turn and took the path toward the city where the renowned Flower Market was still in full swing.

Kati found the incredible assortment of vegetables, flowers, and exotic plants impressive. They stopped in front of a stall, where Uncle Sándor pointed out the different types of olives available in dozens of colors varying from pale yellow to coal black.

A young African, carrying long strands of antique white necklaces in one hand and bracelets in the other spotted them as they walked past the stands. He followed them close behind and was so insistent in offering his wares, that Kati felt compelled to buy from him. Since both Kati and Uncle Sándor spoke French, they soon learned that he was a student from Kenya and was trying to earn extra cash by selling jewelry made from ivory of his native land. Kati examined his wares and was certain that the jewelry was fake, made of beige plastic, but she chose several items anyway. They will make nice gifts for her girlfriends in Cleveland. The student was evidently pleased with the sale. He grinned broadly and waved while his dark eyes were already on the lookout for his next customers.

Their next stop was the *Acapulco Restaurant* where Walter was already waiting at a table near a window. The waiter recommended the famous local specialty *soupe au pistou* and *salade nicoise.*

"All right, I'll order that," Uncle Sándor decided to take his word for it. Kati loved French food, so she ordered the same menu.

They were served in no time at all, and they ate in silence, at a loss about what to say. Kati found Walter's presence annoying. He seemed agitated and watched Kati with a special gleam in his eyes. She tried to strike up a conversation.

"I really love it here. I still have five weeks left, so I want to enjoy every minute. That is, until I get back to Cleveland," she added and her face became somber for a second. Cleveland seemed so dull, compared to this...

"You will," Uncle Sándor assured her. "But there's something very important I want to talk to you about." He looked at Walter, hoping that he would take the hint and leave after they had finished their lunch.

But Walter only frowned and made no effort to leave the two to themselves. What would I do without Uncle Sándor, Kati wondered. This guy is out to get me. Her uncle's presence gave her a feeling of security, and since Walter was with them during the entire meal, they were forced to engage in small talk only.

"There's one more site I want you to see," Uncle Sándor said, after paying the waiter and giving him a generous tip. "I remember how your Aunt Irén loved the part of the city called *Cimiez,* located on top of the hill in the northern section of the city."

The trip to *Cimiez* was especially enjoyable for they could see from close the hundreds of luxury apartments and hotels that lined the *Boulevard de Cimiez,* and they got out of the car in front of the *Hotel Regina* to look at the statue of Queen Victoria, a frequent guest at the hotel. They also stopped in the Roman amphitheater and when they finally reached the top they inspected the monastery of the Franciscan Friars, surrounded by a beautiful rose garden. Kati was impressed by the unusual colors of the roses. One that was a shade between pink and orange especially caught her eye.

It was finally time to leave Nice, so they took a road called *Moyenne Corniche*, considerably removed from the seashore. After a ten-kilometer drive, they reached the medieval village of Eze.

Kati was fascinated. She had never seen anything like this before. The castle was built on a steep cliff surrounded by the sea on three sides. Although its walls were already in ruins, the houses of the surrounding village stood intact, built very close together, having withstood the wear and tear of centuries of Germanic, Arabic, and Turkish invaders.

Walter parked the car at the bottom of the mountain.

"I've been here before, so I won't go up with you," he said roughly.

Kati was relieved. She and Uncle Sándor strolled up the narrow streets, stopping to inspect the quaint shops filled with tourist items and local art work of pottery, woodwork, as well as oil and aquarelle paintings of the local scene.

On their way up they noticed several restaurants and cafés in the village and Kati stopped at the studio of an artist whose paintings attracted a great deal of attention. She walked inside to browse and found that he was a thin-faced, gray-haired Pole by the name of Sedek. He was absorbed in listening to a lanky American tourist, who stood in front of a large canvas painted bright orange with a black and white eagle in the center, negotiating a price.

They soon reached the *Jardin Exotique* located near the top, and after buying the entrance tickets, they walked up to admire the variety of trees and plants, most of which were of the cacti and palm families. Then they took the narrow stone steps to the very top.

The amazing view that lay before them was another scene which Kati wished she would remember forever. The protruding rock with the tall narrow houses of the fortified village stuck out of the sea like a sand castle in the desert. Several similar formations on the seashore, covered by bright green vegetation and tall trees, were part of the magnificent panorama.

As she looked around on all sides, Kati's eye was caught by a small restaurant located about half-way down the mountain. Its open terrace overlooked the sea and several small tables with chocolate-brown tablecloths stood in perfect order, inviting exhausted tourists for a much-needed rest.

"That is the most picturesque location I have ever seen for a restaurant," Kati remarked. Uncle Sándor had similar thoughts for he suggested that they stop there on their way down. Kati stood still for a few moments, admiring the white and pink geraniums in wrought iron planters that surrounded the terrace. They provided a sharp contrast to the brown tablecloths and the blue-green sea below.

After leaving the *Jardin Exotique*, they descended several narrow steps and found themselves at the entrance to the café restaurant, *Chateau Eze*. They stepped out on the terrace, and sat down at one of the small tables, joining several tourists who were already enjoying their refreshments. A smiling waiter was soon at their side, and Uncle Sándor ordered two glasses of lemonade.

Kati's face glowed as she surveyed the view. She could not get enough of it.

"This is the most romantic place I have ever been to in my life," she said. Suddenly, her thoughts turned to László, and she wondered what it would be like to be here with him. She pictured him smiling at her from across the table, his shirt open at the collar, his eyes gleaming with anticipation.

"When you're young, you think that life is made of beautiful places and romantic moments," Uncle Sándor observed. "How far that is from reality."

"I don't have any illusions about life," Kati replied thoughtfully as she took a slow sip of the lemonade. "Maybe young people today are more realistic. They don't expect so much out of life."

"Maybe. But I'm not so sure they're happier than we were at that age." He looked at Kati closely.

"Look at you, Katika. You're young, brought up with solid traditions of the past." He smiled and his eyes twinkled. "At least from what I know about you."

"Yes," Kati agreed, "My parents were very traditional. Sometimes way too strict. But so was everyone else in the community where I grew up."

Suddenly, Uncle Sándor's face became somber as he searched Kati's eyes.

"Katika, there is something very serious I want to talk to you about."

Kati listened, wondering what he would say.

"I've been wondering whether you had really found the right partner for life." A dark shadow crossed his face. Then he blurted out, "Are you sure you want to marry that American?"

Kati was taken aback. It's none of Uncle Sándor's business, she thought, annoyed. She appreciated his concern about her future, but why was he so much against her marrying Michael?

"Yes, I'm sure," she replied. He had no idea what Michael was like. Was it because he wasn't Hungarian? What difference did that make?

There was a grim look on her uncle's face.

"Your Aunt Sári and I are both worried about you. We think you should wait before settling down."

"But we're engaged and our wedding date is set."

"I wish we could meet him. Then we could see whether he's right for you."

Kati's heartbeat quickened and her face turned red.

"I'm old enough to decide for myself," she said, herself surprised at her harsh tone. She took another sip of the lemonade, fiddling with the straw.

"I'm sure you think so. But that's not enough," Uncle Sándor frowned and shook his head. "Believe me, growing old is not fun. But age often brings wisdom."

"I'll learn from my own mistakes."

"You could spare yourself a lot of heartbreak."

"Why do you say that, Uncle Sándor? You know nothing about life in America. You know nothing about Michael." Kati retorted, angry.

"But I know about life. We never told you this, but our only daughter Margit married a fellow from Kenya in the late 1950's. He was studying civil engineering in Budapest. He said he came from a prominent family since his father was the chief of his tribe." His face turned dark. "Well...."

Kati sat still, speechless. She had no idea that Uncle Sándor even had a daughter.

"We opposed the marriage to the bitter end, but Margit would not listen," he continued in a solemn tone. "Although they got married in Budapest, and lived in Hungary for a while, Mobutu got homesick and wanted to move back to Mombasa. Margit didn't want to go, but he finally convinced her and since they both got jobs there, they packed up and left." His eyes became moist. He stopped and looked away from Kati.

"It was OK for the first year. Then Mobutu began to go back to his old tribal ways. Margit felt very uncomfortable and wanted to come back." He sighed deeply. "But he wouldn't let her."

Kati's eyes opened wide; she was still in shock.

"They quarreled a lot. She wanted to contact the Hungarian Embassy in Kenya, but he wouldn't let her. I still have her letters pleading for help. Finally, Mobutu got so angry that he sold her for three cows." A tear rolled down his cheeks. "As you can imagine, we were totally devastated. That's when we lost track of her..."

O my God, Kati's heart raced. What a story! She had never heard anything like this before.

"I still don't know where our daughter is, whether she's dead or alive," Uncle Sándor continued. "There were rumors that when a European wife gets sold for three cows, her price later on becomes one or two cows, than a goat or two." He looked so sad that Kati wanted to hug him. But she just shook her head in silence.

"I just told you Margit's story because it shows that it's better to marry from your own culture," Uncle Sándor straightened up in his chair.

"Think about it," he added in a solemn tone.

Kati had never seen him so agitated. But how could he compare a guy from Kenya to an American? After all, American culture is not so far removed from European customs and values.

Kati did not move. She was boiling inside.

"I appreciate that you two are concerned about me. But I'll make that final decision. After all, it's my life," she retorted.

"We just want to spare you from heartache," Uncle Sándor said quietly. "Margit didn't listen to us either..."

"I'm so sorry about your daughter," Kati said trying to calm her anger.

A long silence followed. It seemed like they had nothing more to say to each other. Kati turned toward the sea, taking in the beautiful view. Oh, please, dear Mediterranean Sea, calm my soul, she pleaded silently.

How strange life is, she mused, I am at this amazing place and I have to be disturbed by such awful stories. But her heart went out to Uncle Sándor. How horrible it is to lose one's child, and under such morbid circumstances...

Uncle Sándor sat motionless, deep in thought. Then she heard his voice, as if coming from a distance.

"By the way, dear, László spoke about you before he left that afternoon when you were so angry with him."

"He did?" Kati could not mask her surprise. The mention of László brought a faint flush to her face.

"He said some nice things about you," Uncle Sándor continued.

"He did?"

"Yes, he said that he enjoys talking with you, and he is intrigued by your views about America and Hungary. He said he would like to get to know you better."

"Really?"

"You know, he decided to accept the lecture invitation of the Hungarian Academy of Sciences. He told us that he finally took your advice to heart and thought he should visit Hungary."

"He didn't tell me that."

"You didn't give him a chance, little Kati. You stormed out of the room," Uncle Sándor reminded her. "Anyway, he'll be leaving for Budapest soon. He's flying from Rome."

"Oh."

Kati's heart skipped a few beats. She was not used to talking about László, so she didn't ask any questions, although thousands rushed to her mind.

She was still upset with what Uncle Sándor had said about Michael, but thinking of László lightened her mood.

"I hope you're not angry with me, Katika," Uncle Sándor said. Kati smiled and shook her head, thinking about what her uncle had just said.

They finished their lemonade, and after buying a few post-cards and a bottle of the fragrant perfume made of local flowers and herbs, they made their way to the parking lot. They wondered whether they should follow the coastline and drive back to San Bartolomeo on the Via Aurelia, or take the *autostrada.*

"Let's take the *autostrada,*" Walter suggested. "It would take hours to get home on the Via Aurelia. Siesta is over, and we would have to drive at a snail's pace."

Since they were tired from the long day of sightseeing, Kati and Uncle Sándor welcomed Walter's suggestion. They settled into the back seat and in a little over an hour they were standing in front of the Villa Tokay. Both stayed around in the drawing room for a while, hoping for a phone call from Miklós. But there was no word from him.

Later that night Kati's thoughts were completely occupied with László again. Uncle Sándor's remarks puzzled her. Maybe she had misjudged László, and had treated him unfairly... She finally fell asleep, thinking of him, speculating about when he'll return to Rome and when he'll visit San Bartolomeo again.

*   *   *

Miklós called the next morning, and told them that Aunt Sári would be operated on in three days. He gave the phone to Aunt Sári. She sounded very depressed.

"She must be under heavy sedation," Uncle Sándor remarked after their conversation. But Miklós had assured them that things were going all right, and the tests showed her condition to be less severe than originally thought. That piece of news relieved their anxiety, and they spent the following days walking, reading, and swimming.

The time flew by quickly and Miklós called every day to tell them of Aunt Sári's condition. On the day after her surgery, his voice sounded particularly muffled and sad.

"Unfortunately, there had been some unexpected complications and Aunt Sári is in critical condition."

"Oh no," Kati and Uncle Sándor cried out at the same time. Since their daily mood depended primarily on her state, they spent the next few days in complete depression until two days later Miklós told them some good news.

"Aunt Sári had passed the critical mark. She is now in stable condition," he said with a note of cheer.

Relieved by the news they began taking note of the outside world again and Kati watched a few hours of television each day. She found nothing worthwhile on the Italian TV stations, although she admitted she should be watching Italian programs to improve her language skills. She was surprised that most of the channels broadcast American films and TV series, and she could even watch such programs as "Dallas," "Dynasty," and "Little House on the Prairie" in synchronized Italian.

They made it a point to watch the evening news, and one night, twelve days after Aunt Sári's departure, after they had listened to the results of the newly held Italian elections, they suddenly became conscious of the word *"Budapesta."* They listened closely.

The newscaster announced that there had been an accident at the Budapest Ferihegy Airport. As the Alitalia flight to Rome was taking off and the aircraft was in midair, its left engine stalled and a fire broke out, injuring several passengers and leaving four dead. The injured had been taken to nearby hospitals, the announcer continued, promising to give further details as soon as they were available.

Kati and Uncle Sándor looked at each other in alarm, exchanging looks of panic and fear. Kati immediately thought of László. This was about the time that he was supposed to return to Rome.

"I hope to God that László wasn't on that plane," she said, not in the least trying to conceal her tears.

"We should call the Budapest airport immediately," Uncle Sándor suggested as he tried to remain calm.

"If something happened to him I'll never forgive myself," Kati said. "I'm the one who urged him to take this trip."

She sat motionless, engulfed by worry. Now that Aunt Sári was recovering, she thought to herself, we expected nothing else to go wrong. But now, there's this...

"Oh God, I hope he had taken another flight." she said, no longer afraid to show her emotions.

Uncle Sándor called the Alitalia office in Budapest several times, but no one picked up the phone. He finally reached the manager of László's apartment in Rome, but the man had no idea of the *Signor Professore's* date of return. It was already late in the evening, and they had no way of contacting officials at the university, so they gave up for a while.

They were just about ready to retire for the night, when the piercing sound of the telephone startled them. Kati ran to pick up the receiver.

It was Angela. She came right to the point.

"Kati, do you know whether László was on that Alitalia flight from Budapest?" There was concern in her voice. She spoke in English, but her accent was much heavier than before.

"We don't know, Angela. All we know is that he was to return to Rome around this time."

Kati could hear her deep sigh at the other end. Having gotten the information she wanted, Angela hung up quickly, leaving Kati to wonder about her relationship with László.

Kati thought of the worst, imagining László dead. Losing a loved one had become a familiar event in her life.

"Oh God, let László be OK," she said aloud. She hoped and prayed that he would not share her parents' and Uncle Tibor's fate.

"We'll find out tomorrow, little Kati," she heard her uncle's solemn voice as he tried to console her, but his worried look revealed his own anxiety and fear.

*   *   *

Kati hardly slept a wink all night, tossing and turning in her bed. Even the glass of warm milk she brought to her room from the kitchen didn't help her fall asleep.

The next morning she was the first customer at the news stand. The Rome papers printed the list of passengers on that ill-fated plane. László's name was among the injured.

Kati ran up the steps of the Villa Tokay like lightning. She was so relieved about the news that it didn't even occur to her that László might be seriously injured.

He is alive, she kept telling herself and ran to share the good news with Uncle Sándor. She found him already dressed, ready to step out for the morning paper.

"László is all right," Kati ran to Uncle Sándor and handed him the paper. There were tears of joy in their eyes as they entered the breakfast room and told Aunt Juli about the list of survivors.

"Kati dear, what do you say to our flying to Budapest as soon as possible?" Uncle Sándor asked unexpectedly as they sat down to breakfast. "László would be delighted to see us, I'm sure. And we know that Sárika is well on her way to recovery..."

Kati was stunned by his suggestion.

"Do you think we should?" she asked, overwhelmed with joy at the prospect of seeing László again.

"Let's hope he wasn't seriously injured," Uncle Sándor remarked, after reading the article stating that *Professore Dottore* László von Temessy was taken to the Central State Hospital in Budapest.

Later that day Miklós called, and assured them that Aunt Sári was doing well. He also asked about László. He had read about the Alitalia accident in *The New York Times,* and wondered whether they knew when he was returning to Rome.

"Tell Sárika that Kati and I decided to fly to Budapest for a few days to see how he was doing," Uncle Sándor said.

"You mean you're going to Budapest just to see him?" Miklós sounded incredulous.

"Yes," Uncle Sándor replied calmly.

"What was László doing in Budapest anyway? He swore he would never go back as long as those commies are there."

"Look, Miklós, I still live there. I know what's going on."

"Well, good luck," Miklós slammed down the receiver.

But nothing would stop Uncle Sándor.

That afternoon they walked over to the nearest travel agency. There were no seats available on the Genoa-Budapest flight the next day. They would have to wait another two days because there were only three weekly flights to Budapest, even during the summer months. They bought two tickets for the next flight. The day of their departure arrived quickly. Walter drove them to the airport. He dropped them off at the terminal and carried their luggage inside.

"Uncle Sándor, I feel so uneasy about leaving Walter here, alone with Aunt Juli."

"Now that you mention it, I have a strange feeling too. But it never occurred to me when I thought about flying to Budapest," Uncle Sándor replied, clearly worried.

"Maybe I'm imagining things, but I noted a look of self-satisfaction in his beady eyes, as if to say, 'I'll show you,'" Kati said, alarmed. "There's evil lurking inside that man."

But they shrugged Walter off; their concern for László was greater.

"I hope Aunt Juli will be all right," Kati said as they boarded the plane.

9

Flying to Budapest

Budapest

Kati and Uncle Sándor sat squeezed into the seats of the Soviet-made plane of the Hungarian Airlines, MALEV. Kati would have preferred to fly with Alitalia, but the travel agent at *the Agenzia Viaggi Igotours* convinced her that the two-hour flight in such close quarters was bearable. She had flown with MALEV before, from Frankfurt, when as a teenager she spent several summers at Lake Balaton with her parents. She recalled that MALEV was the only airline that served wine *gratis* with meals and snacks. She decided to try a glass of *"Szürke Barát,"* a dry white wine which had been *Apuka's* favorite.

As she sipped the wine she thought of her last meeting with László and their quarrel at the *Hotel Ondina*. Strange, how the incident seemed far away, as if it had happened many years ago, and to someone else. Their disagreement seemed trivial now that László's life had been threatened. Kati felt embarrassed for having acted so childishly, ignoring his presence and losing her temper at the Villa Tokay. Maybe he was interested in her, after all. She remembered Uncle Sándor's words when he told her that he wanted to get to know her better...

Yet, she doubted the wisdom of her trip to Budapest. It seemed like an excellent idea at the time Uncle Sándor had suggested it, but the more she thought about it, the more uncomfortable she felt.

Kati sat gazing out the window, staring into space. Uncle Sándor turned to her. He had a worried look on his face.

"You don't look too happy, Kati dear. What's wrong?

"I don't think I should be visiting László."

"What do you mean?"

"He may think I'm running after him."

Uncle Sándor looked puzzled. "He's part of our family and he's in trouble. I'm sure he'll be glad to find that we're concerned about him."

Kati did not reply. Her gloomy expression remained unchanged.

Uncle Sándor touched her shoulder to take a closer look. "But little Kati, you're blushing."

Kati turned red in the face, but she did not say anything. She picked up a magazine pretending to search for an article to read.

Her attraction toward László was growing with each day, she mused. For the hundredth time she went over every detail of the times they had spent together, remembering his kisses and his embrace. The sensations were overwhelming. She felt like a naughty child who knew the wrongness of her actions, yet did them anyway, hoping that things would turn out all right in the end.

She thought of her life in Cleveland and Michael. She had read his letters several times. He complained about her staying longer, and wrote that ever since she had left, his days passed slowly. "I feel totally miserable. I miss you terribly, and I don't know what I'll do if you don't come back," he wrote, "Kati, I love you so much. Why did you have to go to Italy?"

Kati felt awful. Did she really love him? What would he do if she didn't go back? Poor Michael, he's thinking of the worst that could happen to him. She had noted a touch of gloom in his personality, but as long as she was around, he was always upbeat and looked forward to their life together with anticipation and joy. She recalled Uncle Sándor's blunt question, "Are you sure you want to marry that American?" And although she had replied with a definite "yes," she began to wonder.

A new thought flashed through her mind. True, they came from different cultures, but that can be bridged with understanding and care. But there was something else missing... the spark, the excitement of being together, of being truly in love. No, I had not felt that way about Michael, Kati admitted. He is a very nice and caring person who helped me when I needed emotional support. But it is almost as if I feel only gratitude toward him, and not much more...

Kati felt terrible about this new possibility. Michael deserved so much more.

Then thoughts of László in the flight accident and the possibility of his being seriously hurt came to mind. His life being in danger had crystallized her feelings. I must be falling in love with him, truly in love for the first time in my life...

She admired László for his successful career, and his concern for Aunt Sári filled her with warmth. How nice that he had trusted Uncle Sándor enough to confide in him. Yet, she was prepared to accept the worst, that László was not in the least interested in her. She would just have to forget him once she returned to America, when her visit to Italy, and with it László, would become nothing but a memory, something to remember for a long time to come.

On the other hand, Uncle Sándor's comments at the *Chateau Eze* gave her hope. Maybe László did like her, just a little. Her emotions leaped from hope to fear, while feelings of doubt plagued her.

"What will László think of my visit?" She asked anxiously.

"He'll be very happy to see you. Don't worry. Try to relax," she heard Uncle Sándor's reassuring words, as the old man turned toward her again, noting that his grand-niece looked very pretty in a sky-blue dress with matching jacket.

"He'll be flattered by the visit of a pretty girl, straight from the Riviera, with a beautiful tan," Uncle Sándor added with a wink, "And don't forget, this is a family trip, nothing else." His eyes flickered with merriment.

"Too bad we couldn't get through to the hospital to find out about his injury," Uncle Sándor continued. "I'm sure they would have notified his nearest relatives."

"Is Aunt Sári his nearest relative?"

"Yes, I think she is."

Kati remembered their many attempts to call László at the hospital. Uncle Sándor even tried to contact the son of an old friend, Dr. Endre Szabó, an internist at the Central State Hospital. But Dr. Szabó was never available, and the nurse told him that she was not allowed to share information about patients with other than close relatives. So, even three days after the accident, they had no news about the severity of his injuries. At least this uncertainty justified her visit in her own mind.

She finally decided to take her uncle's advice to settle back and enjoy the flight.

The two hours flew by quickly. The stewardess announced landing at the Ferihegy Airport, and Kati joined the tourists who clapped when the plane landed on Hungarian soil. Deplaning was tedious as usual. A rickety bus took them to the terminal. A half hour later their luggage finally appeared on the baggage conveyor. They took a taxi to Uncle Sándor's apartment located on No. 8 Maros Street, near the Southern Railroad Station.

Kati peered through the dirty cab window on their way toward the center of the city, noting the new roads and several apartment complexes that had been built since her last visit. She was glad to be back, and considered her unplanned visit to her favorite city a pleasant addition to her European trip.

"László has no idea we're here," Uncle Sándor remarked. "He'll be really pleased to see us."

They were on the brink of crossing the Danube on the Chain Bridge and Kati recognized the familiar panorama of Castle Hill with the new *Hilton Hotel* on the Buda side. She turned around and admired the neo-Gothic Parliament Building and the colossal Intercontinental Hotel on the Pest side.

"When do you think we should go to see him?" Kati asked, trying to conceal her eagerness.

"I'll try to call Dr. Szabó again to find out what's going on. Maybe we can visit László tomorrow morning." Uncle Sándor saw that Kati was not up to facing László too soon.

"That's a good idea."

"Let's settle into the apartment first and rest a while," he suggested.

Kati gladly agreed. Suddenly, her eyelids felt heavy, and she could hardly keep her eyes open. She needed time to regain herself.

"Do you have dollars, marks, or shillings? I can give you a good price." The harsh voice of the taxi driver brought her back to the present. "I know you live outside the country just by the way you're dressed."

Uncle Sándor shook his head. "We'll get our forints at the bank," he declared.

The driver stepped on the gas pedal in anger. Apparently he was used to dealing on the black market and hoped that he could make a deal with them.

It was exactly three o'clock when the cab stopped in front of Uncle Sándor's apartment. He paid the fare and gave the perturbed driver a generous tip.

"If I can't get a hold of Endre Szabó, I'll call his father," Uncle Sándor broke the silence as he opened the outside gate and they walked up the dingy steps. Several trash cans filled to the brim lined the right wall of the area that led to the front door of his apartment.

"His father is a good friend of mine from long ago," he continued. "He should be able to tell us how we can reach his son.'"

Uncle Sándor had told Kati that the Central State Hospital was reserved for dignitaries and important state officials and one needed "socialist connections" to get information on patients. His attempted calls from Italy were largely made for Kati's sake, although he had hoped that by some lucky coincidence he would be able to obtain information about László's condition.

Kati watched Uncle Sándor as he assumed the role of the host, moving with the same ease in the cramped two-room apartment as he had in the palazzo at San Remo. She marveled at the adaptability of such men and felt a new admiration for her uncle, as she recalled that he had never complained about having to give up his past life of luxury.

She surveyed the tiny apartment with interest, noting that remnants of the past were in every corner. Fine oriental carpets in rich shades of blue, dark red, and chocolate brown lent an air of elegance to the close quarters. An ornate credenza with glass doors displayed several Sterling silver trays, an exquisite Meissen porcelain coffee service for twelve, and several expensive Chinese vases. Three large oil paintings by Hungarian and French masters graced the walls of the larger room that was used as a combination living room and dining room.

"You take the room in the back," Uncle Sándor suggested. Kati settled in, and by the time she had emerged from a long and refreshing bath, he had already made a phone call, and had been to the corner grocery store. He was busy preparing tea in the kitchen.

"I was finally able to speak to Dr. Szabó," Uncle Sándor said. His eyes sparkled. "László is fine, although they have to do further tests on him during the next few days. Thank heaven he was not seriously injured. Just a sprained wrist and elbow..."

"Oh, I'm so glad it's nothing serious," Kati burst out. Happy to hear the news, she gave Uncle Sándor a big hug.

But the next moment she was overcome with doubt. Now her presence will be much more difficult to justify. What will László think of her? At least if he had been really injured, there would have been a reason for her trip.

Then she realized the ridiculousness of her thoughts. How could she think like that? To wish serious injury on László out of sheer egotism, so that she wouldn't appear pushy in his eyes.

"Let's call László right now," she suggested. "Let's tell him we're here. He shouldn't be surprised by our visit."

"I think we should surprise him!" Uncle Sándor disagreed.

A few minutes passed. They looked at each other questioningly when they heard the shrill ringing of the telephone. Who could be calling so soon?

"Hello," Uncle Sándor hesitated as he picked up the old-fashioned black receiver. His eyes widened in surprise.

"László? Well, well, is that you?" Uncle Sándor asked.

"Yes, yes, I'm here," he continued, "And I've a surprise for you. Katika is here too. Looks like Dr. Szabó didn't waste any time telling you. We were going to surprise you..." He was all smiles. "We had no idea about the extent of your injury. You should have notified us in some way." There was a pause. "You couldn't? Why not?"

Kati's heart jumped and her face flushed with excitement. She felt like a school girl expecting her first call from a boy, the object of her infatuation. What will it be like to hear László's voice again? What could she say to him?

"László wants to talk to you," Uncle Sándor held the telephone at arm's length, placing it into Kati's hands. Kati was shaking.

"Oh László, I'm so glad you're all right," was all she could say.

"And I'm so glad you came, little Kati. I've thought a great deal about you lately."

Kati gasped. "Really?" she asked, holding her breath.

"You wouldn't know this, but I came to Budapest because...
because you suggested it."

"You make me feel terribly guilty," she said.

"We'll talk about that tomorrow. Then we can decide what
you can do to make amends for your mistake..." László replied in
a half-serious and half-joking tone.

"All right." Kati smiled. "See you tomorrow. Good-bye."

She slowly replaced the receiver. A feeling of joy swept her
whole body. "I'm so glad you came." László had said, she
recalled wistfully.

Following their supper of cheese and cold cuts, including
Hungarian Herz salami and yellow bell peppers, they watched
television for a while. Kati was thrilled to hear Hungarian
spoken on television; it was a rare opportunity for her, although
the news was filled with anti-American propaganda, exalting the
greatness of the Soviet Union.

Nevertheless, she was relieved at the turn of events. László
had called, and he wasn't seriously injured. And he looked
forward to seeing her...

"Let's go to bed," Uncle Sándor suggested wearily after the
news broadcast. He pulled out the bedding from the box under
the couch and began making his bed for the night.

"Good night, Uncle Sándor," Kati gave him a kiss on the
cheek. She had a hard time hiding her excitement. As she lay on
the narrow bed in the small back room, she thought about
tomorrow and was no longer sorry that she had followed Uncle
Sándor's suggestion to accompany him to Budapest.

*   *   *

The next morning Kati woke up to the aroma of freshly-
brewed coffee. She dressed quickly and made her bed. When she
glanced at the coffee table that stood in front of the couch on
which Uncle Sándor had slept, she noted that he had already set
the table for breakfast.

Before falling asleep the night before, she had decided to wear another of her new outfits that Aunt Sári had bought her in San Remo. The light-green summer dress, with a short-sleeved jacket seemed just right for the occasion. She wanted to look her best for László. She expected something special from this visit, but didn't have the slightest idea what this "something special" would be.

Uncle Sándor, although accustomed to his niece's good looks, looked at her with admiration.

"You look especially beautiful this morning," he remarked as he poured Kati her coffee. "But a little nervous too. Am I right?"

Kati cast down her eyes and blushed. "Yes, you're right."

"The taxi will be here in a half hour," he said. "Relax, little Kati. You'll see, everything will turn out all right."

As Kati and Uncle Sándor sat in silence in the back seat of a City Taxi cab, a 1500 Lada, both were lost in thought. The bearded cabdriver made several attempts to strike up a conversation with Kati, but gave up after a while, concentrating on battling the morning traffic.

Kati watched with interest as they drove past Moscow Square, bustling with activity. Men carried leather briefcases, while women toted colorful cloth shopping bags. The square was overrun by blue and white-collar workers in perpetual motion. They hurried past cars, buses, and streetcars, while some ran toward the entrance of the subway that was the most efficient means of transportation in the city.

"It seems like the whole population of the city is out this morning," Kati remarked. She was glad that she didn't have to push her way through the crowd. They soon left the busy square, driving on Szilágyi Erzsébet Ave., past the circular building of *Hotel Budapest.* They turned left, and then right to a wide street called Kútvölgyi Street. A few minutes later the huge building of the Central State Hospital loomed in front.

"Here we are. The place for big wigs," the cabdriver remarked sarcastically. They ignored his comment. He reached out his hand toward Uncle Sándor, thanked him for his generous tip, but looked puzzled by their apparent haste. They must be visiting some important commie, his look said.

Kati and Uncle Sándor ran up the front steps. They were stopped by the hospital porter who wanted to know who they were and the patient they wished to visit. A quick call to László's private room, an accommodation that was rare even in this hospital, confirmed the legitimacy of their visit. They hurried to the elevator and pushed the button for the third floor. Neither turned back to look at the porter who stood shaking his head with a knowing look in his near-sighted eyes.

Kati's heart beat faster and she even pinched herself to calm her nerves. The moment of seeing László after all these weeks had finally arrived. They hurried toward room no. 373, located at the end of the long and narrow corridor. Despite its length, it seemed light and airy, lit by closely-placed, large windows on one side.

The doors of the rooms were left wide open, and nurses dressed in white hurried in and out, carrying either food trays or bedpans. The door to room no. 373, however, was closed. Uncle Sándor knocked three times, and since there was no sign of activity inside, he slowly pushed the door open.

A second later he and Kati stood as if frozen in their tracks.

László, wearing a dark-blue silk house-coat, his left arm in a sling, stood in the middle of the spacious room. With his right arm he held close the voluptuous figure of a raven-haired girl, dressed in a red skirt and flimsy white blouse. Their backs were to the door, and they looked as if their passionate kiss had just been interrupted.

Kati and Uncle Sándor stood mesmerized in the doorway. Kati was too shocked to make a sound. Her eyes began to burn. Disappointment, jealousy, and anger swept over her.

Finally, Uncle Sándor made a rasping sound with his throat.

László turned around, and for a moment he was at a loss about what to do. But he quickly regained his bearing while he removed his good arm from the waist of the girl.

"Angela just arrived ten minutes ago," he murmured, unsuccessful in hiding his embarrassment. His green eyes crinkled as his lips broke into a most engaging smile. "Hello, Uncle Sándor. Hello, little Kati." Kati heard his boisterous voice as he greeted his visitors. He looked incredibly handsome, even in such leisure clothes, and Kati had the feeling he knew it.

Uncle Sándor and László embraced with genuine affection. Kati extended her hand for the customary handshake, but László pulled her hand to his lips, looking straight into her eyes. He displayed the self-confidence of a natural-born *charmeur*.

"As I said on the phone last night, I'm so glad *you* came to Budapest," he whispered, not taking his eyes off of Kati.

Kati's eyes flashed in anger, and she jerked her hand from his lips. For a second, László was taken aback, but he had enough presence of mind to make the best of the situation. Uncle Sándor glanced toward László and shrugged his shoulders apologetically, as if to say, "that's women for you."

"Please, everyone, do sit down," László motioned toward the small sofa and two chairs in the corner of the room.

All the while, Angela beamed with satisfaction. She greeted Uncle Sándor and Kati warmly, exchanging a few pleasantries with them. Because of her, the conversation had to be conducted in English, for it was the only language all four spoke well.

"I had a hard time getting a flight to Budapest," Angela began as she surveyed Kati with a critical look in her dark eyes. "I'm sure you did too. I finally flew from Milano."

Kati returned her gaze and noted jealousy in Angela's every move. It was crystal clear that the beautiful Italian girl considered her a dangerous rival who could steal László's hard-earned affection from her at any moment.

László seemed to revel in the attention of the two girls. He's probably not interested in a serious relationship with either of us, Kati thought. He's continuing to play the field.

Uncle Sándor tried to steer the conversation to a light and cheery subject, expressing several times his relief at László's escape from serious injury.

"You'll just have to use one arm when embracing pretty girls," he joked. Kati was aghast. It was a distinctly man-to-man joke, and considering the circumstances, a tactless one. A wry frown settled on her face, and she found it difficult to join the conversation.

"I'll have to stay around in Budapest for a few more days to get the results of the tests that were done as precautionary measures," László explained, grinning.

"Do they think you suffered internal injuries?" Uncle Sándor's voice sounded worried.

"They just want to check me out. That Dr. Szabó friend of yours has taken me under his wings."

"Well, it's good to have 'socialist connections,'" Uncle Sándor explained. There was irony in his voice. "There's no other way of being treated decently in Hungary. You must always know the right people."

"That's communism for you. I can hardly wait until this is over and I can leave." László said.

Kati noticed that Angela was fidgeting in her seat. She looked like she wanted to say something. She finally interrupted their conversation. "You probably don't know this, but László was named Economic Advisor at the Italian Ministry of Interior," she said proudly, as if it were her accomplishment.

Uncle Sándor turned to László with a wide smile.

"It has always been my belief that many Hungarians make it big, once they leave the narrow confines of this country. I'm so happy you're one of them. Congratulations, László. You didn't even tell us," he reprimanded. He shook László's hands, and gave him another bear hug.

Kati looked at László and murmured, out of politeness, "Congratulations!"

"Thank you. It's really not that big of a deal. Unfortunately, now I'll have to stay here longer than I planned. I hate to be away from my work," László said. "But tell me about Sárika. How's she doing?"

"As you probably know, the operation was successful, so she'll be coming back soon. We'll have to return to San Bartolomeo in a few days. We want to be there when she arrives."

Uncle Sándor made every effort to engage Angela in a conversation, inquiring about her first impressions of the Hungarian capital, so that László and Kati could have a chance to exchange a few words in private. But he soon realized the futility of his efforts. Despite László's attempt to talk to Kati alone, she refused to utter more than a few curt words of "yes" and "no." Both men were soon forced to give up, realizing that there was no way they could alter Kati's mood.

Then Kati did something totally unexpected. They watched in amazement as she suddenly stood up with an assertive, yet graceful movement. She turned to László with forced enthusiasm and a fake smile.

"Thank you for your hospitality, László. It was really nice seeing you again." The sarcasm in her voice was unmistakable. She turned to Angela, who looked visibly relieved at the prospect of their departure.

"Nice to see you too, Angela. I'm sure you'll have a good time in Budapest." Then she added as if it were an afterthought:

"I have some good friends here. I'll make use of my time too." Then turning to Uncle Sándor, she asked: "Remember Gábor Barna, Uncle Sándor? I talked to you about him before. He has a high position with one of the big banks. He'll be delighted to know that I'm in Budapest."

Then she faced László again. "Have a good time. Good-bye, László. And good luck!"

Uncle Sándor watched his niece in amazement. A look of admiration appeared in his eyes. After a hasty good-bye, he followed Kati out of the room, as if ordered to do so.

"You did quite well, little Kati," he told her later as they were perusing the daily menu at the quaint *Kékgolyó Restaurant* near Uncle Sándor's apartment. They had taken a taxi from the hospital, and since it was already lunch time, he suggested they go straight to the restaurant.

"As we were leaving and you made your exit with such grace and determination, I happened to glance back at László. You should have seen his face." Uncle Sándor's eyes twinkled.

But Kati made no comment.

"You know, Katika, I'm really puzzled about László. What I told you at Eze was true. He said he wanted to get to know you better. Yet, what we just saw in the hospital..." Uncle Sándor continued.

"Please don't bring that up again, Uncle Sándor. I'm strong enough to take defeat. Life has hardened me pretty well."

Kati hated to recall her reaction when they barged in on Angela and László in the hospital room. Her feelings of hurt and dismay were too obvious. But now she was proud that she emerged triumphant, putting László in his place.

It was true that she had friends in Budapest. In fact, one of the young men had hinted at marriage a few years ago, although he doubted whether Kati would want to settle permanently in present-day Hungary. That was probably true at the time, she thought now. Yet, if she really fell in love, truly in love, she could live anywhere...

It was no coincidence that Gábor Barna's name came to her lips. He had once told her that he had fallen in love with her. A rising star in the bank industry, he had an important position at the Hungarian National Bank. He spoke several languages and had traveled abroad extensively. In fact, he had visited Kati twice in Cleveland, when *Anyuka* and *Apuka* were still alive. At the time he had been very much in love with Kati, but she did not consider him seriously, perhaps because she was in no way ready to settle down.

It would be good to know what he was doing now, Kati reflected. She decided to call him that evening.

That night as she lay on the narrow bed after several attempts to reach Gábor, she made every effort to put László out of her mind. She recalled the words she had said to him that morning: "Good-bye, László. And Good luck!" She remembered that she had already said good-bye to him before, on that bright, sunny day in San Bartolomeo. But this time she really meant it. This was forever, a final good-bye.

Then she thought of the coming month she was to spend on the Italian Riviera, and of the possibility of László visiting Aunt Sári. She finally fell asleep, but before completely sinking into a welcome state of oblivion, she compared the events of the night before and those of today. What a difference, she sighed.

I was still filled with hope then, she remembered, as tears of disappointment flooded her eyes. She tried in vain to drown her sobs in the crisply-ironed, snow-white pillowcase.

*   *   *

When Kati and Uncle Sándor had planned their trip to Budapest, they made their flight reservations so that they could spend at least five full days with László. Now that things failed to turn out as expected, both would have preferred to return to Italy sooner. There was no chance for that, so they decided to make full use of their time.

During the day, Uncle Sándor visited friends and ran errands, while Kati took shopping trips into downtown Budapest. She spent most of her time in book stores that sold old and new books. She never ceased to be amazed at the excellent quality of the books that the Hungarian press produced. She bought several copies of prose and poetry, both by classical and modern authors, and she was especially pleased when she found a copy of Péter

Ruffy's *My Hungary* in English. It was a large and very impressive volume, filled with fascinating photographs. She planned to take it back to Dave Johnson, as a token of her gratitude for consenting to extend her stay in Europe. She felt lucky to find an exquisite porcelain figurine called the "Madonna of Kalotaszeg" in one of the antique shops, manufactured at the renowned porcelain factory of Herend in Transdanubia. She bought it for Aunt Sári, for she noticed that her aunt didn't have it in her otherwise extensive Herend collection. She also selected several smaller and less expensive artifacts of Hungarian folk art, embroidered tablecloths with matching napkins and carved wooden boxes. They would make great gifts for Michael and her friends and colleagues in Cleveland.

She chose a particularly attractive wall-hanging for her friend Kriszta, remembering her with fondness, for it was she who had talked her into taking this trip.

Both Kati and Uncle Sándor avoided discussing the events at the hospital. Only once, two days after their visit, did Uncle Sándor mention László's name.

"I thought László would give us a call," he remarked casually as they sat down to their evening meal. Kati didn't say anything. That afternoon she had contacted several of her friends, and had set up a date for each afternoon and evening, either to meet with girlfriends, some of whom were already married, or to have dinner at one of the fashionable restaurants. To her disappointment she had been unable to get a hold of Gábor Barna, although she did have dinner dates with two other male friends.

On the last day of their stay, when she was walking across *Vörösmarty Square,* she suddenly noticed Gábor as he stepped out of the main office of the Hungarian National Bank. He looked lost in thought, but when he glanced in Kati's direction he recognized her immediately.

"Kati! Kati Mátrai. Is that you?" He shouted excitedly as he ran toward her and gave her a friendly hug. He kissed her on both cheeks.

"How are you? What are you doing in Budapest?"

"Oh, Gábor, what a coincidence. What luck," she said, out of breath. "I called you a few times a couple of days ago." Then she added with reproach, "But you were never home."

"I just got back from Geneva last night. Oh, Kati, it's so great to see you again. What are you doing here? What are you doing tonight?"

Kati was touched by his display of affection. She noted that Gábor looked quite handsome in his well-tailored light-gray summer suit. The years they had not met had been kind to him, for he acquired that special demeanor of a man of the world. His boyish good looks seemed more appealing now, and he had a distinct masculine air. He certainly made a more favorable impression than a few years ago, Kati thought.

"You look great. Things must be going well for you."

"I can't complain. With this new 'goulash communism,' it's pretty good for people like me."

"Oh yes, I heard that expression." Kati said. "I heard it means you work a little, they pay you a little, but then you also have a chance for private enterprise. I even heard that some people refer to it as 'communism with a human face.' How can that be true?"

"Well, it's true, to a degree. There are opportunities for private enterprise on a small scale. And that's a move toward capitalism. Rules are not as rigid as before. And there's also a possibility for travel outside the country. The fact is, there are more opportunities for us than for people in the surrounding states," Gábor explained as he smiled broadly. He moved closer to Kati, and looked around to make sure no one else could hear him.

"It has been certainly good for me. I come and go, and I get to travel abroad a great deal, but..." He lowered his voice when a passerby came too close. "But prices are going up too quickly, and that really hurts the majority of the population. And, there's not much freedom, as in the West, and people still live in fear, to a degree..."

"You know what, Kati, let's not talk about such serious topics," he added playfully. Kati noted that old glimmer in his eyes. She hoped he was not carrying a torch for her. Carrying torches for someone was not exactly a pleasant state. She was beginning to see that.

"Will you have dinner with me tonight at the *Atrium*?" Gábor asked.

"I'd be delighted to," Kati answered and was glad she didn't make plans for her last evening.

"Let's meet at seven o'clock in the *Atrium's* new brasserie called *Clark Söröző*. The food is good there, and the atmosphere very pleasant." He glanced at his watch. "Excuse me, Kati, but I really have to run to a meeting. See you tonight."

Before storming off, he paused for a moment and Kati could just barely make out the words he murmured under his breath, "My, how beautiful and sexy you've become, Kati."

He was gone as quickly as he had appeared.

Kati looked forward to her last evening in Budapest with anticipation.

She wondered about the location of the new *Hotel Atrium*. She knew of several other hotels that had been built recently, and had already seen the *Buda Penta,* a tourist class hotel near the Southern Railroad Station. She had heard of another luxury hotel, the *Forum*, but she had no idea where either the *Atrium* or the *Forum* was located.

It was still early afternoon when she returned to Uncle Sándor's apartment. She decided to start packing, for she expected to stay out late that night.

Uncle Sándor was glad to find her in such good spirits, and was especially delighted when she told him that she had run into Gábor Barna and had a dinner date with him.

Looking chic in a simple black dress, Kati stepped out from the taxi and entered the *Atrium* through one of the revolving doors. She felt as if she had just been transported into another world. The hotel had a unique atmosphere. There was a large fountain in the middle, and to the left, a helicopter was suspended from a ten-story high ceiling. A circular glass elevator was visible in the center of the large open space. A café-restaurant, accessible by escalators was already visible at the entrance, although it was located toward the back of the building. She noticed the *Clark Söröző* to the right on the first floor.

She stood at the entrance, looking for Gábor who was already sitting in one of the booths by the window facing the street along the Danube. She smiled broadly as he stood up and waved, and rushed to meet her. He beamed when the eyes of several guests turned to admire the beautiful girl who was to be his dining companion.

Kati was captivated by the relaxed, yet elegant atmosphere of the place. The restaurant was nearly full and the soft music lent an air of tranquility to the scene. They ordered a "Transylvanian Wooden Plate" for two. It included some of the most tastefully prepared slices of meat that Kati had ever eaten. Gábor suggested a bottle of white wine, *Badacsonyi Kéknyelü* and with such Epicurean delights, they were well set for a most enjoyable evening.

"Are you going with someone?" Kati asked playfully. "Have you found your true love yet, Gábor?"

"No, not yet. I'm still looking," he replied wistfully.

It was evident that Gábor was still interested in her. He didn't take his eyes off her all evening.

She told him about her parents' accident, about her uncle's death, her new job, her trip to the Italian Riviera, Aunt Sári's illness, and finally her plans to return to Cleveland. She even mentioned Michael, but only in passing, and didn't tell Gábor that she was engaged. She had decided to remove her ring for the evening since she didn't feel like having to explain that she was serious about someone.

Kati had mentioned all the people who had figured in her life, with the exception of one: László.

Fascinated by every detail, Gábor remarked, "The last four years of your life sound more like a very sad, but exciting novel."

If he only knew about László, Kati thought, surprised at her own openness, attributing her talkative mood to the excellent wine.

Gábor looked straight into her eyes as he asked in a serious tone. "Tell me Kati, have you met the man of your dreams?" His voice was soft as he leaned across the table and gently touched her hand.

Kati was taken aback by his gesture of familiarity, yet she didn't pull her hand away.

"No. No, I haven't met him yet," she replied flatly. Then, a moment later, as if through some divine intervention, the main entrance of the restaurant, located directly across from their booth, was thrown open. Kati turned pale as she watched László step inside. He was closely followed by Angela and another couple. The hostess wasted no time in hurrying toward them and greeting them with a friendly smile.

As László began searching the place for a vacant booth, he happened to glance in their direction. As his eyes glided toward Kati, his mouth fell open and a shocked expression crossed his face. His eyes met hers, and the two of them were bound together by a deep, penetrating exchange. To Kati it seemed like an eternity, as László, without moving a muscle, gazed straight into her eyes. Yet, he did not give the slightest hint of recognition. Kati returned his gaze, and felt that their souls, the very essence of their being, had been locked together in that long mesmerizing look, never to part again.

She watched as László finally turned away, regained his composure, and sat down in the booth that Angela and his friends had chosen with the help of the hostess. It was only two booths away from their own, and Kati could hear the sound of their laughter, accompanied by lively conversation.

But for Kati, the evening was over. She fell silent and fidgeted in her seat.

Gábor immediately noticed the change in Kati.

"What is it? Is anything wrong?" He asked, clearly worried that he had said something to offend her. He suddenly looked lost and sad, but Kati could not bring herself to appear happy and nonchalant.

"Nothing, Gábor, nothing at all. It's just that I remembered that our plane leaves early tomorrow. I better get home soon." Kati replied and added with a forced smile, "It's way past my bed time, you know."

"I'll drive you home. You don't need to take a cab," he said. "I just got my car out of the repair shop before I came this evening." He looked dismayed and tried to make small talk until they finished their meal.

"I can't imagine what happened," he told her as they were driving across Elizabeth Bridge. "Please tell me."

But Kati refused to explain her sudden change of mood. Once they reached Uncle Sándor's apartment, she said good-bye on the sidewalk at No. 8 Maros Street, and disappeared behind the bulky outside gate.

That night she could not fall asleep for hours. That look in László's eyes continued to haunt her, even in her dreams.

10

Trouble in San Bartolomeo al Mare

San Bartolomeo al Mare and Cervo

The next morning, as they were making last minute preparations for their return trip to San Bartolomeo, it didn't take long for Uncle Sándor to register Kati's foul mood. She said very little during breakfast, and it seemed as if a dark cloud had settled permanently on her whole being. She looked unusually grave and there was not even a hint of a smile on her face.

Last night, Uncle Sándor had already been asleep by the time Kati returned from her date at the *Atrium*. He took a close look at Kati, suspecting that his niece's despondent mood was caused by something that happened the night before. She seemed to have gotten over the incident with László in the hospital room, but something new must be bothering her.

Uncle Sándor chose to ignore her obvious depression. He tried to create a cheerful atmosphere by his customary chatter about Aunt Sári's return from America, the sunny weather in Budapest, the healthy sea air, and all the amenities that life offered on the seashore of the Italian Riviera.

After landing, they entered the familiar surroundings of the waiting area at the Genoa airport. Kati was reminded of her first arrival, when she waited nervously for someone to drive her to Aunt Sári's home. She recalled her surprise at hearing a

Hungarian name announced on the intercom, although she could only make out "László" and not the last name. And with a strange twist of fate, the bearer of that name was to play a role in her life, at least for a while, she mused. She wondered whether the man whose back was turned to her at the refreshment stand had been László. Funny that she had never asked him, and now, she would never have the chance. She thought of her ride with Miklós, how he mentioned a "László" again, and the turbulent events of the past four weeks. She found herself yearning for those quiet times before her trip to Italy when her life was clearly mapped out and her future was all set, and everything seemed bright and uncomplicated.

"Traffic must be pretty heavy," Uncle Sándor remarked as they stood waiting inside the revolving doors at the airport terminal.

As previously arranged, Walter was to drive them back to San Bartolomeo. But over half an hour had passed, and there was no sign of him. Kati decided to call the Villa Tokay, and after several attempts she finally managed to reach Aunt Juli. She sounded upset and distraught, but assured Kati that Gino was on his way to the airport and he could be expected to arrive shortly.

An hour later Gino arrived, a somber expression on his face. He said nothing more than the customary words of greeting, and the three of them made the familiar drive to San Bartolomeo in silence. Kati even dozed off as they were passing through one tunnel after another, but she could not fall asleep. She felt agitated and upset, and her mind was swarming with thoughts of László.

She became more alert as the navy-blue Mercedes made a left turn on the Via Aurelia, and Kati recognized the rows of palm trees lining the street. As they turned to the right, into Via Europa, she was shocked to see a large crowd of tourists at the back entrance of the *Hotel Stella Maris.* There were several cars parked on the street, several of which belonged to the Italian police, the *Caribinari.*

Kati immediately spotted Aunt Juli standing in front of the wrought iron gate, at the back entry of the Villa Tokay. She was talking with three members of the Italian police, conducted in half-Hungarian and half-Italian. To make her points clear, she gesticulated wildly, but when she noticed Kati and Uncle Sándor stepping out of the car, she ran to meet them, obviously relieved by their arrival.

"It's Walter, it's Walter," she cried, gasping for air. "I found him this morning as he was leaving the Contessa's room."

Uncle Sándor and Kati looked at her in alarm.

"He broke in and tried to get a hold of her will," Aunt Juli continued breathlessly. "He found it and saw that Kati and Count Miskolczy were to inherit the Contessa's fortune. He broke her safe open and was just about ready to escape with her jewels and money, when I saw him sneaking down the staircase. I was petrified, and didn't know what to do. I screamed for help. Thank God my Gino was around! He called the police immediately."

She sighed, relieved that she was finally able to tell her story in Hungarian. Then she glanced in Gino's direction, and her eyes were full of pride. A moment later she broke down and began to sob, exhausted from the morning's events.

"They've already arrested him and took him away. Thank God," she said under her breath after she regained herself. Kati, trying to calm the older woman, put her arms around Aunt Juli's shoulders as they made their way through the large crowd and entered the villa.

"They're still keeping the villa under surveillance. Oh, it's so embarrassing. Everyone is staring at us!" Aunt Juli clung to Kati's arms.

"What will your Aunt Sári say?" She asked in alarm.

By dinner time she calmed down a little. Uncle Sándor suggested that they all eat their evening meal in the breakfast room next to the kitchen. He wanted Aunt Juli to feel at ease. She seemed anxious to tell the whole story.

"You know, ever since you two arrived, Walter seemed so agitated," Aunt Juli began. "He often acted like he was in a daze, and even dropped some dishes in the kitchen. Broke some valuable china too." She stepped out to the kitchen and returned with two serving dishes of steaming hot *borjúpörkölt,* veal stew with paprika, and potatoes with lots of chopped parsley on top. After having served the meal, she moved closer and sat down at the table with Uncle Sándor and Kati. "I asked him several times what was the matter. He finally blurted out. 'You'll see, we won't inherit a thing since these two are here. The Countess probably changed her will. If she dies we'll be without a job. And no compensation." Aunt Juli shook her head in disdain. She turned toward Kati and continued.

"He said that he was especially upset with you, Katika. He always referred to you as the 'little fortune hunter.' I still remember his red face as he told me one morning, 'She's young. She'll probably get everything, without having worked for it. While you and I and Gino run around all day, working hard, and trying to please her.'"

Uncle Sándor and Kati sat stunned. Both searched for words.

"When I decided to come here, I knew nothing about my aunt's tremendous wealth." Kati said quietly.

"And how Sárika trusted this fellow. She almost treated him like part of the family," Uncle Sándor remarked. "We all hope to God that Sárika will be all right, and then all this nonsense will mean nothing." A smile appeared on his face. "To think that I would inherit money from my niece! What a preposterous idea!"

"The idea of an inheritance never even entered my mind. Never." Kati said.

"That fellow must have been really greedy! And you know what, I'm sure Sárika thought of him in her will. What a jerk! Now, he'll lose his job and won't get anything."

"And he'll have to serve time in jail," Kati added.

Uncle Sándor looked thoughtful. "You know, there have always been people like him. Even, as we used to say, in the good old "happy peaceful times" when I was young."

"You have to tell me more about those days," Kati reflected. "But now, I'm so exhausted. Do you mind if I take a nap?"

*   *   *

Since Aunt Sári and Miklós were expected to arrive in two days, the members of the household had some time to catch their breath, and to recover from the commotion caused by Walter's unexpected criminal behavior. Although the whole event was shocking and outrageous, Kati was relieved that she would not have to face his smirk and his insolent smile again.

He must have been after Aunt Sári's money ever since he started to work for her. That's why he resented me so much, Kati concluded. She tried to dispel her own heavy-heartedness and made every effort to concentrate on things at hand, worrying more about Aunt Sári's health and safe return than anything else.

That evening, Aunt Juli was already humming happily in the kitchen as she prepared dinner. Although her cheerfulness had a positive influence on Kati's despondent mood, she and Uncle Sándor ate their dinner in virtual silence.

"The house was so empty without you," she told Uncle Sándor and Kati. "In two days we'll all be together again. Thank God!" She folded her hands and raised her eyes piously toward the ceiling. Then she crossed herself.

Kati settled into the comfortable blue and white bedroom that had become home. After dinner, she stepped out on the large terrace, enjoying the glory of the setting sun and the calming effect of the sea.

I still have three weeks here, she sighed, trying to dispel her melancholy. "And I am so thankful for Aunt Sári's recovery." But when the events in Budapest came to mind, she sank into renewed melancholia.

"I'll have to get over him," she thought, trying to convince herself that it would be best never to see László again. The next moment, however, she hoped that he would turn up in San Bartolomeo before her return to the States. Just to see him once more! Yet she wondered why she should care one way or the other. If she saw him again, her feeling of love and expectation would return, and it would take even longer to get over the disappointment.

She was thankful that Uncle Sándor volunteered to accompany Gino to the airport to pick up Aunt Sári and Miklós. She would have a little more time to pull herself together.

To avoid the usual heavy traffic toward the Genoa airport, on the day of Aunt Sári's arrival, Uncle Sándor and Gino left in the early morning hours.

Kati decided to wait for them in the nearby park. She wanted to dispel her depression by reading a contemporary novel that she picked up in Budapest. She hoped it would take her mind off of her own problems. But she was disappointed, for the story was filled with profanity and ungainly characters, and it was written in such brutal style that she could not read any further. Under the pretense of realism, modern writers concentrate on the violent and the crude, she concluded. She preferred to read about the uplifting and joyful sides of life, about heroines who solve their problems and overcome hardships. She considered them just as much part of everyday reality as the harsh realism and tortuous stories about deviates and criminals.

She happened to look up from her reading when around one o'clock the navy-blue Mercedes turned the corner into Via Europa. She closed her book and ran back to the villa, waiting at the back entrance. Under Gino's expert maneuvering the car came to a slow stop on the narrow street.

Miklós sat in the front, next to Gino, while Aunt Sári and Uncle Sándor occupied the back seat. Kati ran to Aunt Sári's side of the car. The side window was pulled down.

She immediately saw that her aunt had changed radically, having turned into a much older, broken woman. Her eyes had lost their usual sparkle, and her cheekbones stuck out more prominently than ever. She looked small and frail as she sat hunched back in the comfortable seat.

"Aunt Sári! Aunt Sári," Kati called as she reached her hand inside the car, touching her aunt's shoulders, and giving her a kiss on the cheek. "Welcome back, dearest Aunt Sári." She held the car door open as her aunt emerged very slowly, assisted by Miklós who ran to her side. Kati tried to hide her astonishment, and gave her aunt a warm embrace and another kiss on the cheek.

"I have changed, haven't I?" Aunt Sári asked as her face darkened. Then she smiled, and for a moment she became her old self again.

"It's so good to see you again, darling Kati," she glanced at her niece with shining eyes. "You don't know how happy I am to be back!"

She stepped between her two relatives, took them by the arm, and the three of them walked slowly through the park to the front entrance of the Villa Tokay.

"How often I dreamed of this place while in the hospital," Aunt Sári continued. Large tears rolled down her hollow cheeks. "There were times when I thought I would never see you again."

She squeezed Kati's arm and turned to look at Uncle Sándor, her eyes shining with gratitude.

Aunt Juli was already in the garden, and ran to meet them. She bubbled with excitement as her shy husband stood quietly in the background. They had agreed not to tell Aunt Sári about Walter yet, so she chatted about how worried she had been, all the preparations she had made for her lady's arrival, the dishes she had cooked, and the cleaning she had done during the past few weeks.

Kati held her aunt's arm as she helped her up the steps. Aunt Sári turned around before going inside. Her eyes swept the beautiful garden and she took a deep breath of the sea air.

"Thank God, thank God," she whispered under her breath.

Two of the small tables in the hall were covered with telegrams, letters, and cards which Aunt Juli had saved during her absence. They were from Aunt Sári's friends and acquaintances who expressed concern and sent best wishes for her quick recovery.

Later that evening Miklós assured Uncle Sándor and Kati that her operation had been successful and there was no cause for worry. Aunt Sári had already retired for the night, and the three of them were relaxing in the cool darkness of the drawing room.

"She had what I suspected all along, subacute bacterial endocarditis," Miklós explained

"Can that be permanently cured?" Uncle Sándor asked. "Sárika does look terrible, you know."

"That will pass. Thank God, her complete recovery is assured. I'm so glad I met Dr. Greenwood at a conference. We became friends and he was willing to take a look at her. He's one of the best specialists in the field, an expert at cardiac surgery for valve repairs. He told me after the surgery that hers was indeed a serious case, but assured me that she would be all right."

"Oh, she looks so thin and drawn. How long will it take until she returns to normal?" Kati's voice was filled with worry.

"All she needs are a few quiet months of rest. She'll be fine if there are no outside circumstances to disturb her peace of mind." Miklós looked meaningfully at Kati.

He thinks my presence here is disturbing, Kati's mind raced, or maybe that I should stay longer. I can't figure him out.

"You can only stay about a month, right?' Miklós asked. "That's better than nothing."

Kati took a close look at Miklós. Lines of worry appeared on his forehead, and he looked much thinner and worn out than when he left. But the customary mockery on his face was softened by weeks of sleeplessness and worry. His genuine concern for her aunt's well-being was evident.

"I wanted to tell you that your aunt spoke of you very often," he turned to Kati. "And I'm sure the fact that you stayed definitely helped her will to live."

Kati was delighted to hear his words.

"Miklós, we really don't know how to thank you for taking such good care of her. For taking off from your busy schedule to be with her," she said. At least her visit to Italy turned out to be of benefit to someone, she thought bitterly.

"And you had to leave your family, Inge and your children," Kati continued. "Thank you so much for being with Aunt Sári and saving her life."

"Really? You're thanking me for saving her life?" Miklós frowned and Kati had the distinct feeling that he was thinking of the inheritance. "I'll see my kids tomorrow," he continued. "I'll stay here overnight. There are two guest rooms next to yours."

Kati was alarmed, remembering that first day when he was so fresh with her.

"By the way, where's László?" The expression on Miklós' face hardened. He became his usual sarcastic self. "I expected him to be here when Sárika arrived," he said with a hint of irony.

"He was in that flight accident, as you know. He had to stay in Budapest for a while," Uncle Sándor explained, although it was clear that Miklós had directed his question toward Kati.

"He'll be flying back to Rome soon. He had to wait for some medical reports." Uncle Sándor glanced at Kati. "I wouldn't be surprised if he turned up in San Bartolomeo soon," he added. Kati stood up and walked to the window.

"And your trip to Budapest? How did it turn out, Kati?" Miklós asked in a piercing voice. Kati did not move.

Uncle Sándor came to her rescue. "Oh, we had a very pleasant time," he said for Kati's sake, but Kati suspected that Miklós was shrewd enough to sense otherwise.

"László will turn up shortly. I'm sure," Uncle Sándor continued, and Kati had the feeling that he said that more for her sake than for his.

During the following weeks Kati spent part of each morning and all of her afternoons with Aunt Sári. They took long walks on the seashore, played cards with Uncle Sándor, and to Kati's great relief, her aunt was visibly responding to the sea air and the tranquility of her own home. She began to regain her former good looks, and to be her cheerful and charming self again. Everything was going well, except for one thing that bothered Kati immensely.

She found that her aunt had become too dependent on her. She expected Kati to be at her side each morning and afternoon. If, for any reason, Kati was a few minutes late, a hint of reproach appeared in her eyes.

"I'll miss you so much, Kati darling," she told her almost every day. "I wish you wouldn't go back to Cleveland."

"But you know I have to. You must understand. My future is there. I have to make it on my own." She added, almost as an afterthought, "You know quite well that my fiancé is waiting for me. Michael is becoming very impatient."

"Ah, that Michael," Aunt Sári gestured with her hand, as if to dismiss Michael as someone who was not to be taken seriously.

"Uncle Sándor can stay as long as you want him to," Kati tried to console her and to ease the pain her departure would cause her aunt. She continued to spend most of her time with Aunt Sári, but there were times when she thought those days would never end, and she became anxious to return to Cleveland. After all, it was inevitable. Cleveland was her home, the home she would soon share with Michael.

One day she mustered enough courage and made a bold announcement.

"I would like to spend a day in Cervo. I've wanted to do that ever since I arrived, but for one reason or another, I never got around to doing it." They were sitting in the drawing room listening to Hungarian Gypsy tunes, Aunt Sári's favorites.

"Of course, go ahead, dear," Aunt Sári said in a resigned tone. "I must get used to your not being here, anyway. Sooner or later."

"Should Gino drive you up? Or Claudio, the new man? He seems very nice and dependable."

It did not take long to replace Walter. One of Gino's friends recommended Claudio who turned out to be an excellent employee, at least so far.

"Yes, he is certainly nicer than Walter," Kati observed. Claudio was always smiling at her and everyone else. "He's so good natured."

"Yes, he is. You know, Kati dear, I still find it unbelievable about Walter," Aunt Sári continued. "I really trusted the man. He seemed to be such an outstanding worker. Always ready to do his job," she noted. "He's in jail now, and he wants to see me. The police just sent me a message. But I'm not ready for that yet." Her face turned somber.

"Aunt Sári, I'd rather walk up to Cervo. Alone. It will do me good," Kati quickly returned to the previous subject. She longed to go up there by herself, to think and meditate about her life, and enjoy the quaint atmosphere of the village. Most of all, she wanted to enjoy the beautiful panorama. For the first and last time.

She had begun to feel annoyed by her aunt's clinging to her, and the constant moral support she expected.

"I feel suffocated," she confided to Uncle Sándor one evening after her aunt went to bed early. "It's so difficult to have to spend almost every minute of the day with her."

Uncle Sándor looked startled, but said nothing.

"I love Aunt Sári dearly, and I am so happy that I could be of help during her early weeks of recovery." Kati continued. "But Aunt Sári has no idea what it is to work for a living and what life is like in America for someone who has to hold down a job. I have to be a little selfish too. I have to think of myself and my future."

"I understand, little Kati. Please give her more time. Until she fully recovers. She won't need you that much then."

Kati wondered when that time will come. She felt restless. Now her future was clear, and she knew it lay in Cleveland with Michael as her husband, and a promising career, as she had originally planned. She had come to Italy to get to know her aunt. She had also yearned for some diversion from her humdrum life in Cleveland. Both goals had been accomplished; she smiled with satisfaction. There were a few unexpected events, of course, but ultimately the result was the same. In the end, her Italian holiday would be nothing more than a fond memory, something she could cherish in the years to come.

My visit to Cervo will be a fitting end to my Riviera holiday, she thought, torn by duty toward her aunt, her desire to make it on her own, and her curiosity about the village and its inhabitants. In a way, she told herself, Aunt Sári's suffocating dependence on her eased the pain of having to part with San Bartolomeo. She knew it would be difficult to leave. She had come to love the place, its joyful holiday atmosphere, the wide quay and seashore, the blue sky and the bright sun.

How I'll miss the sea, she sighed. Each morning when she woke up, sometimes even before seven o'clock, the sun was already shining brightly, and she spent several minutes just gazing out in reverie at the vast expanse of water. Watching the movement of the waves made her realize that she was just a tiny speck in the great scheme of things. A mere speck of sand, nothing more.

The next day she woke up earlier than her usual hour. She slipped into her white jeans, a pink cotton shirt, and put on her well-worn walking shoes. Not wanting to disturb anyone in the villa, she slipped outside without breakfast. It would be great fun to sip coffee on the terrace of one of the cafés nestled into the mountainside, to be carried away by the breathtaking view of white-washed houses and the undulating sea, and to feel the caressing morning breeze on her cheeks.

She decided to take the route along the seashore on the *Passagiata al Mare* as far as she could, and then follow the most picturesque road up to the mountain top in Cervo. The peace of the quay soothed her mood and her tenseness eased as she walked quietly, inhaling the fresh air tempered by the warm rays of the sun. The shops were still closed, the shutters pulled down, and only a few eager fishermen stood silently on the narrow passages flanked by large boulders, hoping to make their catch of the day early.

How I'll miss this place, Kati pondered, always returning to the same thoughts. She shivered when she remembered those long and rainy fall and winter days in Cleveland. A feeling of melancholy began to invade her mood. For a moment she even thought it would have been better never to have come at all.

But at least I had the chance to live in this beautiful sunny place for a little while, she reasoned, longer than most people get to in a lifetime. She tried hard to put László completely out of her mind, making plans for her future in Cleveland.

But everything here reminds me of him, she thought as she passed the remains of the tower and the line of trees where she had seen him for the first time.

She turned left when she reached the creek that flowed into the sea, and then right on the Via Aurelia. After crossing the bridge, she was already in the village of Cervo. Its territory began right on the other side of the creek.

She passed several hotels and shops and decided to turn off the Via Aurelia, taking a wide back road that passed by numerous camping areas such as *Camping Lido*. She reentered Via Aurelia by the *Hotel Salumeria,* and found herself at the foot of the hill on which the old section of the medieval village was built. The mountain looked even steeper and more forbidding from close. Kati wondered which road she should follow to reach the top.

She decided to take the *Circonvallazione a Ponente* that encircled the western side of the village. She stopped often to take in the picturesque view. She had almost reached the top when she turned around again and lost herself completely in the striking beauty of the vast panorama. The grayish-blue sea lay at her feet, and the colorful condos, winding roads, and green vegetation of San Bartolomeo and Diano Marina could be seen clearly. She found it hard to tear herself away, but began to feel a little hungry, so that after reaching the *Piazza del Castello* at the top, she decided to have breakfast in the quaint *Bar Ristorante Bellavista.*

Out of breath, she walked up the steep steps and chose a table with the best view. Only a few Italians were around although it was already ten o'clock. She had really taken her time. She gave her order to the smiling waiter and continued gazing out toward the sea.

The service turned out to be unusually quick. She took a slow sip from her *cappuccino*, and began buttering one of the delicious crisp rolls. Suddenly she noticed a man walking through the arcade that opened to the *Piazza Santa Caterina.* He looked so familiar, but for a moment Kati could not place him. Her eyes opened wide and the butter knife slipped from her hand, she was so stunned by what she saw.

It was László. As she reached to pick up the knife from the cobble stone floor, her heart began to pound, and she felt as if it would immediately jump out of her chest.

Dressed in beige slacks and shirt, and carrying one of those small leather bags so popular with European men, László looked the very picture of the man she had dreamed of as a young girl. The well-fitting slacks and tight shirt accentuated his muscular form, enhancing his natural good looks.

Kati found him more handsome than ever.

She sat still, staring down in his direction, as if completely immobilized by a magic power, beyond her control.

László gave no sign of having noticed her, and she was almost sure he hadn't. He did not even glance her way. He couldn't have seen me, she reasoned, because I'm partly hidden by the profusion of flowers and plants on the side of the terrace. Kati watched him and felt her heart race faster. Should she call out to him? He might simply pass me by, she thought suddenly. She panicked.

But László walked straight toward the steps that led up to the *Bar Ristorante Bellavista.* A second later he was standing in front of Kati's table. He had a broad smile on his face. There was no trace of injury on him anywhere, although Kati expected his arm still to be in a sling.

"Little Kati, your aunt told me I'd find you up here."

Kati sat motionless, still in a daze.

"Do you mind if I join you?" he acted as if there had been no misunderstanding in Budapest, and the two of them were the best of friends.

His question was a mere formality, asked out of politeness, for he pulled up a chair and sat down across the table from Kati. He was smiling broadly.

Kati blushed, and secretly envied his ability to act with such ease in any situation. She had often felt flustered under unexpected and embarrassing circumstances. Now, in his presence, she felt like a school girl at the lunch table when the boy she liked happened to take a seat across from her.

"I was just having breakfast," Kati said, with forced cheer in her voice.

"When was the last time we met?" László asked with a gleam in his eyes that was a deeper green than Kati had remembered. What a ridiculous question, Kati thought. What was he driving at?

"At the *Atrium,* you know quite well." Kati retorted. Realizing her brashness, she asked softly, "When did you leave Budapest?"

"A week after you and Uncle Sándor disappeared."

"How did you know when we left?

"Oh, I have ways of finding out things if I want to."

"I'm sure of that," Kati said.

"I decided to stay around a little longer since I was there already. Don't you think that was a good idea?" He laughed mischievously.

"I'm sure it was."

Did Angela stay in Budapest with him, Kati wondered. But asking that would betray her own feelings.

"And what did you do? How did you pass the time?" She asked in an innocent voice.

"Well, first I did a lot of thinking. A lot of hard and deep thinking about my life and my future. Then I found out that you two had already gone."

László folded his hands, and leaned across the table to be closer to Kati.

"I decided to call on friends I hadn't seen for fifteen years. It was so strange to see them again, but after we sort of warmed up, we talked about old times and reminisced about our days at the university."

"With the exception of one, all of them are married," László continued, with a slight emphasis on the word "married."

"Really?" Kati pretended to be surprised. His friends must certainly be old enough, she thought.

László continued, gazing at her with smiling eyes.

"So I met their families and had dinner with a different one for four or five days."

That means Angela must have left, Kati thought. He would not have let her wander around in Budapest alone.

"Oh, really?" She asked again.

"Then a prominent economist at the Academy of Sciences found out that I had stayed longer," László continued, "so they asked me to give another lecture." He did not take his eyes off her.

Kati returned his gaze. I have nothing to hide, she told herself. I'll be leaving soon, and might as well enjoy myself for the last time. Gradually she began to feel comfortable in his presence. László's arrogant air that had bothered her before was gone; it was only his self-confidence that remained, something that she had always admired in a man. He was definitely more humble and personable than before.

"I'm so glad Sárika is all right. I worried so much about her."

"Oh yes, she's is fine now. I stayed longer because I wanted to help her recover," Kati tried to explain the reason for her longer stay. As if he didn't know.

"When are you flying back, little Kati?" László asked softly, and reached for her hand. She pulled away.

"In three days."

He seemed surprised by the news. Apparently he thought she had decided to extend her stay much longer.

"And I came here to stay for at least a week," he said with regret. "So that I could be with you."

"Oh." Kati swallowed hard. "With me?"

"Yes, with you. I wanted to spend time with you. To get to know you better."

"I can't stay here forever. I have to get back to my job and my fiancé, Michael."

"Oh yes. I almost forgot. You're engaged." László turned away and Kati knew that he had just told a fib. He knew that I am engaged, she thought. How could someone forget something like that?

"Yes, I'm engaged. To a very nice guy," she replied. She sounded like she wanted to convince herself too.

She heard his earnest voice, as if coming from far away.

"Tell me, Kati, and please be honest. Do you love him? Do you love him enough to spend the rest of your life with him?" László's voice was tender, and when he turned his gaze back to her she saw that his eyes were filled with a new softness.

A long silence followed.

Kati could not bring herself to answer his question. She scrutinized the tablecloth as if interested in every detail of its weave. How can I reply when I myself don't know how I feel? For want of a better object, she fixed her eyes on her empty *cappuccino* cup.

But she could not answer his question.

"I knew you would sit way up here, Kati. I knew you would enjoy the view," László, realizing her dilemma, changed the subject.

"It looks like you and I have a lot in common. Similar interests, same background," he went on almost in a whisper.

Kati sat motionless, still gazing at her cup. László continued.

"I come up here often when I visit Sárika. It's so peaceful. Sometimes I even spend a whole day, reading, taking notes and even writing. I can work very well in this atmosphere."

"This is a marvelous place. Just being here calms me," Kati agreed, still avoiding László's eyes. "It's nice to get away from all the commotion and the noise below."

"I know of an even more magical place. It's not too far from here. It's even more secluded and more romantic. Farther removed from civilization." He paused. "In France."

Kati looked up. Their eyes met.

"It's not Eze, is it?" she asked.

"It is. Yes, it's Eze," László's eyes twinkled with satisfaction.

"I was there once with Uncle Sándor. Oh, how I loved it! I never wanted to leave. Never."

László continued to look at her.

"Since you're leaving sooner than I expected, I want to take you there. What do you say to that, little Kati?" That "little Kati" business again, Kati felt frustrated.

"Why do you keep calling me 'little Kati?' I am a grown woman," she said obviously perturbed. She gave him a piercing look.

"Because you have such a gentle, almost innocent air. It makes men want to take care of you, to protect you. Like one protects a child." Kati finally heard an explanation. She never realized that she came across as someone who needs to be taken care of.

"But I'm a pretty strong person," she replied forcefully. "Even if I don't show it. I've had to take care of myself..."

László interrupted her sentence. "I know. You've demonstrated that often enough. And two or three times to me too..."

Kati smiled complacently.

"Well, as I said before, Kati, I would like to take you to Eze. We could have dinner there before you leave. Will you come?"

"I only have three more evenings here. I'm leaving on Sunday morning."

"Then it's Saturday night," he said. He reached across the table again and taking her right hand in both of his, he held it tight. Kati's first reaction was to pull away. But she could not bring herself to do it. This is the moment I have been waiting for, the moment I had dreamed of as a young girl, a long time ago, she thought.

She raised her eyes and met his gaze. She did not say a word. She did not need to. They smiled at each other in silence and she let her hand rest in his, knowing that something had been deeply touched inside the very depth of their souls.

11

Strolling along in Cervo

The Village of Cervo

László's invitation was certainly unexpected, and at first Kati was delighted at the prospect of visiting Eze once more. At least her secret wish to return there would be fulfilled, she thought joyfully, and with László at that.

Her hand was still resting in his, and as she looked at his strong fingers, the warmth of his touch sent a surge of excitement through her body. László must have noticed, for he squeezed her hand gently, and the tender look in his eyes suddenly turned to desire.

Kati sat still, with downcast eyes, afraid to show her own feelings, and uncertain of the outcome of his interest. Then she thought of her aunt and uncle, and a look of alarm mixed with sadness settled on her face.

She swallowed hard and turned to look into the distance, avoiding László's penetrating gaze.

"I really don't think I can go to Eze. Thanks anyway. I feel I should spend my last evening with Aunt Sári and Uncle Sándor. It's only proper."

László was not prepared to take no for an answer .

"I'll arrange it with your aunt and uncle," he assured Kati. "I'll have to convince them to do without you that last evening."

His voice was determined, although his eyes were soft as he searched Kati's face with genuine affection.

His lips parted in a knowing, confident smile, signaling to Kati that he was used to having his every whim satisfied. Clearly, he did not care much about the effect his actions had on other people. He simply expected everyone to comply with his wishes.

Kati had never been an expert at hiding her feelings. The puzzled look in her eyes betrayed her confusion. Why was László so determined to take her to Eze? Why was it so important to spend their last evening together, especially in such romantic surroundings?

Thinking about it made her have second thoughts about another visit there.

"I'll only feel even more sad about having to leave," she said firmly.

László did not answer.

"I really don't think they'll like your idea," Kati continued, "especially Aunt Sári. She really clings to me nowadays."

But László only grinned, and there was a hint of reproach in his eyes.

"It's bad enough that you're leaving sooner than I expected. At least your last evening should be completely mine."

Kati almost asked him why. His sudden interest confused her.

"You didn't pay much attention to me in Budapest," she said as she recalled the events of that disappointing trip.

"I'm much wiser now," László said quietly. "As I mentioned before, I have given my life a lot of thought. About what I want out of life. And," he smiled broadly as he turned toward Kati, "I have thought a lot about you."

"About me?" Kati felt even more confused. Why me, she asked herself silently. I cannot let myself fall for him again. I have to use my head, not my heart.

"We'll talk about it this afternoon," she finally said. She was not prepared to commit herself. She had no right to ignore Aunt Sári and Uncle Sándor. They had both been so kind to her and she loved them dearly.

And I don't want to be disappointed again, she thought. László had caused me enough heartache already. I will not give him another chance.

Yet, she yearned to spend her last evening with him. A farewell dinner in the magical village of Eze would be a fitting end to her visit to the magnificent seashore of the world-famous French and Italian Riviera, the secret dream of tourists around the world.

She slowly lost herself in his seductive glance, her own love rising to the surface. The intensity of her feelings toward him was overwhelming. It came as a shock. Suddenly he meant more to her than she dared to admit to herself. He must not know how I feel, she thought in panic. Unless he feels the same way about me, I would have to suffer the greatest disappointment of my life.

"You know well that I already had more than my share of grief. I don't want any more," she reflected wryly.

A moment later she felt foolish for expressing her misgivings outloud. They were so out of place here. She looked away from László, immersing herself in the sight and sound of the picturesque village of Cervo and the sparkling sea below. She took a deep breath of the cool breeze, softened by the warmth of the sun. I must be strong, she told herself, and resolved to make the most of the last three days of her stay.

Dismissing all thoughts of doubt, worry, and fear, she smiled brightly at László, hiding the pain of their impending separation and the prospects for her future life in Cleveland. She was determined to steer the conversation in another direction.

"László, I'm curious to look behind the walls of this fascinating village. I walked up on the steps that encircle the settlement, so I didn't really get to do any sightseeing. Do people actually live in those ancient buildings?""

"They certainly do. I'll take you around. I enjoy strolling along those narrow streets and steep steps."

Kati noticed that the waiter, standing a few yards away from their table, seemed to be listening to their conversation. His eyes had a look of intense interest, as if he were trying to guess the language they were speaking. He finally asked them.

"*Ah, Ungherese,*" his face lit up as László explained that they spoke in Hungarian.

"*Si, si,*" he exclaimed, grinning, yet it was clear he couldn't make a connection. Deep furrows appeared on his youthful forehead. Then, suddenly, his face lit up.

"*Ah, certamente! Puskás! Calcio! Soccer!*" He cried out, proud that he appeared well-informed.

A shadow crossed Kati's face. So that was the extent of an Italian's knowledge about the land of her heritage. The waiter knew of one famous Hungarian, Öcsi Puskás, the soccer star and coach. What about all the cultural accomplishments of her countrymen?

László must have had similar thoughts.

"You see, that's what the average Italian knows about Hungary. Once you leave the country, there's hardly any mention of Hungary in the West. Hardly any, I am sorry to say."

Kati could not resist a nasty thought that came to mind.

"You know, László, I hate to say this, but during my visits I noticed that Hungarians in the mother country have a tendency to believe they're well-known and important to the world outside. Some even pretend to know everything there's to know outside Hungary's borders."

"Even if they have never left their homeland," László added. "Maybe it's terrible to say this, but I feel more at home here in Italy... And I grew up there..."

"Imagine how I feel. I wasn't even born there, and only spent a few months, during the summer. Yet, I have this love and affection for everything Hungarian, the people, the countryside, the culture. I feel that somehow I belong there..."

"This is a very complex issue," László replied in a serious tone. "But only for those who have deep feelings toward their heritage. Like you and me."

"I agree."

"How about discussing these problems some other time? It's too beautiful and romantic up here..." László smiled and motioned to the waiter. He asked for the bill and gave the waiter a handsome tip. The young Italian looked after them with appreciation as they walked over to the steep staircase that led to the *Piazza del Castello* below.

László took her arm, as he guided her down the steps. His smooth fingers caressed her bare upper arm, making her whole body tingle with pleasure.

This is just a gesture of gallantry on his part, Kati told herself. But she hoped it meant much more.

Having reached the bottom of the steps, László reached for Kati's hand. She was a little taken aback by his familiarity, but she did not pull away. A feeling of contentment swept over her, and at that moment it seemed perfectly natural to be walking hand in hand with the famous Professor László von Temessy of Sapiensa University in Rome.

They crossed the square and walked along the long archway that led to the *Piazza Santa Caterina.* Noticing an old map of Cervo that was fastened to the wall on their left, they stopped for a moment to study it.

Then László led the way up to the *Museo Etnografico a Levante* where they looked at the display of agricultural, trade, and household items in dusty little rooms.

"These people really had a harsh life," László remarked. The tools, implements, and furniture used by the past inhabitants of the village reflected their grueling existence.

Kati's attention was caught by items women used in the nineteenth and early twentieth century. Ancient power-looms, primitive sewing machines, and large wash basins stood as testimony to the roles and duties of women of those times. "I'm glad I was born into the present era. I certainly wouldn't like to spend my life behind a giant wash basin, or an old sewing machine. Or even a kitchen sink," she added.

"You won't have to, little Kati," László replied, as he pulled her closer, tightening his hold on her hand.

They soon left the Museum of Ethnography, and Kati delighted in peeping inside the cozy rooms of the *Locanta S. Giorgio,* located directly on the square. "It would be so nice to dine there once," she remarked as if talking to herself.

"Maybe we'll do that sometime," László replied. Kati was surprised by his gentle tone.

The *Piazza Santa Caterina* was already behind them as they walked down the narrow stone-paved Via Alessandra Volta, and reached another square named after Dante.

"There are people actually living here," Kati remarked, as they came across a group of children running around, playing hop-scotch or tag, while those a little older gathered around a fountain, engrossed in animated conversation. Several women were hanging out to dry their freshly washed, bright clothes, while others hurried across the square, carrying shopping bags, filled with groceries.

"This is a very educational walk," Kati said, looking at each newly discovered detail, enjoying the atmosphere of the medieval village. Good thing she wore comfortable shoes; otherwise it would have been difficult to walk on the cobble stone streets.

"Notice how high and close together the houses are. Actually, one wall supports two structures." László remarked.

Kati took her hand from László's and extended both her arms.

"I can't believe how narrow these streets are," she cried with delight. "I can touch the walls of the buildings on both sides of the street."

As she stood defenseless with both arms extended, László spread his own arms and pulled Kati close in an embrace. His lips searched hers, and suddenly the walls of the ancient buildings began to whirl around her.

"Please László, you're making me dizzy," she said, smiling under her breath, as she tried to tear herself away.

"That's exactly my heart's desire, to make you light-headed and vulnerable," he answered and touched her lips again, repeating the fervor of the previous kiss.

This can't be happening, she thought as she returned his kiss. She had noticed a special look in his eyes all during their walk, but she never thought it would come to this.

They continued their walk, as if their passionate kiss had been the most natural thing in the world. Kati felt embarrassed, and pretended to be engrossed in the unique architecture of Cervo. Both were content in just being close, sharing their enjoyment of the village.

They turned the corner onto Via Cavour, and found that despite the bright noonday sun, it was quite dark in the street below. As they passed under an archway overgrown with purple clematis, honeysuckle, and climbing roses, László stopped suddenly. She had no choice but to stop too.

For a moment they stood in silence. Then László pulled her close again. He held her by the waist, planted a gentle kiss on her forehead, and one on her lips. Gazing at her enraptured, he held her tight.

"*Katikám,* my dear little Kati, I'm falling in love with you," he whispered. "You have no idea how much I've been thinking of you during the past few weeks." Love shone in his green eyes that had a grayish tint in the semi-darkness. He raised one hand and stroked Kati's flushed cheeks.

"I love you, Kati," he said. His voice was gentle, ever so soft.

Kati was so startled by his words and his move that she had no time to pull back. Not that she wanted to, she thought frantically, as she listened to the wild beating of her heart.

"You caught me off guard," she said, feeling helpless. A moment later she was swept off her feet, marveling in delicious new sensations.

Oh, dear God, please don't let this lead to more disappointment, she prayed.

During their embrace and kisses the outside world turned into a dark blur, and for Kati, neither the past nor the future mattered.

Did he really say he loved me? Kati wondered later, as they continued their walk in silence. Or did I only imagine those words? She took a shy glance at his profile, but was afraid to say anything, lest she would break the magic spell of the moment.

László must have had similar thoughts for he was silent too. Once, when he glanced toward Kati, with his free hand he lovingly stroked her hair, shimmering golden brown in the sunlight. His eyes were filled with tenderness and love, and his lips gently curled in an easy smile.

They soon found themselves in another cobble-stone square in front of the large baroque church of *San Giovanni Battista*. It was the two high towers of this church that dominated the skyline of Cervo from afar.

They decided not to go inside, and for a little while they stood, holding hands, in front of the wide steps that led up to the elaborate wooden doors of the main entrance. Then they walked over to the waist-high stone wall that enclosed the courtyard.

They had said nothing since the kiss and embrace in the archway. They stood overwhelmed by the view of San Bartolomeo al Mare and Diano Marina, as both villages lay spread out far and wide on the seashore, directly below them.

"Can you find Aunt Sári's villa?" László broke the long silence.

Kati smiled and nodded "yes." A spoken word would only disturb the magic that had come between them.

They were more than half way down the steep hill when they reached the *Ristorante Serafino.* It consisted of reconstructed and modernized rooms, one of which displayed art objects for sale, ingeniously arranged. They paused for a moment on the wide terrace with another marvelous view of the sea. Kati was tempted to suggest a short rest at one of the quaint tables.

But I would be afraid to have to look László in the eye, if we sat down, she reasoned. And we would have to carry on a conversation. It was much safer to walk beside him. At least they didn't have to talk.

They strolled past the *Palazzo Mocchio*, which served as the main building of the village school. They stopped in front of an unusually small structure, and peeked through a dusty shop window displaying old books and ancient documents. It was the *"Archivum Vecchio Ricordi,"* the sign said.

What peaceful lives the villagers must lead, Kati pondered. Their tranquil existence is truly enviable. Yet, she knew that she could never be content in such surroundings, so far removed from the exciting hubbub of the modern world.

They finally reached Via Aurelia.

"Let's buy some apples," László suggested. They stepped inside the corner grocery store. Apples in hand, still holding hands, they walked until they reached the Via Repubblica. They turned left in the direction of the the Villa Tokay.

Walking with László like this was like being in a dream. They stopped several times along the way in front of shop windows, but as if by mutual agreement, they still did not talk. Kati's feeling of joy and contentment grew with every step. This was one dream that she didn't want to wake up from. She clung to every moment, hoping they would never reach the Villa Tokay.

In three days, I'll be far away from here, she thought sadly, savoring every moment of their walk to the fullest. She didn't want to think of the future, because now she knew that there was no future. There was no future without László. Yet, duty and her life in Cleveland beckoned from far away. She could even picture Michael's welcoming smile and hear his joyous welcome, "Kati, you're back! Thank God."

They found Aunt Sári and Uncle Sándor sitting in the drawing room, enjoying their after-lunch coffee amid pleasant chatter.

"Darlings, so you found each other," Aunt Sári declared in her charming way. Then she stopped, somewhat embarrassed at the hint of the double *entendre*. But she went on as if her words had not even been spoken.

"Isn't Cervo a charming place? It's like going back in time, many centuries. So unlike the busy seashore." She made a face, revealing her annoyance at the swarm of tourists and vacationers who passed in front of her villa each day.

Kati and László nodded in agreement. László looked at Kati, and then turned to his sister-in-law.

"Dear Sárika and Uncle Sándor. This is a good time as any to ask you..."

Three sets of eyes gazed at him in anticipation.

László smiled mischievously, enjoying the suspense he had created. Both Aunt Sári and Uncle Sándor looked at him with questioning eyes.

"You wouldn't mind if I stole your niece away during her last evening here, would you? You see, I invited her to the village of Eze," he grinned. "For our last dinner together," he added, smiling broadly, implying that there was more to it than that.

Aunt Sári and Uncle Sándor exchanged glances.

"Well, we certainly don't like to spare her on her last evening," Aunt Sári turned to Kati, her fondness for her niece evident in her every gesture. Fighting her tears, she added, "It will be so lonely without you, Kati dear."

Then she looked at László and gave him one of her radiant smiles.

"But then, László, you're part of the family. We'll do without her, but only for your sake."

"See, Kati?" László beamed with satisfaction. "We have two wonderful and understanding relatives."

"I would like you to know," he turned to the two older people, "that your considerate little niece didn't think it was right for her to spend her last evening away from you," he explained. "She wouldn't commit herself until you two agreed."

Everyone smiled broadly.

Then a frown appeared on László's forehead and he looked as if he had suddenly remembered something important. His face turned serious as he faced Kati.

"You know what, Katika, I just remembered I've some business matters to take care of today and all day tomorrow, so if you don't mind, I'll pick you up at five o'clock on Saturday afternoon. Then we'll drive to Eze and enjoy our farewell dinner..."

"All right," Kati replied faintly. She could not hide the disappointment in her voice.

She had hoped the two of them would spend the next two days together. Apparently, László had other plans. Maybe, it was just as well. Maybe it was better this way; spending more time together would make parting even more painful. A few last hours together in Eze, and they'll say good-bye, never to meet again. But then, why did he say "I love you" during their walk in Cervo? It must have been a spur of the moment thing, as both were so overwhelmed by the romance of the village.

László became his most charming self as he took his leave of Aunt Sári and Uncle Sándor, kissing both on the cheek. He definitely gave the impression of a man of the world, yet there was a special glow in his every move, as if he were expecting something extraordinarily good to happen soon.

"I'll see both of you shortly," he said to Aunt Sári and Uncle
Sándor. Turning to Kati, he took her hand gently in his, and
lifting her fingers to his lips, he held them much longer than ever
before.

Kati caught his glance.

"I would have really loved to spend the whole day with you
today and tomorrow. But there are some urgent matters I have to
attend to," he said softly.

He was still gazing at her, when Kati thought she detected a
hint of regret in his eyes. Why am I torturing her, his eyes said.
But maybe I'm just imagining things; Kati attempted to dismiss
her idea as she tried to read his mind.

She stood at the back entrance of the villa, looking after him
as he walked through the gate and got into his gleaming red
Porsche. Beige should be his favorite color, she mused. It
provided a striking contrast to his black wavy hair and his tanned
complexion. What a day, she thought to herself, lost in the
reverie of the events.

Kati was so preoccupied with László that she forgot that her
aunt and uncle were waiting for her. She had the feeling they
made every effort to act as if László's unexpected departure was
of no significance, that it was part of the normal course of
events.

She wanted to hide her own emotions, and resolved to put
him out of her mind. Only an occasional trembling of her hands,
or wavering of her voice revealed how she felt. She knew that
Aunt Sári and Uncle Sándor were aware of her feelings and her
disappointment, and she was thankful that neither of them said
anything when she stepped into the drawing room.

She turned to her relatives with forced cheer.

"I guess I'll run upstairs and start packing. I hope you don't
mind. After that, I think I'll take a nap. The outing to Cervo was
a bit exhausting."

"I'm sure it was, Kati dear," Aunt Sári acknowledged.

Exhausting! It was much more than that. Kati was glad Aunt Sári and Uncle Sándor understood. Neither tried to persuade her to spend her last evening with them.

She was ready to dash upstairs, but when she heard Aunt Sári's voice behind her, she stopped.

"Wait a minute, Katika, I almost forgot. You're not going to believe this. I met someone today, and he said that there's a lady from Cleveland who knows you."

Kati was surprised. "Knows me? Who could that be?"

"Her name is Luciana."

"Oh, yes. Of course. It must be Luciana Fabriani. We flew over together."

Kati had thought of her a few times and wondered how she was doing. What was it like for her to come back to Italy? How did she get along with her old love, Giorgio? But then, she was married to Waldo, and had two sons. Her place was in the US, no matter what.

Aunt Sári was eager to go on. "You see, today I finally went to see Walter in the prison. I was told he wanted to see me. I went for old time's sake. I actually feel sorry for him." Her eyes became moist, and Kati would have loved to know what those tears meant.

"There was this prison guard by the name of Giorgio. We began talking; he was so friendly. When I told him that my niece was visiting from Cleveland, he told me that he also had a guest from Cleveland by the name of Luciana."

"Really?"

"Then we figured out that the two of you must know each other. Giorgio said that Luciana talked a lot about a young Hungarian girl who came to visit her aunt. And that's you! When I was leaving after having talked to Walter, Luciana appeared in front of the prison building. So, I got to meet her too."

"What a coincidence," Kati could not believe her ears.

"You know, this Luciana wants to see you before you fly back."

"Me? I wonder what for? I'm surprised she's still here."

"She said she'd drop in tomorrow, early afternoon."

That's all I needed, Kati thought, but wondered what Luciana wanted.

"Really? Well, I'll be around all day Friday. We won't be leaving for Eze until Saturday afternoon." Kati's head was swimming. Why did Luciana want to see her? Did she decide to leave her husband Waldo for Giorgio, her old love?

She was definitely ready for a nap.

"I'll go upstairs. I hope you don't mind," she excused herself quickly.

She dashed upstairs on the familiar marble staircase, skipping every other step in her haste. It would be best to keep busy every minute of the rest of the day, as well as tomorrow, she thought, so there would be no time left to think.

12

Dining at the Chateau Eze

Eze, France

Dinner that night with Aunt Sári and Uncle Sándor turned out to be pleasant. Kati was relieved that neither of them mentioned her imminent departure. Most of all, she was grateful that they made no attempt to convince her to change her mind. At least she didn't have to put up a fight and to go over her reasons for returning. She was also glad that they did not say anything about László.

They chatted happily, in no way revealing that there will be just one more evening that they will spend together as a threesome.

"I look forward to seeing Luciana tomorrow. I wonder why she wants to see me." Kati remarked.

"Who knows?" Uncle Sándor said. "Maybe she just wants to find out how you spent your time on the Italian Riviera, how you liked it here. Italians are usually very much attached to their families and their country."

"I know. You should have seen the big crowd of relatives who turned up when we arrived. It seems like ages ago," Kati marveled, thinking of all the things that happened during the last two months. "My stay feels like a chapter from a story book."

"I feel the same way." Uncle Sándor added. "I certainly had a wonderful time. It will be hard to get used to communist Hungary after all this."

Aunt Sári lit a Chesterfield, and began puffing on it. She looked nervous and impatient, as if she didn't want to acknowledge the fact that her beloved relatives were soon leaving.

"Miklós called today," she announced unexpectedly.

After finishing their dinner, they were sitting out on the terrace, with some sweets on a silver tray and a bottle of Napoleon brandy on the table in front of them. Uncle Sándor was pouring a small portion into each of their elegant crystal glasses.

"He sends his greetings to both of you. He said he was sorry you were leaving, Katika. He really wanted to see you again."

Sure, Kati thought, remembering her first day at the Villa Tokay. She had decided not to mention anything to Aunt Sári. Thank Heaven, there had been no opportunity to be alone with him again!

"He. has such darling children. He should be happy," Kati remarked. Then she posed a most daring question. "Why did he marry someone like Inge? Somehow they just don't fit together."

"I'll tell you a big secret," Aunt Sári smiled. "Inge is a very wealthy young woman, the daughter of a prominent German industrialist. They met soon after Miklós defected from Hungary and he was in medical school in Heidelberg. They dated for a while and she became pregnant. Miklós married her because he felt it was his duty to act honorably. I remember how torn he was. He didn't know what to do. He asked for my advice and I told him that he should accept the consequences of his actions. And so he did."

"But they're not happy together," Kati insisted. Then she thought of Michael. Will she be happy with him? Are they made for each other? Or will her life be like Inge's, not quite right, not the kind and loving relationship that everyone dreams about?

Her heart was torn. Please smile down upon me, *Anyuka* and *Apuka*, she breathed a silent prayer. Please help me accept whatever Fate has in store for me.

Two more nights in the Villa Tokay, she thought to herself. She looked forward to Luciana's visit on Friday, but she was especially excited about spending her last evening with László in the enchanting village of Eze.

She slept well that night in the familiar blue and white room where she felt completely at home.

*   *   *

Around two o'clock in the afternoon, Kati heard the front door bell ring. Everyone in the household was taking their customary siesta, so she opened the door.

Dressed in a bright summer dress, Luciana stood in the doorway. She held out both arms and gave Kati a big hug and a kiss on the cheek.

"I'm so happy to see you," Kati said, returning Luciana's exuberant greeting.

"I hope you had a great time in my beautiful country," Luciana began.

"A wonderful time," Kati acknowledged, smiling.

"I told you so. Remember?"

"Oh, yes, I remember quite well. I was rather unhappy about coming here because there was no one waiting for me at the airport. "Let's go outside and sit on the terrace"

She offered Luciana coffee and a slice of walnut cake that Aunt Juli had baked the day before. After some lively chatter about the beauty of the Italian Riviera and the friendliness of the population, Luciana came right to the point.

"Kati, dear Kati! I'm so glad you're still here. I wanted to talk to you before you flew back to Cleveland."

"To me? Why?"

"Well, I don't know how to tell you this." She pursed her lips, and was silent for a moment. "Kati, I'm not going back," she announced in a somber tone, waiting anxiously for Kati's reaction.

"Not going back?" Luciana's words were like a thunderbolt from a clear and sunny sky.

"What about Waldo, your husband? Your two sons?"

"My sons are all grown up. They can come and visit me after they get over the first shock. After all, they're half-Italian." Luciana smiled complacently.

"And your husband? You mean you're leaving him?"

"He'll feel more comfortable with his own kind. He's an American, through and through. Football and baseball are his only loves."

Kati was stunned. She was searching for words.

"I would like you to take this letter to Waldo. Give it to him personally. I didn't want to send it through the mail. Maybe you can explain things to him."

"How can I do that? I don't even know you that well." Kati paused and took a deep breath. "And I certainly don't know him."

"Well, you know Italy, and the lifestyle of our people. We like to have a good time, and not work all the time..."

"That's no reason to leave your husband," Kati interjected.

"Well, no, but I found my true love here. Giorgio and I picked up where we left off over twenty-five years ago. He's such a doll, although rather domineering at times. And he tells stupid jokes. But we still get along so well... We understand each other's thoughts..."

Kati was speechless.

"So, Kati. Would you do me this great big favor? Would you give Waldo this letter and this package? You don't live far from our house."

Kati hesitated. She felt terribly uncomfortable. I certainly don't want to get involved in this, she thought to herself. But I cannot think of a reason to refuse.

"All right. I'll do it for you," she said reluctantly.

Luciana was visibly pleased. "Thank you, Kati dear, thank you," she beamed.

After a few more minutes she stood up.

"Good-bye, Kati. Come and see me on your next trip to Italy. We'll be glad to see you. After my divorce from Waldo, Giorgio and I are getting married."

Kati was still in shock. How could someone do this after more than twenty years of marriage? She felt terrible for Waldo. But then, maybe he saw this coming. Maybe their marriage wasn't so great anyway. But at least Luciana should tell him in person, not just through a letter. She was definitely a coward, Kati concluded and tried hard to put Luciana out of her mind.

*   *   *

The day before her return flight to Cleveland was finally here. Kati had gotten up early, and the morning hours flew by quickly as she immersed herself in the tedious job of packing. She could barely get all her clothes into her two suitcases, since Aunt Sári bought her so many new ones. She decided to leave some of her old dresses behind, piling them high on an easy chair.

She was engrossed in trying to decide what to leave behind, when she heard several knocks on her door.

"Come in," she said, wondering who it could be.

The door opened, and Aunt Juli stood in the doorway, with a well-stocked lunch tray in hand. There were dark circles under her eyes. Her smile was forced, and her voice was shaking.

"So kind of you to bring me something to eat," Kati said although she was not at all hungry. She gave Aunt Juli a big hug after she put the tray down on Kati's desk. Without waiting for an invitation, Aunt Juli sat down on one of the easy chairs, and turned to Kati with apprehension in her voice.

"Dear little Kati, so the time has come for you to leave us."

"Yes, Aunt Juli. It's for the best."

"I wish you could stay. Why don't you?"

"I really can't. Cleveland is my home. I have a career there, and also friends. And Michael. I told you this many times before..."

"I just wish that...that... László..." She began, but she could not finish her sentence as a sob escaped her lips.

"Please don't cry. I'll come back yet. Maybe next year. You'll see."

While she was determined to console Aunt Juli, Kati tried to fight back her own tears. She turned away from the housekeeper, closed up her large suitcase, and placed it outside her door in the hall. She did not want Aunt Juli to see her face, so she stepped inside the bathroom, and turned on the faucet to dab cold water on her eyes and cheeks. Since she left the door open, she could make out Aunt Juli's words.

"Dear little Kati, I wanted to tell you... I just heard that Angela is engaged. She's getting married soon."

Kati gulped, and her heart sank. She continued splashing her face with cold water. It couldn't be, she panicked. Angela couldn't be marrying László. She thought of his words in Cervo. It just couldn't be true!

"Kati dear," Aunt Juli continued, "She's not marrying László. She found someone else. Another foreigner, a guy from Sweden. I just wish that..."

Suddenly, Kati realized that Aunt Juli had been harboring romantic dreams for her and László. But she did not reply to the news. She dried her face, powdered her nose, and put on some lipstick while Aunt Juli continued.

"I just wanted you to know that we all love you here. Now that Walter is gone, I'm sure you feel more comfortable with us."

"Oh yes, Walter. Why did he dislike me so much?"

"Well, I guess he saw you as a threat. He told me once that he harbored dreams of getting some of your aunt's money. With you and Uncle Sándor being here, that possibility vanished. At least in his mind."

"Oh, but how could he expect something more from my aunt? He was well-paid."

"Yes, that's true. But he thought that he was one of you. That he belonged to your family, your class. He always thought he was better than us, Gino and me. And he felt he had done a great service for your aunt."

"What do you mean?"

"When Mr. Kálmán and Annie disappeared, he really spent a lot of time trying to find them. But to no avail."

Kati had a hard time paying attention to what Aunt Juli was saying. Her thoughts were miles away. She was thinking of tonight's dinner with László and her impending trip back to Cleveland.

"Your Aunt Sári really loves you," she heard Aunt Juli's voice again. "Now that thank God she's cured, she's thinking of the future... She is devastated that you're leaving for sure."

"She's been asking me to stay, but I really can't. You know that, Aunt Juli." Ah, Aunt Juli is thinking of herself and Gino, of course, Kati realized again.

"Maybe she didn't make herself clear enough. Your aunt has always been shy about expressing emotions. She always hides her feelings, and wants to appear in control of things," Aunt Juli insisted.

"I'm sorry, Aunt Juli," Kati shook her head and tried to take a few bites of lunch. She found that she had no appetite. Her arms and legs felt heavy as a surge of exhaustion came over her.

"I'm so tired, Aunt Juli," she finally said.

"I'll leave so you can lie down a bit. I just wanted you to know about Angela."

Aunt Juli quickly left the room, teary eyed, realizing that her mission was not accomplished.

Kati decided to take a nap. Lying on the wide comfortable bed, she folded her arms behind her head, and stared at the ceiling.

Maybe I should stay here a little longer, she thought. After all, everyone wants me to stay. She was tempted to change her plans. But she couldn't do that. There was her job and there was Michael... Once she had made a decision, she should stick to it. She learned that from the past.

But it's so difficult to leave now, she admitted, just when László has become so attentive, so interested. She could still hear his words, "Dear little Kati, I'm falling in love with you," and a little later he said, "I love you, Kati."

She pondered about how things were turning out, and she wondered whether Luciana made the right decision. A feeling of sadness came upon her; a sense of loss overwhelmed her heart. What should I do, she asked herself in desperation. Her spirit was torn. Her mind told her to leave, while her heart urged her to stay.

In the long run, it would be best to leave right now, she finally concluded. The sooner the better. She would just be postponing the inevitable.

She thought of her date for the farewell dinner in Eze and soon fell asleep, trying to convince herself that she had made the right decision. Her place was in Cleveland, with Michael, she told herself. She had always thought of herself as a woman of principle. Now she had to prove it.

Kati soon woke up from her short nap. It suddenly hit her that she just had one more day in San Bartolomeo. She decided to take a leisurely walk along the familiar quay, and to say a silent good-bye to the tiny shops and cafés she had learned to love. As she passed the tightly-packed *Lido Bar* and the *Hotel Ondina*, she remembered her quarrel with László.

Now, even that seemed insignificant, and anyway, she thought, they had made up since. She recalled their stroll through Cervo, cherishing every minute they had spent together. The fervor of his kiss and embrace returned, sending new ecstasy through her body and soul. Why was he so loving toward her? Why did he say he loved her, and why did he disappear during her last two days here?

Worry and uncertainty lay heavy on her heart, yet a feeling of expectation took the better of her, as she turned around and made her way back to the Villa Tokay.

*   *   *

By five o'clock Saturday afternoon Kati was standing on the terrace that opened out from the drawing room. The sea below her glittered in the brightness of the Mediterranean sun, and she watched the throng of bathers as they lay on the beach and on rocks covered with colorful towels, soaking in the welcome rays of the sun.

A sense of loss mingled with serenity came over her. She felt at peace. It must be the soothing effect of the sea, she concluded. The perpetual movement of the waves subdued her agitation, and in the immense design of things, she realized now, she was but an insignificant speck, a grain of sand, whose fate mattered to none but to herself.

She was prepared to accept her destiny, whatever it was to be.

The loud chime of the doorbell woke her from her thoughts. She hastened inside to open the door. She knew there was no one around. Aunt Sári and Uncle Sándor were still taking their afternoon naps, and Aunt Juli had gone shopping a few minutes before.

She opened the door and smiled.

"Hello, László."

László's eyes shone with admiration.

"Kati, you look absolutely gorgeous," he whispered as he stood in the doorway, spellbound. His eyes took in every curve of her body, perfectly dressed in an Oscar de la Renta creation of powder blue chiffon.

"Thank you, László. I feel great. I wanted so much to return to Eze once more, and now you're taking me there."

László did not take his eyes off her.

"This dress looks so perfect on you. It complements the azure of your eyes."

Kati blushed. Her softly curled golden brown hair swayed gently on her shoulders, and when she pushed her hair back with her right hand, the delicate silver pendant earring that matched her necklace came into view.

A peculiar glow emanated from her whole being, a combination of inner strength and serene acceptance of life.

"I have never seen you look this beautiful," László remarked as he guided her out the door.

They stepped out of the villa, and after Kati locked the front door, they strolled through the public park. László led the way to his Porsche parked at the back entrance of the Villa Tokay. It stood waxed and shined, ready to take them to their destination.

The drive to Eze seemed more like a final journey, a last pilgrimage of joy which people make before resigning themselves to an unpleasant, but inevitable future.

I feel so vulnerable and weak in his presence, Kati thought as they settled comfortably into the bucket seats. László's closeness made her lose her bearing, and she made a special effort to avoid his gaze when he happened to turn toward her.

She glanced in his direction only once, afraid that he would guess how she felt. But he was forced to lose himself in battling the heavy traffic on Via Aurelia.

"Looks like the whole population of the Italian Riviera is driving through San Bartolomeo," she remarked.

"Yes, they must have some urgent business to take care of," László agreed and his eyes had a special shine.

They finally reached the *autostrada* by traveling northward on various winding roads, and from then on, their journey was smooth and without excessive traffic.

Kati became so engrossed in taking in every detail of the spectacular sight that opened up before them that she hardly noticed László's frequent glances in her direction. The panorama was familiar to her by now. The sparkling sea below and the soft curves of the mountain range with lush palms and olive trees, and the enchanting villas and mansions that broke the monotony of the countryside had all become part of what she had come to love and to cherish.

"This is my last chance to enjoy all this," she said.

László must have guessed her thoughts.

"You look a little sad, Katika," he remarked. He noted Kati's bewildered expression. "What's the matter? Is anything wrong?"

"Oh, it's nothing. It's just that I ... I love the Riviera so much, and I'll miss it so...." Her throat burned. Her hands lay folded in her lap, and she pinched her palm with her nails. László should not know how unhappy she felt.

They crossed the French border without waiting, and by six o'clock, they were already driving toward the seashore, in the direction of Eze, "*Eze - village - medievale*," as the sign said.

They left the Porsche in the parking lot at the foot of the mountain on which the village was built.

"The walk up will do us good," László said. "I hope you can walk in those high heels."

He reached for her hand as they made their way on the wide road that led to the wall around the settlement. Inside the village they stopped several times to admire the doorways and window sills covered with a multitude of flowers in full bloom. Climbing roses in pink, red, and white, purple and white clematis, and petunias in all the colors of the rainbow grew profusely, everywhere.

They passed the small shops, cafés, and restaurants, and Kati wondered which restaurant László had chosen for their farewell dinner. They finally stopped at the entrance of the fanciest one, the *Chateau Eze.* "This is a good omen," Kati thought. It was the same café-restaurant where she had enjoyed a glass of lemonade with Uncle Sándor several weeks ago. But then, a good omen for what? What was she expecting?

"I thought this would be the perfect place for us this evening," she heard László's voice, as he guided her inside.

"Yes, it's perfect," she agreed.

As they entered a wide arched doorway, they were greeted by the head waiter, a short, middle-aged man dressed in a white tuxedo and black bow tie.

"*Professore Dottore,*" he said in rapid Italian. "We've been expecting you." He smiled at Kati with admiration in his dark eyes. They followed him as he led them through several small rooms in which the tables were set for dinner in anticipation of the evening crowd. He did not stop until they reached an isolated corner on the terrace at the far end that faced the panorama of the sea.

"I thought it would be more pleasant to sit outside," László said as he pulled out Kati's chair, and stood behind her until she was seated. "We can enjoy the splendid view from here and also have some privacy."

Kati noted that the former chocolate-brown tablecloths had been replaced by white linen, and the terra-cotta umbrellas at each table had been removed. The tables were set with white bone china and shimmering silverware. A single red rose in a slender vase stood in the center, enhancing the festive atmosphere of the evening.

"Let's have a cocktail before dinner," László suggested, as he reached across the table and touched Kati's hand. His hand rested on hers. Kati felt a sudden surge of excitement dashing through her whole being.

"A Pink Lady, please." she blurted out. For the moment she could not think of the name of any other drink.

Lines appeared on his forehead. "A Pink Lady? Oh yes, I remember now. I drank one in New York once." His eyes brightened. "I'll try one too."

The waiter looked puzzled. László motioned him closer and spoke to him in Italian. The waiter's eyes lit up.

"*Oh, si, si!*" he smiled and left.

All along, Kati was gazing in the direction of the Mediterranean. It was a calm late afternoon, and the smooth indigo ink surface was broken only by tiny drops of light that glistened on the undulating waves in the setting sun. An occasional yacht appeared below. Even a few motor boats raced past, but their sound never reached them. They were a thousand feet above the sea.

Kati tried hard to concentrate on the beauty of the scene. She knew herself well; her feelings always showed on her face. She remembered how her Italian holiday had begun by hearing the announcement of a "László" on the intercom at the Genoa airport. It was a strange twist of fate that it was also ending with a "László." She was curious to know whether this "László" was the same one...

"I've always meant to ask you. Were you at the Genoa airport about two months ago?"

László looked thoughtful.

"Yes, as a matter of fact, I was. I had to meet two professors from the U.S., from Cornell University and Stanford. That's why Miklós went to pick you up, although Sárika first asked me to do it."

So it had been László whom she saw from the back. How strange life was!

"After having met you, I definitely would have preferred to pick you up instead of them," László said with a gleam.

"Well, that was cleared up quickly," Kati reflected and tried to smile. "And tomorrow I'll be on my way to the Genoa airport again," she added.

László reached across the table, squeezed her hand, and Kati had the feeling he was going to say something important. But he only whispered, "Little Kati, look over there."

Kati turned around and saw the head waiter carrying a silver tray. A foamy pink liquid glistened in two crystal glasses. He was followed by another waiter, almost hidden from view by a large bouquet of red roses.

"Here you are, *Signor Professore and Signorina*," the head waiter motioned to the one carrying the bouquet. "Let's put them in a vase." He smiled knowingly. "I hope you like them."

Kati was overwhelmed. "László, you didn't..."

"Yes, I did... Six dozen roses. My gift to you on your last evening."

How thoughtful, Kati thought. A feeling of warmth swept over her.

When the waiters left with wide smiles and many bows in their direction, László's expression became grave.

"Little Kati, I have a confession to make. When I first met you, I thought that you were just a pretty girl on holiday at my sister-in-law's. I never gave you a second thought. I even took advantage of you a few times."

He avoided Kati's eyes.

"But then, when I got to know you better, I realized how different you are from all the women I know. A young girl, all alone in the world. Yet, you have determination and high goals. I began to think of you more often."

He paused but did not look at Kati.

"I even took your advice, and flew to Budapest. Something I didn't want to do because I hate those communists, and I can't stand that regime."

He fell silent for a moment. The graveness of his voice betrayed that he was very serious.

"But I learned something from my trip," he continued quietly. "I found that so many people detest the government. But they also have to live and to support their families. And to build their careers. Of course, there are many opportunists around, but the majority have no choice but to try to make it in a system they despise. I realized how lucky I am. I defected because I wanted to have a choice about my life and future."

Kati listened intently but did not answer. László still avoided her eyes. "But I made many mistakes too. I made bad choices. All kinds. One of them has to do with you. I don't want to remind you of your hospital visit..." He took a deep breath.

"There I saw you as a young woman of character, one who has a will of her own."

Kati sat motionless, anxious to hear what he had to say next.

"And then, finally, when I saw you at the *Atrium* that evening, with that young man, my heart stopped for a moment. That night I realized that I would be absolutely crazy to let you go." He paused for a moment.

Kati listened with every nerve of her body.

"But I didn't want to do anything rash. And I have never been in favor of marriage." He grinned. "Maybe too many have failed around me."

He paused for a moment.

"Then the more I thought about you, the more certain I was that I was falling in love with you. Truly in love, for the first time in my life."

"Of course, there had been women in my life, and I have sown some wild oats. I am old enough," he smiled, alluding to his age. "But I have never felt about anyone the way I feel about you."

He turned back to Kati and looked into her eyes. His tender look spoke of love.

"I began to think. We come from the same culture. Our backgrounds and values are very much alike. I knew then, that if I didn't catch you before you leave, I would regret it for the rest of my life. I would be letting go of a precious jewel, one that could never be replaced."

"László?" Kati whispered. "You told me you loved me at Cervo, remember? And I didn't answer. I didn't say anything because... because I was afraid of being used. But now..."

"*Katikám,* my sweet little Kati," László said softly, taking Kati's hands into his, caressing it gently. "Little Kati, I love you so much. Will you marry me?"

"How can I? I'm engaged." Kati's heart pounded.

"That can be changed, can't it? Engagements have been broken before."

"I know, but..."

They must have had the same thoughts, for without a word, they stood up from the table and walked to the far end of the terrace. They stopped behind the tall palms and philodendrons planted in large boxes along the rail.

Kati felt László's touch on her shoulder. They faced each other and his eyes told her everything she longed to hear. But her thoughts raced as the image of Michael glared at her from the back of her mind. How will she tell him? She'll have to fly back to Cleveland and let him know that she's sorry... so sorry... but... He deserved much more than a "dear John" letter.

"Kati, promise me you'll never say good-bye to me as you did at the *Hotel Ondina* and in the hospital room. Promise me that."

"Never, never. I'll never say good-bye to you again," she whispered.

He took her in his arms, holding her as if he would never let go. Their lips met, and her fears, doubts, and frustrations vanished. She could finally melt into his arms, to lose herself in his embrace. She knew she would never have to leave the place she had learned to love.

Her summer in Italy will never have to come to an end.

Epilogue

Kinga finished reading the manuscript. She had read feverishly through the night. She placed the black binder on the night stand and stared into space, deep in thought. She was heartbroken, but no tears came to her eyes. In this, she was unlike *Édesanya* who cried easily, and was always embarrassed when she could not hold back her tears.

She was shaking inside. A deep sadness settled on her whole being. This was her mother's story, a story she had never told her children. Nor her husband. How happy she might have been with László von Temessy. They were a perfect match, same view of life, same culture and heritage. And they found true love in each other. Her children's lives would have been different too.

But it was not meant to be. Kinga wondered why their love had gone unfulfilled. What took place after her mother's return to Cleveland? Did something happen to László? Why did she change her mind? Or was it László who backed down? There was no answer. It was like tramping through a jungle, searching for a rare exotic plant that was hidden from view, nowhere to be found.

She reached for the binder, her fingers relishing the touch of each page. Gently, she caressed the names "Kati" and "László," hoping that one day she would learn the truth.

Should I let Father read this, she pondered. No, it would be better if the secret were left untold. But keep the life of Kathleen

Mátrai Keller alive in your memory, she reminded herself. And pass it on to your children some day... The story of a great lady, whose life on earth ended too soon, and her journey was forever sealed on that fateful evening twenty-two years ago in far away Eze, on the French Riviera.

She took the manuscript and wrapped it lovingly in brown paper. She vowed not to touch it until it was time... Time when her own children would be curious to read about an exceptional person, the grandmother they would never know.

Kinga stood up and glanced into the mirror above her mother's dresser. She felt *Édesanya's* presence, and could almost see her mournful eyes staring at her from far away. There had always been a distinct resemblance between mother and daughter. The color of Kinga's hair and eyes, her high cheek bones, the gentle curve of her brow were all reminiscent of Kathleen Mátrai Keller.

I hope that I will always have her spirit, she sighed. And her strength.

She knew that the time had come to fulfill her mother's last wish, to scatter her ashes into the Mediterranean Sea, right by San Bartolomeo al Mare. There, perhaps she may even learn the secret that prevented the union of the beautiful Kati Mátrai and the dashing László von Temessy, her true love, the man of her dreams.

Suddenly, Kinga remembered the words her mother had whispered during her last visit at the Cleveland Clinic. "Kinga darling, please never forget that I had a good life. In spite of everything." Kinga had searched her eyes, puzzled at what she meant.

Now she understood.

She pondered about fate and life, and was reminded of her own future, thankful for the opportunities America provided for her and her brother Tom.

Plagued by guilt and regret, she lamented the days gone by when she could have had heart-to-heart talks with her beloved mother. Now she had no choice, but to continue selecting *Édesanya's* belongings. A part of her mother went with every item she had to discard.

I'll never forget her and I'll never forget her story, Kinga vowed. She felt a burning sensation in her eyes. With her right hand she wiped a teardrop rolling down her cheeks.

Then she broke into uncontrollable sobs.

About the Author

Ágnes Huszár Várdy is a literary historian, novelist, professor, and the author, co-author, and co-editor of eleven volumes and over ninety articles and essays on literature and culture. Her highly acclaimed social-historical novel, *Mimi*, is being used in history and literature courses at several universities in the United States and Europe. She currently teaches Non-Western World Literature at Duquesne University in Pittsburgh, Pennsylvania.

Forthcoming in 2007

Ágnes Huszár Várdy: Mimi - a novel (**3rd edition**)

— Compelling saga of wealthy young baroness during World War II Hungary

— Story of scandal, suicide, forbidden love, Nazi occupation, Soviet conquest, loss of homeland

— Novel captures unique social relationships and historical aspects of era

Comments by Readers of 1st and 2nd Editions:

* "The book is so enjoyable that I couldn't put it down until 4:00 am." *S.A. Los Angeles, CA*

* "I enjoyed every single word; I practically relived the past." *E.V. San Diego, CA*

* "The characters are so alive that I could almost see them and could share their joys and sorrows." *S.S. Cleveland, OH*

* "I found *Mimi* captivating. It held my attention to the very end." *B.P. Tucson, AZ*

* "The characters are well-drawn. The story flows naturally, presenting a uniquely realistic portrayal of Hungarian society in the '30s and '40s." *P.F. Sarasota, FL*

* *"Mimi* is an excellent book and very difficult to put down." *G.M. Budapest, HU*

* "I finished the novel with tears in my eyes." *E. Ch. USA/Sao Paulo, Brazil*

* "I would like to express my sincere gratitude and admiration for your writing this book. Thank you for providing me with such a broad background of what was previously untold." *F.M. Haarlem, The Netherlands*

* "I read *Mimi* and I loved it." *E.B. Washington, DC*

* "Thank you for sending me this gem of a book." *C.B. Pécs, Hungary.*

* "I truly enjoyed the story... Your writing is, without any doubt, exquisite...it felt as if a motion picture was being shown on a screen in front of me. Many descriptions read like a screenplay for a movie... The way you write dialogue is masterful." *W.F. Allison Park, PA*

* "The authenticity of the book is outstanding... I myself lived through what Eszter and her family experienced. Ágnes Huszár Várdy has written a beautiful book, giving readers pleasure and a lot to think about." *AVP, eyewitness and survivor, Charlotte, NC*

Mimi can also be ordered from the author:
5740 Aylesboro Avenue, Pittsburgh, PA 15217
Tel/Fax: 412-422-7176; e-mail: AHVardy@aol.com

Forthcoming in Spring 2007

Steven Béla Várdy and Ágnes Huszár Várdy,
Stalin's Gulag: the Hungarian Experience

— First complete summary and analysis of one of the most dreadful outcomes of Soviet occupation in Hungary after World War II

— Mass deportation of hundreds of thousands of innocent civilians -- including teenagers and pregnant women to Stalin's slave labor camps -- the **Gulag**

— Extermination of as many as 45 million people in Stalin's death camps, among them c. 250,000 to 400,000 Hungarians who perished under the most gruesome circumstances

— Authentic exposé of suffering and inhuman treatment of victims of **Stalin's Gulag**

— Volume based on previous scholarship, official documents, memoirs, and personal interviews

Dear Readers,

I would be happy to attend any book club that chose either of my novels, *Mimi* or *My Italian Summer*.

In the Pittsburgh, PA area, I could attend in person; otherwise, I would call in.

I would be delighted to meet my readers and talk to them in person!

Sincerely,
Agnes Huszár Várdy